MAGICAL MOR

DAUGHTERS OF DUSK

EMMA SHELFORD

DAUGHTERS OF DUSK

Kinglet Books
Victoria BC, Canada

Cover design by Deranged Doctor Designs

ISBN: 978-1989677292 (print)
ISBN: 978-1989677308 (ebook)

www.emmashelford.com

First edition: February 2021

CHAPTER I

I was handcuffed in a police cruiser with a pounding head and a woolly mind all because I'd been mouthy to a cop. Turns out they didn't take kindly to being called dirty pigs.

The cop was still jabbering on about my rights, his eyes raking curiously over my muddy clothes, but I tuned him out and took stock. Despite bruises and a throbbing head that felt as if it were pressed in a vise, I felt amazing. The chronic ache in my back was gone, my bad knee—courtesy of my ex-husband—wasn't protesting from its bent position, and I felt like I could leap out of the car and somersault without needing physiotherapy afterward.

I shouldn't have felt this good. I was fifty-five years old, and my body usually took masochistic pleasure in reminding me of my years. Maybe it was a side-effect of whatever trauma had recently befallen me. I couldn't remember much beyond a few minutes ago, when the cop had fished me out of the mud with clear disregard for my bruises. I raised a hand to my face, where it encountered skin stretched over bone structure that was not mine. The nose was pointed and narrow, the lashes long, and the cheeks tight and full. My eyebrows were thicker, and the mole beside my mouth had vanished.

My breathing came sharp and shallow, and I cast my eyes around to distract myself. Unmoving bodies littered the shoreline beyond the windshield and did nothing to dispel my mounting panic. The scents of dirt, blood, and the salty tang of the ocean mingled in my nose. What had happened here? I glanced at my hands and didn't recognize them. Their nails were bitten into a jagged mess, and the knuckles were slender with youth.

I shuffled over to catch a glimpse of myself in the rearview mirror. A young woman stared back at me with dark eyes amid a muddy face that might have been beautiful if clean. Brown

1

hair shone between clods of dirt, and shapely shoulders peeked through the stretched neck of an overlarge sweatshirt. Strange, insubstantial strands of gossamer silk wiggled around her head, glowing burgundy, silver, and green. I swatted at them, and the woman waved her hand in front of her face.

"Stay still," the police officer warned me from his post at the cruiser door. He, too, was surrounded by writhing strands of a brilliant aquamarine. His admonition concluded, he turned to a nearby uniformed woman and left me to slump in my seat with astonishment.

Somehow, in the mess of all that came before, my conscious had left my old body and landed in this new one. Through the fogginess of my mind, memories surfaced as if from a fleeting dream.

My old body had been possessed by an elemental earth spirit. My mind had been trapped in a prison, unable to break free but unwilling to die. I had seen occasional glimpses of the outside world when the spirit possessing me had been careless. Finally, a great struggle had pushed out the intruder, resulting in the carnage outside.

"What happened here?" I interrupted the police officer. My voice was annoyingly high-pitched. How could anyone take me seriously?

The officer frowned.

"You tell me. You were here."

"I don't remember anything."

At least, nothing beyond the last few minutes after the officer had pulled me out of the mud. I tried for a doe-eyed, innocent look. I was out of practice—middle-aged women could rarely pull it off, and I'd never been the meek, pouty type, even in my youth—but it seemed to work, because the officer's face softened.

"Memory loss? We'll take you to the hospital after we get your statement. Assuming you're ready to cooperate."

I nodded with an inward sigh and looked around. I'd have

2

to evaluate the situation with my own eyes if he wouldn't tell me anything. If I wanted something done right, I'd have to do it myself. It was the story of my life.

The cruiser was parked at the bottom of a steeply sloping driveway that meandered to a building by the sea. My Vancouver-raised mind immediately calculated the probable price of this piece of real estate, and I swallowed a whistle. I was no stranger to opulence—my own properties in this expensive city attested to that—but the size of this waterfront lot was astonishing.

For the first time, I fully examined the building to my left, and my jaw dropped. It towered over me in an expanse of rough-hewn stone, reminding me of the ancient city of Petra in Jordan. My ex-husband had taken me there once. That trip had been a highlight of some dark years.

The building was both eerily beautiful, despite a section of destroyed façade, and entirely out of place next to the neighboring house with its plate-glass windows and expansive wraparound balcony. The eeriness was compounded by a network of multicolored strands that swirled in mesmerizing patterns over the entire surface of the structure. My eyes traveled over the shifting colors in wonder then glanced around. Every person was similarly surrounded by a different color of strands, nearby trees had their own green trailing threads, and the breezy sky was full of shifting silver motes.

I shivered. What was I seeing? Was it a side-effect of my body transfer?

It must have been the middle of the night, because everything was lit up by huge spotlights. Bodies were sprawled in front of the building, some clearly dead and some being carted away on stretchers to waiting ambulances. The spirit possessing my body had been powerful. By the looks of it, the battle to remove it from my old body had been intense. I hoped that meant that the spirit was gone from the physical world. I wanted it as far away from me as possible. There was no way

I would share my body again.

The police officer dropped heavily into his seat with a sigh and started the ignition. His partner slid into the passenger's side and slammed her door shut.

"If you're taking me to the station, I'm not going to be much use," I said from the backseat. "With the memory loss and all."

"It's procedure." The driver twisted to back out of the driveway between other cruisers and ambulances.

I sighed and slumped in my seat. After the destruction outside, being detained by the police for some polite questioning was the best-case scenario. I could get through this. Soon enough, I would be alone and free to discover my new self.

When we arrived at the station, the female officer escorted me by the elbow through a side door toward a long counter.

"Name." The officer behind the counter kept her eyes on an empty form in front of her.

I stared at the woman, flummoxed. What was my name? I had no idea what moniker this body used when she had full control over herself. In my old life, I was called March Feynman, but I had dozens of names in previous lifetimes. Who was I?

The woman behind the counter didn't know, and neither did I. The freedom of this notion stole through me like the heat from a warm bath, comforting and intoxicating all at once. I could be anyone. No one knew me. No one had any expectations of me. No one looked up to me, relied on me, wanted to be me, wanted to have me, wanted to control me. I could be whomever I wanted to be.

"Name," the woman repeated. The officer behind me cleared his throat impatiently.

"Morgan," I said. "Morgan Leigh Feynman."

"So, Morgan," the female cop said, a reassuring tone to her voice. We sat across from each other in an interrogation room, with the male cop pacing behind her. "I'm Officer Lee, and this is Officer Marston. We have a few questions for you about the incident."

"I'm happy to help however I can, Officer Lee." I pasted on a smile. "But I really can't remember anything."

Warmth stole through my chest when the officer called me Morgan. A little soul-searching, with some magical help, had previously opened my eyes to my past lifetimes. Back in the Dark Ages, I had been the woman Morgan, sister of Arthur, the Arthur known in these times as an ancient king. It was all water under the bridge, now, and my memories of those times were fuzzy at best. Still, it tickled me to be called that early name once more.

"We'll ask you questions, and answer if they trigger anything, okay?" Marston said gruffly. I narrowed my eyes at him, my stomach twisting with inexplicable anger at his reasonable question.

"I'm not a medical expert, but is this really the correct procedure for a victim of probable head trauma and amnesia?"

Lee must have sensed my antagonism toward her partner, for she quickly intervened.

"A few quick questions, then we'll drive you to the hospital. Whatever you can tell us will help with the investigation. There were many casualties at the temple today, and we appreciate your help bringing the perpetrators to justice."

"Of course," I said. The anger that Marston's words had strangely triggered in me faded. "Fire away."

Lee looked relieved at my composure, and she folded her hands together on the table. When Marston opened his mouth to speak, she quelled him with a look.

"What is the last thing you remember?" she said.

5

My brow furrowed. That was a good question. The last clear thing I remembered was grappling with Merlin—a magician from my earliest memories of Morgan and Arthur, immortal and miraculously unchanged over the centuries—in Stanley Park until he forced an elemental spirit into my body. After that, I had only vague impressions of unknown faces and places until I had awoken at the temple site.

"It's all very fuzzy," I said with regret. "I don't remember much before a few weeks ago. I'm sorry."

"That's fine," Lee said with a smile that softened her otherwise stern face. "You're doing great."

I almost raised my eyebrow at that statement, but then I remembered my appearance as a young woman, clearly in need of emotional support.

My stomach lurched and my head fogged but just as quickly cleared. I blinked rapidly. What was that? Maybe this new body was prone to indigestion. Would I have to learn a whole new set of quirks? My previous body had been growing old with its own problems, but at least it was the devil I knew.

Lee asked a few more general questions in the hope of prodding my recalcitrant brain into action, but it had nothing to recall. I wanted to yawn—my new body was reaching the end of its rope—but I resisted with an iron will I had cultivated over the years.

"One more question," Lee continued. "Do you know a man named Merry Lytton?"

My hands clenched under the table. Marston looked confused, but I knew who Lee was talking about. Merry Lytton was the current name of Merlin. Most of the memories from my past lives were foggy at best, but he had cropped up in almost every one, and usually not for the better. That immortal meddler was one of the first in a long string of faithless men. I had a vision of taking all their throats in my hands and squeezing the life out of them like they had done to me.

The overwhelming rage shocked me into sobriety. How had

that emotion reared its ugly head? I prided myself on my calm reason.

I couldn't see how admitting I knew him would do me any favors, so I settled on looking politely puzzled.

"The name doesn't ring a bell."

Lee narrowed her eyes at me, clearly not buying my denial. A knock at the door saved me from further questions. Marston answered it and spoke briefly before closing the door again. He handed Lee two pieces of paper.

"Do you recognize this man?" she said, passing me one page across the table.

I took the paper and examined it. A woman with limp brown hair and pallid skin had her arm around a young man who looked remarkably like her—he must be a brother—but her smile didn't reach her tired eyes. With a start, I recognized my new body.

How did they have this picture? Were they searching for my new body and pulled this photo from a missing person's report?

"No," I said truthfully. "I don't."

"Your name is Fiorella Provenza," Lee said quietly. Her eyes searched my face for a reaction. "Your brother reported you missing a few days ago. With your permission, I will contact him to let him know his sister is safe."

"No," I said quickly. This day was already complicated enough. I didn't need long-lost brothers bursting in on the scene. "No, I'm not ready to do that. I'll call him in my own time."

"Okay," she said with a nod of sympathy. "Thank you for your cooperation. We will likely be in touch in the future as the investigation continues. Please contact the station if you remember anything, especially about Merry Lytton." She eyed me, clearly reluctant to let me go after my reaction to Merlin's modern name. "We can take you to the hospital now."

"I would much rather see my family doctor," I said. All I

wanted was to be alone to clean up, look in the mirror, and delve into my memories in private. At any rate, I doubted the hospital had much experience with body transfers. "Could you drop me off at my house on Marine Drive?"

"Nice part of town for someone your age," Marston said.

I bit back my retort when I recalled my new face.

"It's my aunt's house," I invented. "Please, I feel fine. I would much rather visit my own doctor."

Lee sighed and rubbed her chin.

"Okay," she said. "Why not. Jim, would you get a waiver form for Ms. Feynman to sign? I'll take her to the cruiser."

The strange, woozy feeling of indigestion came over me again in the police car, and I closed my eyes and swallowed hard to push it down. It wasn't a long drive to my main residence, and I opened my eyes when the cruiser pulled to the curb.

"This the place?" Marston peered into the darkness through the windshield at an impenetrable hedge that hid the house from prying eyes roadside. The neighbors had a tasteful display of red and green Christmas lights outlining their peaked roof, but my residence wasn't illuminated.

"Yes, this is it." I opened the door and stepped outside, grateful for fresh air.

"Maybe I should walk you to the door, make sure your aunt is here," Lee said.

"No, that's fine," I said quickly. "It's so late. She'll be asleep. I'll go rest and call my doctor in the morning. Thank you for the ride. Good luck with your investigation."

"Thanks. You're not the only one who's confused about all this. We'll reach out later." Lee nodded before the car pulled out into a break in traffic. She might reach out in the future, but my name wasn't the only falsification I put on the form.

I faced the gate with a happy smile. I was home. It had been a while.

I noticed with displeasure the twisted metal of my wrought-iron gate. Someone had wrenched the bars apart last month, and in the chaos of the last few weeks, I hadn't yet phoned the repair shop. I pushed the gate open, and it sailed inward on well-oiled hinges. My groundskeeper must still have been working despite my absence. Thank goodness for automatic deposit.

Overwhelming wooziness overtook me, and I gripped the gate with whitened knuckles and gasped for breath. It took a full minute to pass. Before I could stumble through the gate, a male voice called out.

"Excuse me, miss, do you need help?"

I hadn't been called a miss in decades. Was he trying to be funny? I whirled around, ready to tear a strip off him, and a lock of long brown hair whipped me in the face. Right. I wasn't myself.

The man stared at me with concern, his face sweaty above a ratty old tee shirt and jogging shorts. He must have been out for a late-night run. My heart thumped in an unsteady, pounding rhythm. Men were all the same. My ex-husband had been so good at faking concern, too. Even at the bruises he had put there himself.

"I'm fine," I said in a clipped tone.

"You don't look well," he pressed. "Can I help you inside?"

Really? I wasn't impressed with this younger body that I had somehow landed in. The invisibility of a middle-aged woman had its perks. *Can I help you inside*—how stupid did he think I was?

"Back off," I said. "I told you I'm fine. Don't make me say it again."

The man took a step back, hurt and confusion in his face. Nice try, buddy. I could recognize emotional manipulation when I saw it.

Guilt washed over me when I walked through the gate. What had come over me? The man was clearly trying to be nice, even if it were an odd time of night to be jogging. Why had I flown off the handle? I almost turned back to apologize but stopped. I didn't need help, and I certainly didn't want to explain myself to anyone else. I had too many questions and not nearly enough answers.

In fact, I needed answers now. It was time to discover what I knew.

This body had no keys, of course, but there was a spare key hidden above the mudroom entrance. I wobbled around the side of my Tudor-style house whose dormers were barely visible in the darkness of night. The rain had stopped a while ago, but clouds were still threatening. I ignored the front door under the portes-cochères, skirted a rhododendron to find the side door, then ran my fingers above the doorjamb. The key was where I'd left it, and it slotted easily into the keyhole of the mudroom door.

I thought I would take a moment to regroup once inside, delve into my memories of the last few weeks, and generally allow myself to fall apart in the privacy of my home. This new body I was inhabiting had other ideas.

It started with a tingling in my stomach, then an odd push in my mind. I opened my eyes, and silver threads swirling around my body danced in agitation.

I released the door handle, adrenaline pumping my heart like an overbalanced washing machine. What was happening to me?

With a pulling motion that felt like a suction cup on my skin, the silver strands rose on their own and formed the rough shape of a human head and torso. I held my breath. The strands that formed eyes opened their silvery eyelids and looked at me.

"What are you doing in this body?" The shape spoke in a sharp whispery voice that reminded me of hissing gales and roaring hurricanes. "I found it first. It's mine."

I stared at the silvery shape that swayed in a nonexistent breeze. Everything slotted into place. Somehow, this body that I had jumped into was already inhabited by an elemental spirit.

For years, I had worked toward this very goal—inviting a spirit traveler into my body to gain elemental powers—and, for the second time, I had achieved my dream.

The problem was, I didn't want it anymore.

CHAPTER II

I narrowed my eyes at the shape emerging from my arm, even as a sliver of fear pierced my heart. I had spent the last few weeks with an elemental inside my old body, and the spirit had taken over my entire existence. I couldn't go back to that, not again. I couldn't be under someone's control.

"Think again, traveler," I snarled. "This is my body now. Flutter away and find yourself another. Or, better yet, go back to wherever you came from."

"I was sent here on a mission," the elemental hissed. "I must stay and complete it. Besides, this body was prepared for me. I cannot simply jump to another one."

"Well, neither can I."

I watched in horrified fascination as the shape's features melded and sharpened into the head, arms, and torso of a man. He looked vaguely familiar.

"Is that what you normally look like?" I said, my guardedness momentarily suspended by the elemental's antics. His eyebrow strands moved into an approximation of a frown.

"I took the shape of the last person you saw so that you might feel more comfortable taking orders from me. I have access to your memories."

His face was a replica of the man who had asked if I needed help at the gate. The elemental's words sunk in, and my head jerked back.

"You're in my mind? Get out. I didn't give you permission to poke around in there."

"It isn't about permission. We are linked since we share this body. For now, at least. When you leave, you will take your mind with you."

"When you leave, you mean."

My brain raced through all the spells, chants, and rituals I had studied throughout my life. I'd always been fascinated with the world beyond, and a year ago, my beliefs were validated when I'd finally discovered evidence of an elemental realm. Elementals existed in a parallel plane to our physical world and were intimately connected to natural processes on Earth.

Despite foggy recollections of arcane studies in my past lives, I had never discovered the true nature of magical power. I'd since learned there were four branches of elementals, each corresponding to a phenomenon found in nature. Fire elementals controlled forest fires, lightning, magma, and the sparks of rocks colliding. Earth elementals were called forth from landslides, pebbles rolling on the beach, and the shifting of plate tectonics. Water elementals rolled with ocean waves, fell from the sky in raindrops, and ran down bodies in sweat. Air elementals raced in the wind, flowed out of lungs with each breath, and lifted the wings of birds as they flew.

There had to be a way to regain control of this body. So many religions throughout history had invented magical or spiritual ways to interact with the natural world, and many rituals directly influenced the elementals. I had compiled a vast arsenal of spells in my mind, most of which were untested. Surely, one of them would banish an elemental from my new body.

To give myself time to think, I kept him talking.

"What kind of elemental are you?"

"Air," he whispered. I didn't know if he were trying to be mysterious or whether his voice always sounded like that. I suspected the latter. "You can tell by the color of my threads."

The strands were silvery gray. I glanced at my body, where burgundy and green threads twisted together.

"Which ones are mine?"

"The dark red ones are yours. The green threads are from my new body," he said pointedly.

My lip curled, but I ignored the hint. My mind was still racing through possibilities.

13

"What's your name?" I asked.

"Elementals do not have names."

"If we'll be sharing a body, I can't refer to you as 'the protrusion from my arm'."

"We won't be sharing the body for long."

I ignored the comment and searched for an appropriate name. I didn't spend long since my mind was busy with the spells.

"Caelus," I said. "It has the Latin root meaning air. That will do."

"Caelus," he said slowly. "What do I do with a name?"

"Answer to it, mainly."

"I won't need to for long." He looked at me sharply. "Cease your searching. You cannot banish me from this body. I am too powerful for you."

Damn. He was in my head. I'd forgotten about that. Luckily, I had found a spell. I hoped it would work.

"We'll see about that."

Without further warning, I reached my hand out to grasp the threads at his torso and pulled up and out. Caelus' face contorted before it dissolved into a writhing mass of silver strands that boiled around my hand. They pierced my skin like a thousand bee stings, but I didn't let go. This was my chance to remove this parasite before he removed me.

I pulled hard, but the damn strands were as sticky as molasses and twice as annoying. After a few seconds of pulling and feeling like my hand would fall off from the pain of Caelus' attack, I switched tack. If I couldn't remove him from this body, then I sure as hell would be the one in control.

I chanted a spell from an ancient Malaysian text and pushed Caelus' strands into my stomach. If Caelus wanted to stick around, he would have to be quiet about it. I would bring him in and suppress him the way the other elemental had done to me. I couldn't allow myself to lose control again.

Caelus tried to struggle, but those ancient Malays must

14

have known their business because the stinging sensation faded until all I felt was a faint queasiness in my gut that soon settled. I breathed hard and rested my hand against the door. A cluster of silver threads was knotted below my ribcage with green and burgundy strands flowing freely around it, then all strands faded from my sight. Caelus' active presence must have allowed me to glimpse the elemental threads. Now that he was contained, I didn't have that ability.

I allowed myself a brief smile of satisfaction before I turned the door handle. People who underestimated me always regretted it. At least these days they did. My early years had been the opposite.

I might have felt guilty at suppressing Caelus, but my previous experience under the thumb of a powerful spirit had squashed my previous goodwill toward elementals. Having Caelus in my body was a huge risk, and I couldn't let him gain the upper hand.

I pushed open the door and my eyes fell on the comforting sight of the washer and dryer across the hall from the mudroom. Not that I did much laundry—I had a housekeeper for that—but it was still home. I kicked off my filthy shoes next to the umbrella stand, ran to the laundry room, stripped my clothes off, and took a clean towel from a rack to wrap around myself. A shower and sleep were my first priority, then I needed to sort out my future. March Feynman was dead, but Morgan needed to live on something. After running three successful businesses and acting on the board of directors for many more, working as a barista or waiting tables didn't appeal. Not that I was too proud for it, but—well, maybe I was too proud. In any event, I might as well use what I had made in my old life to fund my new one.

I padded across wood floors gleaming from streetlights filtering through the entryway's windows, through the quiet hall, and up carpeted stairs. I passed three of my favorite watercolors, bought from an up-and-coming artist who used the sales of her art to sponsor her niece, whose boyfriend had run away after their baby had been born. My bedroom was as I had left it weeks ago when I'd first interacted with the elemental who had eventually possessed my old body. I hadn't brought the spirit to this home, needing a sanctuary away from elementals.

I was glad I hadn't, for the house was untouched. I strode into the bathroom, anxious to step into hot water pulsing through the two jets set at exactly the temperature I liked. The wall-to-wall mirror over the bathroom counter stopped me short.

This was my first good look at my new body. Mud-streaked brown hair hung in ragged tendrils to my shoulder blades, and large eyes blinked in a fawn-like way. I narrowed them and they grew a little more worldly. That was better.

I let the towel pool around my feet. No complaints there. The breasts were small and high on my chest, and my hips were slender below a flat stomach. I turned to look at my bottom, which was nicely rounded. My reflection smiled back at me. This second chance had more than one perk.

Ribbons of white on my arms caught my attention. I held them out and examined thin scars that crisscrossed each forearm. My mouth twisted. Had the woman whose body I now inhabited cut herself in the past?

For the first time, I let myself wonder about Fiorella. Who was her brother? Did she have a job? Had there been trauma in her life or deep-seated depression? What had led her to the site of the earth spirit's temple tonight?

I felt no other presence in this body, and I believed Caelus' assurance that she was gone. A stab of remorse hit me for the waste of this young woman's life. It had been my own bad choices that had subjected me to the other elemental's control, but had it been her choice to be possessed?

The only small consolation I could offer myself was that Caelus had possessed her first. It hadn't been at my instigation that Fiorella was gone. I closed my eyes and quieted my mind, anxious to find some hint of the woman who used to inhabit this body. If she were still present, could we share her form?

Gooseflesh had erupted on my skin by the time my eyes popped open again. All was silent in my inner being, and the quiet confirmed my fears. When a powerful elemental took control of a body, the previous owner would die. The only reason my old body hadn't perished, and my soul flown to whatever awaited beyond, was that I had taken magical precautions. This woman had not.

I turned away from the accusing eyes of my new body and stepped into the shower. There was nothing I could do now to undo the events of the past. All I could do was move forward with decision and purpose.

Purpose doing what, I wasn't sure.

I collapsed on the bed after my shower and instantly passed out until gloomy daylight forced my eyelids open. December in Vancouver was often rainy, and today was no exception.

My body ached, but I pushed myself out of bed despite its protests. The discomfort was from bruises and muscle-work, not the aches of age, so it was far more bearable. I could get used to this.

I chose my most casual clothes from the walk-in closet—this body would attract more unwanted attention in a crisp power suit than too-big jeans—and vowed to go shopping today. But first, I needed money.

I paused on my way downstairs. On my vanity—a piece of furniture I had purchased on my first trip to Barcelona post-divorce—hung two rings on a slender gold chain. The yellow diamond of the engagement ring was ostentatious, and the wedding band was heavy and studded with more diamonds. I had never liked the color of the engagement ring, but yellow diamonds cost more, and Peter always needed to show off. The rings had shackled me to my ex-husband tighter than a collar, and even now, years after our divorce, I kept them as a reminder. Never again would I let a man—let anyone—rule me the way he had. Never again would I allow someone to manipulate my mind and emotions to trap and control me. In the years since, I became a strong, confident, independent woman, but I never forgot where I came from, and those rings reminded me of what could happen if I let my guard down. Never again.

I swiped the chain off the vanity on a whim and swung it in my hand on my way downstairs. Once in my office, I dropped the rings on my desk, booted up the laptop, and reached for my reading glasses with an automatic motion. When I slipped them over my ears, they rested on my nose in the wrong place. I blinked rapidly at the blurriness and ripped the glasses off.

My mouth curled up. No need for reading glasses anymore—that was a perk I could get used to. Gone were the smudges, the lost pairs, and the extra set in my purse. For another few decades, I could be free of those awful accessories.

My computer was ready, so I checked my bank accounts. A few were completely dry—the elemental in my body had spent far too much money on constructing that ridiculous temple—but my offshore account was untouched, enough for what I planned. I transferred the maximum allowable funds into one of the accounts for Sweet Thing, the cupcake shop I owned that had been a front for the secret organization I'd led dedicated to magical research. Sweet Thing was a handy company to siphon money to and from.

I pulled open my desk drawer and rifled through the contents until I found a debit card for my Sweet Thing account. Now that March was dead, access to my old personal accounts would soon be frozen. The Sweet Thing funds were not under March Feynman's name and so would be unwatched except by my business partner who didn't have access to this account.

March's last will and testament would divide her assets between my sister August and multiple women's centers in town. August lived in an assisted living home since she was mentally incapable of caring for herself. Interest from the trust that would be set up after March's death would keep her living in comfort for the rest of her life. I spared a moment of sadness that I wouldn't see her again—she would be terrified by a stranger—but she barely recognized March and wouldn't miss her.

I wouldn't have nearly the cash I used to hold—I'd be a relative pauper—but I would have enough to live on comfortably for a time while I found my feet. Now, Morgan Leigh Feynman needed to become a real person. March's cellphone was long gone, and I thanked my former self for not giving up the landline. My contact in the government picked up after the second ring.

"John Preston, Department of Employment and Social Development."

"Hello," I said. My voice was higher pitched than I was used to, so I deepened it to sound more like my old self. "It's March Feynman. How are you?"

"March." John's voice was pleasant but guarded. I had helped him in a sticky legal situation a few years ago, and he knew I was here to collect. "I'm well. How can I help you?"

I clenched my fist. This was the part where I learned exactly how indebted to me John was. I hoped he was properly grateful for the favor I had granted. Loose morals wouldn't hurt, either.

"I need a falsified social insurance number," I said. No way to sugarcoat it. "My niece was living off the grid with her father and has never been registered. No birth certificate, nothing. It's a long story. I want to help her out now that she's finally entering society, but I don't want to wait for the proper channels, investigations, all that nonsense."

The phone hissed as John pushed air out forcefully through his lips. I waited.

"Okay," John said, his voice restrained. "Okay, I can do that. Email me the information and a contact."

"Mmm, the contact is difficult. I'll give you a mailing address instead." I added the address of a condo I owned and sent the email with a steady click of the mouse. "Sent. Thank you, John."

"Are we done?" he said stiffly. This task was grating on his moral compass, I could tell, but he would do it.

"For now." I didn't want to leave our relationship entirely complete. Who knew when I might need his services again? "Take care, John."

I hung up and allowed myself a small smile. Morgan Leigh Feynman was on her way to becoming a real person in the eyes of the law.

What did that mean? Suddenly, I was struck by a jolt of unease. Who was Morgan, this new person I had decided to become? What were her goals? What did she want?

As March, I had always been purposeful. I'd had businesses to run, charities to oversee, and secret organizations to manage. Slowly, those activities had eroded away as I passed the reins of my businesses to competent partners, and my organization devoted to connecting with elemental spirits was destroyed by meddling Merlin.

I still had my charity. Although I couldn't play a sponsor's role at the woman's center any longer, funds would be paid in perpetuity from the interest payments of the trust that would be set up once my will was finalized. And there was nothing stopping me from volunteering. Maybe later today I could visit.

My eyes fell on the rings and their chain draped over the surface of my desk. March had been bound by restrictions, propriety, and reputation. Morgan had none of those shackles. Peter, my ex-husband, had sailed away from our divorce relatively intact, unlike the emotional and physical scars he had inflicted upon me.

My gut suddenly filled with molten rage at the sight of the rings, and I itched for vengeance against Peter. Some small, rational corner of my mind cried out that I was being unreasonable, that I had healed from Peter's wounds years ago, but it was quickly enveloped by the mystifying fire. Visions of vengeance flitted through my mind, each wilder than the last.

A key rattled in the front door. I shoved the rings in my pocket and stood, my heart pounding, to see who disturbed my peace. Who had a key?

CHAPTER III

Whistling soothed my jangling nerves. It was Rose, my cleaning lady. It must be Friday.

My calm didn't last. She wouldn't recognize me. What was I going to tell her? I could spin the long-lost niece story, but Rose was more suspicious than John Preston. She and I had always got on well.

Maybe I should leave, sneak out while she wasn't looking. I tiptoed to the door but stopped in my tracks at a male voice.

"How long will we be here, Ma?"

My toes curled. What was Rose's son doing here with her? He was hardly a child anymore.

"It's a big house, Jayden," Rose said sharply. "It will be a while. Find a spot on the couch and get comfortable. But for goodness' sake, don't put your feet on it. We'll be here even longer if I have to clean spots off the furniture."

The boy grumbled, and footsteps traveled to the living room. Rose's feet padded to the downstairs bathroom, and water started to pour.

This was my chance, but I dithered. I didn't like Jayden here. I didn't trust him. What if he snatched something? I wanted him out of my house. Rose, I liked and understood. Her son was an unknown quantity.

I took a deep breath and let it out slowly. This wasn't my life anymore. This house wasn't mine. I needed to let it go and move on. It was full of March's memories and concerns. I wasn't that woman. I was Morgan now.

The repetition of my new name brought back old memories of ancient times. They were so indistinct, like a dream that slipped away the more one tried to remember it. I shook my head impatiently. I didn't have the patience to live in the past. I wanted a new future.

One of March's holdings was a condo in East Vancouver,

bought for investment purposes and currently unoccupied. It would be sold off once the executor finalized my will, but nothing was stopping me from living in it while the paperwork was slowly dealt with. My condo beckoned, a more fitting abode for a twenty-something woman. It was time to move on.

I took the condo keys and all the money from my stash of bills in the kitchen drawer, slipped on a pair of boots that my smaller feet swam in, and shuffled quietly out the mudroom door. Once outside, I took another deep breath.

"A new life," I reminded myself. "A new start."

The house was far from any shops, but after a few minutes a lone taxi trundled by, and I waved it down. After the driver dropped me at the nearest mall, I proceeded to buy clothes more fitting for someone my age. The saleswoman's eyes twinkled with interest when I told her what I wanted.

"I can dress you in whatever I think will suit you?"

"You have—" I counted half of the money in my pocket. "Five hundred dollars. Go."

She clapped her hands in delight and scuttled off. I had to veto a few of her choices—the woman tried to insist on yoga pants, which I couldn't bring myself to wear, even if I now had a perky bottom to pull them off—but at the end of the hour, I was dressed in skinny jeans, a fitted blouse, and a belted, hip-length raincoat. Bags containing the rest of my purchases swung from my arms. After a stop at a phone kiosk, where I purchased the cheapest phone I could find, and a quick visit to the food court coffeeshop and a shoe store, I was ready to take on the world.

A park bench outside called to me, and I sipped my coffee and bit into biscotti while my thumb dialed my best friend's number.

"Hello?" Anna Green answered with a question in her

23

voice.

Who was I trying to fool? Anna was my only real friend. According to the memories of our past lives, much of which were fuzzy, we had been friends for centuries. I trusted her as much as I trusted anyone in this life.

"Hello, Anna," I said, painfully aware of my higher-pitched voice. "I know this will come as a shock to you, but this is March. March Feynman."

Silence echoed in the phone line.

"Who is this?" Anna said with anger. "Why would you say that? If you think it's a joke, it's not funny at all. My friend is dead. Doesn't that mean anything to you?"

"Anna, Anna," I said quickly. "I know it's crazy, but it's true. When the earth elemental took over my body, I was trapped for weeks. Then, something happened yesterday, and my essence jumped into a new body. I woke up at the temple, covered in mud, surrounded by bodies. What happened? Are you safe?"

More silence, then a sob.

"March? Did it work? Is it really you?"

A relieved smile slid across my face. Just because I was starting a new life didn't mean that I had to give up everything. Anna was important to me.

"It's me. I know, I can hardly believe it either."

"It's so good to hear your voice. Well, not your voice, but your words. Oh, this is so strange. Yes, I'm fine. I'm just so relieved to hear you're alive." She sniffed. "I planted that amulet on your old body in the wild hope you could escape your possession, but I didn't really believe it would work. I'm so happy for you."

A vague memory of reaching out to someone with the name of a book of spells came to me. Somehow, Anna had received my message while the spirit still had control of my old body, and she had understood and acted on my plea for help. Anna had created an amulet that had allowed my soul to escape my flesh-bound prison. My heart swelled with gratitude for Anna.

"I'd love to meet up," I said. "When are you available?"

An indistinct male voice filtered through the speaker. Anna must have covered the microphone because her answer was muffled. When she came back to the phone, her voice was brighter, and she spoke quickly.

"I can't talk now, we're heading out. But coffee in a few days? I'll text you."

"All right," I said slowly, bewildered by her change of tone.

"Okay, great. Bye!" Anna chirped and hung up.

I stared at my new phone for a long moment. Was Anna trying to hide me from whatever man she was with? My growing feeling of betrayal was washed out by gratitude at Anna's quick thinking. Of course, I should hide my old identity. I was Morgan now, the new and improved version. I didn't want anyone to know the truth except Anna.

My condo was in the Cormorant Drive district, which was too far away to walk to. It took a few minutes to wave down a taxi, and five buses passed me in that time. I patted the contents of my pocket where my quickly slimming bundle of bills resided. Maybe I should act my new age and take public transit.

Luckily, a taxi pulled up to the curb, and I was spared the conundrum of packing myself into a sardine tin with the rest of the populace.

I must have been smiling out the window because the driver glanced at me in the rearview mirror.

"Having a good day, looks like."

"Yes," I said to my own surprise. "This is a day of new beginnings. I'm ready to seize the moment."

"Good for you, kiddo," he said.

I bit my tongue. The last person to call me a kiddo had been my ailing father twenty years ago. Part of me was amused, but the other, stranger part railed at his presumption. I took a deep breath to curb this impulse and looked out the window. Why was I reacting so oddly to innocuous people? Surges of irrational anger filled my body at the slightest offense, and I didn't understand why. Was my new body overriding my mind's emotions?

The taxi dropped me at the curb of a quiet side street near busy Cormorant Drive. There were very few condo blocks in this neighborhood, but my building was one of them. It was only a few years old, built close to the new Skytrain line. I had bought it as an investment property recently, and my property manager hadn't yet rented it out. For now, it would be Morgan's.

I dug the key fob out of my pocket and let myself into the carpeted lobby. A wall of mirrors shocked me again by the young woman walking in my shoes. When would I get used to that sight?

The elevator delivered me to the third floor which was populated by six units. Mine was at the far end of the hall, but before I could insert my key into the lock, my neighbor's door opened. An evergreen wreath holding a cartoonish snowman figurine with a goofy grin wobbled on its nail.

The middle-aged man who emerged brightened when he saw me. His bushy salt-and-pepper hair wiggled, desperately in need of a trim.

"You must be the owner of unit thirty-two," he said with a cheery voice. "Welcome to the building. I'm Doug."

He thrust out a hand to me. I took it after a moment's hesitation, my new suspicion overtaken by years of training in social graces.

"Thank you." I didn't offer my name. I had no idea who this man was, and I wasn't ready to get friendly with him. As a rule, I kept myself to myself.

"Oh!" His eyes widened. "I just remembered. Your unit

didn't have its balcony painted. They came through a few weeks ago to do it, but no one could get hold of you. They left a tin of paint. I'm sure I can dig it up for you somewhere. I'm on the strata council, you know. Bunch of busybodies, most of them, so someone has to lighten things up around here." He winked at me, and my mouth twitched in amusement despite myself.

Was he as friendly as he seemed? My gut was warning me that people often had ulterior motives, and men more often than not. It was time to end this conversation.

"Thanks," I said. "Whenever you find it is fine. Have a good day."

I escaped into my unit and left chatty Doug in the hallway.

The unit was fully furnished in a plain but serviceable manner, and I sighed in relief. The door opened to a short hallway that widened into a living room with a balcony and kitchen nook. A bedroom was tucked to my right with the bathroom beside it. It paled in comparison to my Marine Drive mansion, but it would be comfortable enough. It was a good base in which to learn who I wanted Morgan to become.

After a ten-minute poke around the cupboards and closets, and a five-minute perch on the squishy couch, I leaped up and strode to the door. There was nothing to do in this condo, and if there was one thing I detested, it was inactivity. I had to do something to fill my time.

My hand paused on the door when a thought struck me. One of the women's centers that I donated to was right around the corner. Why not give it a visit?

I strode purposefully down narrow side streets lined with graceful trees, bare in this season. Occasional glimpses of skyscrapers in the distance peeked between houses. The small women's center had been converted from a tiny bungalow on the corner of a busy intersection. Its white trim was freshly painted and a cheery poster depicting a sunrise festooned one window. It was welcoming, and I nodded in satisfaction. I was proud to support this and three other centers in town. For women in need of help, the centers provided a safe contact point, emergency supplies, counseling resources, computer access, legal aid, and support with finding childcare. If I had known of a center like this years ago, I might have left Peter sooner.

I pushed the door open and breathed in deeply. The scent of pamphlets, mints, and baby wipes was familiar. As March, I had visited this center many times to oversee improvements from my funding. Greta, a plump woman with glasses and a smiling face who volunteered regularly, looked up from speaking with a girl with bright purple hair and a worried expression. A worn-looking woman with faded jeans and a chubby baby sat beside a rack of pamphlets and a scraggly fake Christmas tree with red and green twinkle lights.

"Welcome to Grandview Women's Center," Greta said. "Feel free to look around. I'll be with you shortly."

She continued to speak quietly to the girl, pointing at a piece of paper between them. I strolled to the hallway, contrasting my arrival today with the past. As a patron, I was fawned over when I visited, but today I was just another woman in need of help. I didn't mind the anonymity. This new life was strange and bizarre, but I was quickly getting used to it.

Three desktop computers were squeezed into a converted bedroom, and two were occupied by intent women staring at the screens. A young boy played with a toy truck in the corner. The next room was closed, but a paper sign said that legal assistance was in session and to speak with Greta at the front desk for a meeting. The back room had shelves of supplies— cans of food, packages of diapers, a stack of winter coats—and a cot pushed against the window. Everything was as it had been during my last visit.

I retreated to the front room after my exploration and sat next to the waiting woman. She jiggled her baby, her thoughts clearly elsewhere. Anxiety rolled off her in waves, and it was clear that the jiggling was only just stopping the baby from bursting into tears, despite its fascination with the Christmas lights.

"I was here, once," I said softly. The woman glanced at me in confusion. "Or wished I were. My husband had turned me into the smallest possible version of myself. When he started hitting me, I left. Not right away, of course. It took months to work up the courage to leave. But when I did, I never once looked back."

The woman's eyes raked my face. She bit her lip, but the tense set of her jaw relaxed somewhat.

"I'm happy for you," she said. "Maybe one day I can sit where you are."

"You came to the right place."

Greta's voice called the woman up, but her features were softer than before, and the baby was calmer. After ten minutes of their conversation, Greta led her into the supply room then came back for me.

"Thanks for being patient, dear. What can I do for you today?"

"I'd like to help," I said spontaneously. I hadn't planned my words, but they felt right. "Volunteer, I mean. I really believe in what you're doing here."

Greta's already pleasant face widened in a smile.

"Wonderful. We always welcome volunteers. You'll have to do a background check, of course."

I hesitated. My government identification hadn't yet arrived.

"I'd be happy to submit to a criminal record check," I said finally. "But my government ID is currently being processed, so I can't show it to you."

"That should be fine." Greta nodded firmly then smiled. "We just won't leave you to lock up the place for a while, that's all."

We discussed different roles I could perform and arranged for me to come back tomorrow to orient myself. I left my name and contact details, then walked out of the little building with a lighter heart. Helping the women who came to the center felt like a good start to my new life.

CHAPTER IV

I fell into a solemn mood a few blocks from the center, unsure what my place in the world was. My new volunteering position was good, but it was only a small start. Finding my path would be less simple than I had hoped.

I wandered down the main drag of Cormorant Drive, absentmindedly skirting other pedestrians and sandwich board signs advertising local businesses. The flat streets of this delta city were easy to walk along, aided by my nimble new body. I took a deep breath, and a faint hint of salt air tickled my lungs from the nearby strait. Despite an autumnal chill, the skies had cleared today in a rare patch of good weather. Locals flocked to the streets to take advantage of the sun.

I passed a hair salon called Cut Right and a Lebanese grocer whose windows were filled with olives and feta cheeses. My stomach rumbled, but I wasn't sure what I wanted. Across the street, a bakery named Upper Crust caught my eye. Yes. Something baked was exactly what I craved.

I crossed the street on newly agile feet, dodging bicycles and a delivery van in my quest to reach the bakery. The window was piled with an assortment of fresh breads, glazed doughnuts in rows, and a mountain of profiteroles which made me reminisce about a visit to Paris years ago. Peter had been busy that trip, and I'd had an unusual amount of freedom to roam and sample all the edible attractions the City of Lights had to offer.

A bell tinkled when I entered the busy bakery. There were four tables squished against the side with happy patrons scarfing muffins and coffees, but most of the business was in bread sales. There must have been a rush just before I arrived, for the line was five deep although no one entered after me. The young woman at the till looked friendly but harried. Another woman worked the coffee machine, and a muscular man in the dimly lit kitchen beyond kneaded dough with vigorous motions.

My eyes feasted on the display case. Maybe I should get one of everything. Now that my metabolism was thirty years younger, I might as well take advantage of it. I knew what was coming, after all.

The Eccles cakes appealed, filled with currants and sprinkled with sanding sugar, as did the massive cheese scones. Even decorated cookies in the shape of reindeer held a certain allure. But when I spotted the lemon tarts, that was it. Something deep in my gut craved those round, flaky tarts filled with deep yellow custard.

Why? I had never particularly enjoyed lemon desserts before. What had changed? I looked down at my unfamiliar hands. If lemon was suddenly on my must-have food list, what other surprises did this body hold?

A craving for lemon tarts had an easy solution. I would worry about further complications as they arose.

"A loaf of sourdough, please. And lemon tarts," I told the woman when it was my turn.

"How many would you like?"

"One," I said then amended my answer when my body growled in annoyance. "Dozen."

The woman nodded her braided head as if my request were perfectly reasonable. I almost called her back, but I resisted. My stomach purred in anticipation.

The man in the back lifted his head and stared at me, but I ignored him. The woman carried back my loaf of bread and the box filled with tarts, and my mouth watered at the sight. I hastily shoved cash at her and snatched the baked goods with a shocking lack of decorum. It wasn't like I had a reputation to uphold. Who cared if I were a little overeager?

I walked to the side to make way for further customers, but I didn't hesitate. My trembling fingers slit the box open and grabbed a tart. I shoved it in my mouth, and the sweet-sour flavor exploded on my tongue.

"Mmm," I groaned quietly. With every bite, more sensation burst across my taste buds. Too soon, the tart was gone, but I had a solution for that. My hand greedily thrust into the box once more.

"I don't think anyone has ever complimented me like that before," a male voice said from behind the counter. "You're going to make me blush."

My eyes darted to the speaker. The man previously kneading dough now stood behind the glass case. He was built like a bear, a full head taller than my not insubstantial new height and with muscles to match, although they were carefully hidden underneath a baggy polo shirt with an unfashionably buttoned collar. He was young, maybe in his late twenties. I swallowed my bite and considered. That wasn't so young anymore, was it? My current body was about the same age.

He had a narrow face with a strong jaw and thin lips that turned up in an easy smile. His sandy colored hair was partly shaved on the sides and swept back on top. He was certainly handsome and appeared kind, but I never went by looks. Too often, it was the innocent-looking ones that had the most to hide. Peter had looked positively angelic when I'd first met him. My brain firmly put me on my guard.

My body, however, had other notions. A hot flush suffused my skin, and my gut tightened with pleasurable firmness. Oh, hell. I was attracted to him.

I was far beyond this whole-body hormone reaction and had been for years. Not that I didn't find men attractive—I took likely candidates to bed if I felt so moved—but that race of butterflies and surges of sensation had been mercifully relegated to my youth. They had only gotten me into trouble with Peter, and I had no use for emotions that betrayed me so thoroughly.

Now, I was back in the thick of it. Oddly, it wasn't an entirely unwelcome feeling. It, more than any long looks in the mirror, made me feel young again.

No. I snapped my mouth shut and stood straighter. I was stronger than this. It didn't matter what my ridiculous new body felt. My mind held the reins.

"They're really good," I said honestly. A moment of embarrassment flushed over me at my silly high voice. I needed to coach myself to a lower tone or no one would take me seriously.

Wait, why did I care what this man thought of me? My lips tightened. Had he been trying to pick me up? My body tensed at the implications. A part of me was utterly confused. Was I attracted to him or fearful of him? The mixed signals from my body and my mind were hard to deconstruct.

"Don't worry," he said. "I make them every day. There will be more tomorrow. They're not going out of fashion."

He turned away after a parting smile to me. Despite his initial approach, I didn't get a sense of threat from him at all. My shoulders relaxed, and I retreated from the bakery, another tart already in my mouth before I exited. The promise of more tarts tomorrow made me memorize the bakery's location. I would be back.

I wandered around the bakery and down a sloped side street toward a scruffy playing field, munching my third tart. It felt almost reckless to ingest another of the sweet treats, but my body was eager for them, and it was hard to resist.

Something tugged at my senses, but I couldn't identify it. I shook my head and stopped at the intersection, unsure of where to go now. Back to my condo? Out for a walk? My newfound freedom was both liberating and daunting.

I turned down a side street without thinking, and it wasn't until I passed a narrow alley behind a row of shops that the tugging pulled me again. My eyes scanned an alley with dumpster bins and a high fence between back lane and neighbors. What was my body trying to tell me? When I took a determined step away from the tugging, I heard a thump and

34

a woman's high scream.

My senses went on high alert. I shoved the pastry box and loaf of bread on a tuft of grass beside a telephone pole—there might be danger ahead, but it could wait two seconds while I saved my tarts from being dropped—and raced with my reactive young legs to the source of the scream.

Two figures struggled behind a green dumpster. A young woman with her face twisted in concentration threw a solid punch at a man with a leather jacket and buzz cut. He didn't duck quickly enough, and his lip split open.

Despite the wound, he ignored the punch. The woman's next blow landed on his arm, then he grabbed her shoulders and threw her to the ground. She kicked her slender legs, but the man straddled her with one hand pressing against her shoulder to hold her down and the other scrabbling at her neck. Her fiery red hair thrashed against the asphalt like orange snakes. More blood on the man's temple and a ripped sleeve indicated that the woman had given him a fight.

Blood rose in my body until all sound was muffled. This was what I fought against at the women's center. The woman had no chance, and the man had all the advantage in the world to do whatever he pleased with her. My heart thundered in my chest, and my breath panted with rage.

Wriggling purple threads emerged from the air around the thug, and turquoise strands were frozen around the woman. I looked down in surprise.

The previously coiled silver threads at my stomach now danced around my hands. Had my agitation released Caelus from his bonds? Fear dampened my rage, then my inner opportunist took over. I had seen Merlin fling around power with his bare hands often enough, and all he had was the ability of an elemental. Why shouldn't I do the same?

I had no idea how, but that didn't stop me from trying. Newly instated youth or not, I was no physical match for this brute. I had no weapons, no real strength, and running for help would only leave the woman at his mercy. I needed to act now.

All the threads of the world now appeared in my vision since Caelus was waking. Silvery strands whisked past my face and twisted in loose spirals with the breeze. What if I pulled them the way I had heard Merlin describe? What would happen?

I pinched a cluster between my fingers and tugged. Wind gusted down the narrow alley, and the thug looked up in confusion. I had a glimpse of glazed eyes under thick brows. Was he on drugs?

An idea hit me. I reached for threads that flew past a recycling bin and yanked, instinct telling me how hard to pull.

A sheet of newspaper flew out of the bin and sailed across the alley. With another instinctual tweak of threads, my fingers directed the newspaper into the thug's face. It wrapped around his head, and he jerked upward, pulling frantically at the suffocating paper.

I wasted no time darting forward. The thug's hand flailed wildly and caught my cheek in a nasty backhand that whipped my head around and made me gasp at the blossoming pain. When I turned back, my fingers pressing the wound, the man still struggled with the newspaper. I kicked him in the chest with a satisfying thud. When he tumbled off the woman, I yanked her to her feet, and we stumbled out of the alley. I quickly scooped my tarts and bread from the ground and fled down the road.

The other woman stopped after a couple of blocks, breathing heavily and looking behind her at the empty sidewalk. The thug was out of sight, and she sagged against a nearby fence.

"Thank you." She looked at me, pale blue eyes in an even paler face filled with residual fear of the man and worshipful awe for me. "I don't know what you did, but thank you."

"I will always help a woman being attacked by a man," I said firmly. "I'm only glad I got there in time. What did he

36

want, do you think? Your purse? Sex? Did you know him?"

"I've never seen him before." She reached to her neck and touched a large locket on a gold chain with an unconscious gesture of reassurance. "I don't know what he wanted."

"Do you want to press charges? I didn't get a great look at him, but still."

"No, no." The woman shook her head. "Don't call on my behalf."

I frowned at her but said nothing. Why didn't she want the police involved? Maybe she was hiding something. I wasn't about to protest since I had no desire to encounter the police again so soon.

My stomach protested, and I suppressed it with my will. Caelus was trying to escape after my use of his powers, and I wouldn't let that happen. My head pounded from the blow and my limbs were heavy—maybe using Caelus' powers took more out of me than I had thought—but I had a responsibility to see this woman safe.

"Do you want me to walk you anywhere?" I asked. "I don't mind."

"My car isn't far," she said. Her tone was grateful. "Maybe a block. Thanks."

We walked for a half-block in silence. I contemplated the depths to which some men would sink. The young woman at my side fidgeted with her necklace.

"I'm sorry about your cheek," she blurted out. "My name's Amanda."

"Morgan," I replied, smiling to myself at the use of my new moniker. "And the cheek will heal."

"What did you do back there?" Amanda glanced sideways at me. "That newspaper wasn't an accident. You did something with the wind."

I gave her an incredulous look, because I had no intention of telling her that I currently shared my body with an elemental spirit, the same body that I had only recently occupied. That wasn't normal, and I didn't want to crop up on anyone's radar.

To my surprise, Amanda smiled.

"It's okay," she said. "I understand. You're nervous telling people about your powers. But I'm part of a group that gets it. We have some small abilities of our own. We could use someone like you. Would you like to visit Rosemary? We call her our mother hen." Amanda chuckled. "She looks after us and pecks those who get out of line. She's lovely, though. She could explain everything much better."

What were the chances that I had encountered someone who understood the power inside me? I remembered the tugging on my body that had led to Amanda. Had I somehow sensed her own abilities?

However, I had no intention of joining a clandestine organization that used magical powers. Partly because I knew nothing about my so-called powers, and the source of them was currently locked in my strands. The other reason was because, as March, I had been the leader of my own secret organization dealing with the occult, and it had ended with possession by an elemental and a body switch. I wasn't keen on traveling that path again, not so soon after my new start.

"I'm sure she's lovely and you all do wonderful things," I said. "But I'll have to decline."

Caelus waited until I had said goodbye to Amanda and walked down a side street before he made his move. Maybe he was annoyed at me wresting his power from him then shoving him back into his containment spell. I certainly would have been.

Beside a picket fence painted in a rainbow array, Caelus struck. Every nerve in my stomach screamed at me with the pain of a thousand hailstones in a howling storm. I dropped to my knees, clutching the fence like it was a lifeboat beside the

Titanic, and squeezed my eyes shut while I recited the spell of containment. I could barely remember the words through the haze of pain.

With a dreadful ripping sensation, I was pushed aside. Not physically—I could still see through my body's eyes and hear through the ears—but I had no control over its limbs.

Caelus was driving now.

CHAPTER V

A satisfied feeling stole over me, layered on my fear and anger. It wasn't my emotion. Caelus smiled.

"Finally," he said, using my new body's mouth. "I have control. You have kept me from my mission for long enough."

He lurched upright, and I could do nothing as he wandered back to Cormorant Drive, bread and tarts in one hand. Now that Caelus controlled my eyes, threads of the world swayed from every living thing, and the wind danced with air strands. I was a helpless passenger in my body once more, and the only improvement over last time was that I could see what was happening. During my previous possession, I had existed in a fog of nothingness.

I debated if this were better. It was infuriating being aware of my lack of control. There was nothing I could do. Nothing, except...

I focused on pushing my conscious into the body's arm. It took a bit to master the trick, but eventually something clicked in my understanding, and I flowed downward. With a mental push up, I formed a thread torso as Caelus had done before. I could even make sounds, although I didn't know if anyone could hear me except Caelus. It didn't matter. That was who I needed to talk to.

"What the hell do you think you're doing?" I hissed. "Give me my body back."

"Technically, I was in it first," he said calmly through our body's mouth. "You are the usurper. I'm ashamed it took me this long to take control from you, but it couldn't be helped. You have knowledge that my superiors didn't expect a human to have. Never mind. It won't happen again."

I started to speak, but Caelus interrupted me with a frown.

"I am thoroughly displeased with you," he said. "Not only did you contain me in this body and keep me from controlling it, but you stole my abilities for your own purposes. You may stay here, if you wish, but keep quiet and let me complete my mission in peace. Now that I have the agency to find artifacts on my own and don't have to nudge you in the right direction from the inside, I will take full advantage."

With our left hand, Caelus slammed the top of my strand head and pushed me into our arm. It didn't hurt, but everything jolted and shook. My vision flickered and narrowed until I saw through our body's eyes once more but still as a passenger.

Had Caelus been the one directing me to Amanda's attack? Had he sensed some power that she held and pushed me to follow her? I was both indignant at his control and intrigued about Amanda's abilities.

I took a few minutes to recover from the shock of Caelus' force and watched as he strode purposefully along the road. I pushed at Caelus' strands with my own, but he merely rubbed our stomach at the sensation and pushed me down. Cormorant Drive was growing busier at the evening hour, with brightly lit restaurants full of patrons and late-open businesses hopping with customers. The Lebanese grocer was doing brisk business selling baklava to the after-dinner crowd, but Caelus whipped past and turned abruptly into the next doorway.

It was a pawn shop, filled with old stereo equipment, televisions, game consoles, musical instruments, and other items that their previous owners hadn't considered necessary for survival. An older man with greasy gray hair in a low ponytail was counting bills behind the counter, clearly preparing to close shop. Ruby red strands drifted around his body. His baggy eyes looked us over.

"If you have something to sell, you'll have to come back tomorrow. I'm closing."

"Just looking."

Caelus swept past him to a glass case beside the counter. Inside were valuables—rings, necklaces, earrings—and Caelus raked our eyes over the lot. A few of the pieces had colorful threads waving gently around them. What was he searching for? As soon as I framed the question in my mind, the answer floated to the forefront. I had forgotten that our minds were linked.

Caelus was searching for artifacts. I probed deeper to find out what that meant. Caelus shook our head in irritation but didn't stop me from snooping.

Artifacts, according to Caelus' thoughts, were physical objects imbued with the power of an elemental spirit. Unlike amulets, which were objects with magical properties from human-made spells, artifacts were far more powerful. They had all been made thousands of years ago when elementals had walked freely on Earth. And, as Caelus' emotions clearly revealed, they did not belong on Earth. Their presence on our plane of existence threatened the balance of the worlds.

I didn't understand what that meant, but I knew one thing.

You won't find ancient relics in a pawnshop, I thought at him loudly. *Look in a museum.*

Caelus jerked our head up at my pronouncement, and he wrinkled our forehead.

"Damn it," he muttered.

"What was that?" the man behind the counter said. "Can I help you find something?"

"No," Caelus said brusquely. "I'm done here."

He marched to the door and flung it open. Our body took a deep breath and let it out in a frustrated sigh. I pushed my threads out of our arm again.

"Is that your grand mission?" I asked. I tried to keep my sarcasm in check but didn't succeed. "The master plan? Check in every pawnshop for ancient relics that might or might not have powers? You'll be here for a while."

"You wouldn't understand, petty human," he snarled. "Humans know nothing of balance."

"Touchy. Is that why you made me follow Amanda? Did she have an artifact?"

42

"Only a pitiful amulet," he said. "A human-made magical object, too weak to upset the balance."

"Too bad you didn't have a human ally who could help you complete your mission. Someone who knows a lot about magical objects. Someone who has been studying them her whole life." I gave an exaggerated sigh—a token gesture since I wasn't breathing in my strand form—and shrugged. "I wonder where you could find someone like that."

Caelus' arrested look was the last thing I saw before I slid back into our body and concentrated my strands at our stomach. I corralled my thoughts so Caelus wouldn't know what I was planning. I gave him three seconds to ponder my comment. Two. One.

I struck. With the words of a pre-Colonial Oromo spell racing through my mind, I spread my strands outward and surrounded Caelus' silver threads. I squeezed tightly, forcing his silver into the center of our body and shouting the words of the containment spell in my mind. I was surprised it worked, but Caelus hadn't expected me to fight.

Within seconds, he was subdued. I repeated the spell once more for security, then added a short adjustment of my own invention to make sure Caelus stayed quiet.

I panted with my hands on my knees, but a triumphant grin stole over my features. I was in command once more. Never again would I relax my guard. I couldn't have Caelus control my life.

It was getting late, so I took my loaf of bread and tarts and wandered back to my condo, stopping at a corner store for butter and jam. I could have used a larger dinner—fending off potential rapists was hungry work—but I didn't feel like waiting in a restaurant. Sampling from food trucks in a nearby park was too classless for my liking, and I would never touch fast food, so bread and jam would have to do.

My footsteps dragged as I shuffled into the elevator and pressed the top-floor button with a sigh. Day one as Morgan

Leigh Feynman had been tiring. I still didn't know what I would do with my new lease on life, but I sure as hell would do something. Working at the women's center was interesting—I enjoyed connecting with that woman and her baby today—but it didn't feel like enough.

Now that I was young again, I wanted to grab life by the horns. I wanted to throw myself into everything I could find. I couldn't let fear and propriety rule my life like it had for decades. Even in the last few years, when I'd started the organization that had drawn the elementals to Earth, I'd still been fettered by the ropes of societal pressures and self-expectations. I didn't want to regret the things I hadn't done.

But what did that mean? What would I do with my second chance at this wild and precious life?

The glow of awe and gratitude on Amanda's face struck me. I wanted to make that happen again. I wanted to make a real difference in other women's lives, something bigger and bolder than the center. I wanted them to feel safe.

I still didn't know how to make that happen, but I would figure it out. I had been avoiding mirrors today because it was such a shock to see that youthful, unfamiliar face staring back with my eyes. Now, in the elevator's mirrored wall, I glanced at my image. Instead of the stern nod of resolution I'd been planning to give myself, my eyes narrowed.

Goals were all well and good, but a haircut was first on my list for tomorrow.

I polished off the rest of my sourdough loaf in the morning. It was the perfect blend of airy and chewy with a crust to die for. Plus, my slender waist dared me to finish it. I'd promised myself last night that I would take more risks and say no less. It started with that gorgeous bread.

Stomach satisfied, I dressed and left my condo. The day

was waiting, whatever it might hold. Haircut first. Then, who knew? I would figure it out.

I almost tripped on a can of paint outside my unit's door. I cursed and leaped aside, grateful for my youthful nimbleness. I picked up the tin and peered at it in puzzlement. Someone had taped a paintbrush, stir stick, and note to the top. The note read:

Nice to meet you yesterday, neighbor. I found the paint for your balcony! Have a great day. Doug.

A strange sensation wriggled in my stomach, and it took me a minute to realize it wasn't Caelus acting up. Guilt for my behavior toward Doug yesterday stole through me. I had been borderline unpleasant, and I still wasn't sure why. What if he had simply been trying to be neighborly?

Some part of me protested that this gesture didn't rule out ulterior motives. He could be lulling me into a false sense of security. I shook my head to clear it of the intrusive thoughts, tucked the paint tin inside my door, and walked to the elevator with a spring in my step from the kindness of strangers.

I walked to the salon I had spotted yesterday, Cut Right. It was only two blocks away, and I felt refreshed when I arrived despite threatening storm clouds swirling from the north. There was a wait for drop-in customers, so I settled in a chair to pass the time. With a grin, I pulled out my phone and touched the search bar. If I looked twenty-something, I might as well act my new age. Besides, I had things to investigate.

A quick search brought me to a police report listing, and I scanned it for incidents of assaults against women. I would love to find more women to save like I had Amanda. The problem was, I didn't know how to be at the right place at the right time. The report listing was for events that had already occurred and didn't help me now. There were some obvious trouble spots—as a Vancouverite, I could name a few alleys and parks that were off-limits to sensible women—but the only other option was to hang around at night like some grown-up

Peter Parker. I amused myself for a moment by imagining potential costumes.

Maybe I was coming at this from the wrong angle. Could I get creative? Where else were women frequently disadvantaged? I could ask women at the center for addresses of their abusers, or maybe I could act as behind-the-scenes pressure during divorce trials.

Neither option was particularly attractive. I might have abilities—if I could contain Caelus—but I needed a better focus for them. I tucked my phone in my pocket and leaned back. The answer would come to me eventually, I was sure. Opportunity often came dressed in overalls and looked like work, but I was never afraid of getting my hands dirty. I would have to keep my eyes open, that was all.

The salon was full of the sound of hairdryers and women chatting. One hairdresser chopped locks of black hair from a young girl's shoulder-length bob, another painted dye over foil on an older woman's wet tresses, and another rubbed shampoo into a man's scalp at the sink. A disgruntled looking teenage girl swept hair off the floor.

"Don't forget the corner behind the sinks, Miranda," the woman painting dye instructed the sweeper. Her wavy brown hair was carefully pulled into a high ponytail, and her soft features in a round face were belayed by sharp eyes. "I don't want to find hair over there like I did yesterday."

Miranda nodded with a tight mouth and shuffled to the indicated corner. Her pale brown hair was pulled back with a hairband so that her annoyed features were visible. There was clearly no love lost between those two.

The first hairdresser finished up with the young girl and walked over to me with a smile. She was plump with a friendly look. Her hair was styled in a bouncy array of long, platinum blond curls. While I admired the cut, I decided against getting my hair colored today. It was too wild for me.

But that wasn't what I had told myself this morning. What

had happened to not saying no? A little hair dye was hardly a huge risk, but memories of Peter's chastisements when I had colored my hair for the first and only time during our marriage echoed over the years. I firmly pushed them aside and answered the woman's smile.

"Hello, and welcome to Cut Right. I'm Joy."

"Good morning. I need a new look. I'm open to suggestions."

Joy's eyes gleamed.

"Right this way."

Joy flipped through a few books and pointed to one hairstyle after another. It was overwhelming, so I pointed at one at random.

"That one will do. Whatever color you think would look good."

I clenched my nails into my palms at giving the reins to Joy. She rubbed her hands together with undisguised glee.

"Not too wild, Joy," the woman with the dye said. "I'm watching."

"You're always watching, Rosemary," Joy said with a roll of her eyes. "Spare me the lecture. Have I ever had a customer complain?"

Rosemary huffed but went back to her foils. Joy leaned down to whisper to me.

"You're in good hands, I promise."

I smiled weakly and bit my tongue.

It took a couple of hours to dye, wash, and cut my hair. I avoided watching the process and instead studied the hairdressers. They were all young, ranging from Miranda the sweeper at seventeen or eighteen to Rosemary at no more than twenty-five. They were clearly close, with the rapport of siblings, but there was tired animosity under the jibes. I wondered how long they had all been working there.

Joy chatted incessantly, sometimes to me, sometimes to Rosemary or the other hairdressers, sometimes to other customers waiting at the front. I often tuned her out, but when she mentioned a recent incident, my ears perked up.

"I heard it on the news this morning, I have the radio on my phone, you see, it makes the bus ride go by so much quicker, I tried those streaming apps for music, but I really like morning talk shows and the radio is great for that. They said there was an explosion in Kitsilano, on some beachside property where they were developing a crazy big house. Some of the workers were killed, even. Can you imagine? Going about your work and suddenly boom! Just like that."

"Did they find out who it was? Who caused the explosion?" I asked, interested. If I weren't mistaken, that "crazy big house" was the temple where I had awoken in my new body the other night. I was curious what the news was reporting about the incident.

"Doesn't really matter, does it? They'll find out, I'm sure. Likely it was an accident, but even if not, well, there's a demon and an angel on everyone's shoulder, isn't there? I know I struggle with mine, it's like a tug-of-war up there sometimes." Joy laughed lightly.

I would have to look up the news later. I liked to stay informed, and while Joy's opinion was sweet in her innocence, I knew there were always those who leaned more toward the demon than the angel.

CHAPTER VI

After Joy's ministrations, the woman in the mirror was gorgeous, confident, and stylish. Gone were the limp, dull locks with ratty split ends. Instead, she sported thick, mahogany tresses with subtle lowlights that cascaded in loose waves. My shoulders straightened as I left the salon, and my fingers ran through my smooth hair. If that were what saying yes felt like, I could get used to it.

I wandered down the street, unsure of my destination but enjoying the fresh breeze. Rain hadn't yet materialized, although billowing clouds were closer than ever, and a haze over the North Shore told me that my hair wouldn't look good for long. Maybe my next stop should be at a store that sold umbrellas.

My eyes were drawn to a large wooden sign hanging above a shop window. It was for the bakery, Upper Crust, and the name was carved into wood and painted cream and brown with the relief of a loaf of bread adorning the bottom.

My stomach rumbled. I was out of bread after my indulgence this morning, and lemon tarts called to me with their siren song. I ran across the road on light feet between traffic and pulled open the tinkling door with gusto.

The pre-lunch crowd was light, and only two tables were occupied. I ordered a loaf of cheese bread that I couldn't resist and three lemon tarts, mindful of the baker's teasing yesterday. After I paid, I found a table and opened my box of baked goods with eager fingers.

"Back already? I'm flattered," the baker's voice said.

I looked at the baker's face. It was a long way up to see his half-grin. My betraying stomach fluttered at seeing him again, but I squashed the sensation with an iron will.

"What can I say? They're addictive," I said. "Maybe you laced them with something."

49

I had meant it as a joke, but the baker's face tightened before he forced out a laugh.

"Yeah, that must be it. Not my baking skills."

I smiled and waved at the empty seat across from me. Normally, I wouldn't encourage a man to be so forward, but I was in an open mood. *Don't say no*, I reminded myself. Besides, I felt bad about the drug joke that he had taken badly. My invitation had nothing to do with the squirming in my gut.

He graced me with a smile that lit his whole face and sat with a contented sigh.

"I'm Jerome, by the way." He held out his hand, and I took it.

"Morgan," I said. The name came easier to me today. Saying the name aloud brought a fuzzy memory of long red skirts and a small boy with a mop of curly brown hair. I shook my head to clear it of the intrusion.

He leaned forward with a frown.

"You're hurt," he said. "Your cheek. Are you okay? What happened?"

I touched the bruise with self-conscious fingers and turned my head away. It was an unconscious gesture from my married years—for the last few months, Peter's abuse had slid from emotional to physical—then I grew angry with myself. I had nothing to be ashamed of, not then, and not now. I straightened my head.

"Got into a fight," I said lightly. "You should see the other guy."

He let out a huff of laughter, but his eyes were still worried.

"You sure you're okay?"

I nodded.

"There was an assault. A man had pinned a woman in a back alley a few blocks from here. I ran to help. He smacked me, but I managed to fend him off and we got away."

Jerome looked impressed.

"That takes some balls." He looked embarrassed. "I mean,

that was brave. Did you call the cops?"

"She didn't want to," I said. "I respected her decision."

"Rough streets," he said with a shake of his head and a sad look in his eyes. "I'm sorry you had to go through that." He glanced back at the kitchen then stood. "I need to go, my bread is almost done. It was nice meeting you, Morgan."

"You too."

He walked behind the counter and strode to the sink to wash his hands. I took a bite of lemon tart. Even after my invitation to sit, Jerome was still nothing but a gentleman. It surprised the new, suspicious part of me. Did he truly have no motive? Surely the demon on his shoulder would turn up sometime, as it seemed to with all men eventually.

That afternoon, I went back to the women's center as promised. I hoped that helping at my favorite cause would spark some ideas. There was a need for laundry duty that day, and I dug into my chores with zeal. Many years had passed since I'd worked a washing machine, and I found the simple task monotonous but invigorating. My life, although uncertain and wholly new, felt more authentic than my old one ever had.

I shopped for necessities the next morning then went back to the center in the afternoon, and they gratefully accepted my willing hands. At dusk, I waved goodbye to Mary, the head volunteer coordinator with whom I had only ever dealt as a sponsor before, and stepped into the gathering gloom with my new umbrella. It had been a much-needed purchase, as the rain in Vancouver never sprinkled when it could pour. Tonight was no exception, and the air was heavy with cold dampness even under my umbrella.

I vowed to stop at a Thai restaurant for takeout. It was a decent establishment, but I pointed my steps toward it with mild trepidation. My meals for years had been cooked by a chef or myself in my well-appointed kitchen, and I wasn't used to mucking in with everyone else at a popular eatery.

I squared my shoulders.

"No regrets," I told myself firmly. I wanted to do more, not less. I couldn't let fear rule me. Not anymore.

I braved the takeout counter illuminated with cheery Christmas décor and hustled home through pelting rain. A smile crossed my face as I turned my key in the lock. My little condo felt like home now. Only a few days had passed, but I was more comfortable here than in my mansion on Marine Drive. Morgan suited me.

But winter evenings were long, and after my Thai food had disappeared into my hungry mouth, I was at loose ends. There was no work to distract me, no books to read, and the only entertainment was my phone. After five minutes of reading insipid news, I leaped up.

"New life, new me," I said out loud in the quiet room. "Take life by the horns."

I raced to my closet and drew out the heavy-duty raincoat I had purchased. It was black, fitted with a hood, and completely impermeable to the weather. Too bad I couldn't say the same for my pants, but jeans dried. I slipped on rainboots and ventured into the dark.

I had laughed earlier about pulling a Spiderman, patrolling the streets at night for wrongdoers, but here I was, peering down dark alleys in hope or fear of finding trouble. I didn't know what I wanted: to discover that my new neighborhood was a peaceful one, or to step in and stop a crime. I vacillated between the two.

My taste of Caelus' power had been intoxicating. Although I was far from an expert, indeed had only pushed around a bit of wind, I could still imagine the possibilities. And, with my modified spell keeping Caelus contained, I should have access to his powers without the threat of him taking over. In theory, anyway.

52

At that thought, I raised my hand and summoned silver strands from the tight cluster at my stomach. My burgundy threads teased them out and brought them to my hand through willpower alone. I watched, elated, as they twisted with my own. That was easy. I could get used to it.

With a few silver threads released from their bonds, my vision filled with the threads of the world. The air around me danced silver and blue from rain and air. A passing stranger was draped with rusty red strands, and a tree in the sidewalk glowed with threads of sinuous green that snaked around white twinkle lights wrapping each branch. Two flies buzzed past, trailing tiny purple strands.

It was beautiful, foreign, like I was witnessing something I shouldn't, peeling back the curtain on a play and discovering the pulleys and cables that moved the set. I reached out and pulled on a silver strand in midair. A gust of breeze hit my cheek, and my face cracked in a smile. A few more tugs, and wind pelted rain into my face. I laughed and let go, and the gust halted.

This was power. I had been searching for this for years. Gaining abilities like this were why I had created my ill-fated organization. In fact, scanty memories of my past lives told me that I had been searching for powers like this for centuries, ever since I had met Merlin in fifth century Wales and he had shown me his tricks. From the little I could remember, I had longed for them.

I hadn't cared about manipulating the elements. It was an interesting ability, to be sure, but minorly so. No, I had wanted what it symbolized: freedom. The freedom to choose my own path, the freedom to escape oppressors, the freedom to be who I wanted to be. Although I couldn't remember much from my past, many of the memories I did have were of a woman struggling to break free of her bonds. History had rarely been kind to a strong-willed woman.

But with superhuman powers, I would be the one in control.

No one would stand in my way.

What else could an elemental of the air do? I pulled a few air threads in experimentation. Water strands from the ever-present rain followed them, and an idea crossed my mind. I concentrated with intent, twisted my fingers, and held my breath.

A cloud of condensation twisted sinuously before my face like a tiny tornado in midair. A huff of laughter burst out of me, and a passerby peeked from underneath her umbrella to stare at the woman laughing by herself. Quickly, I waved my hand through the air and dispersed the tornado's air threads, and the woman walked on.

My stomach rolled over and my shoulders tightened. Caelus was stirring. I chanted the containment spell under my breath and the sensation slowed. If I wanted access to these strange powers, my new life would have to be a careful balance between using my new abilities and keeping Caelus in check.

I kept walking. The streets cleared as people finished their dinners and shopping and wandered home. The windows of a row of shops were decorated with white winter scenes drawn with artificial snow, but the back alley behind the row was empty and cheerless. Rain hammered against my hood, and I turned my steps toward the condo. This was silly. Wandering the streets late at night would accomplish nothing. I would have to think harder about how to make a difference in other women's lives.

A crash and a muffled shout reached my ears even through the pounding rain. My heart thumped loudly, and I raced toward the sound. Was my vigil not in vain?

CHAPTER VII

Light streamed from the open back door of a shop. Two figures struggled, and the scene was eerily similar to Amanda's attack. A man held onto the woman's forearm while he groped her neck. She punched and scratched whatever she could reach, but he didn't react at all. Was he high like the last one must have been?

The woman kicked her opponent's knee with a practiced foot. The man's leg buckled upon impact, but his face remained stoic, and he kept hold of the woman's arm with an immovable grip. The only indication that the kick did any damage was that he favored his good leg. How could he not react to the pain?

The woman screamed in anger and slammed her hand into the man's nose then twisted her arm with an efficient motion to dislodge his grip. It was clear she knew what she was doing, but the man's imperviousness to pain was hampering her. He merely grabbed her forearm with his other hand without a visible reaction to the blood streaming from his broken nose.

The woman screamed again, but now the sound was tinged with fear. The man reached for her neck and she twisted wildly like a feral cat.

I pulled Caelus' silver strands, and they flowed to my fingers. The thug was surrounded by magenta threads, and the woman writhed with spiky cream strands that pulsed with her fear and anger. She wore a red apron from the coffeeshop behind her. She must have been taking the garbage out when the thug attacked.

At the sight of the woman's mistreatment, a pulse of rage zinged through my body like an electric current. The emotion was unfamiliar to my normally calm and controlled self, and I took a second to wrestle with my anger toward the thug before I threw the nearest air strands toward him.

A gust of wind shot toward the two, visible to my eyes as a boiling mass of silver strands. It hit the thug in the back, and he spun to the ground with a thud. The wind spilled over to pummel the woman in the face and sent her countless black braids flinging every which way. I vowed to practice my skills tomorrow.

"Go!" I shouted at the woman. She gave the man a terrified glance before scrambling to her feet and stepping into a fighting stance beside me.

I wanted to grab her arm and run to safety, but blood pounded in my ears and my stomach tightened into a knot of rage. Why should this scum walk free when I had the power to stop him?

Silver strands on my arms bubbled and twisted. Caelus was trying to emerge. I shoved him back with a snarl, but in my moment of distraction, the man stumbled to his feet and hobbled away from us. I threw another blast of rain-soaked air at him. He stumbled but kept shuffling away and was soon out of sight.

I heaved a breath, not sure whether to be glad he was gone or disappointed that I had missed my opportunity for justice.

"He's gone," the woman said in a wondering voice. Her shirt was plastered to her body from the pelting rain, but she gazed at me with awe. "You did that. Thank you. I'm Denise."

"I spooked him, I guess." I didn't want to explain about my powers, but Denise shook her head with a smile.

"No, you're the woman who helped Amanda the other night. She figured you had an amulet of power, a really strong one. Our very own Cormorant Drive vigilante. How could we be so lucky?"

Damn it. Another member of this secret society. How could I be so unlucky? I backed away.

"You're welcome. I need to go home now. Good night."

"No, wait." Denise seemed genuinely distressed at my rapid exit, so I halted. "Please, come see Rosemary. She really

56

wants to meet you. She says it's for a good cause. Please, just come and talk to her?"

I had intended to say no firmly but kindly, but Denise's pleading face and her promise of a good cause tugged at my heartstrings. I did need something to do, something I was proud of doing. I doubted this Rosemary held any answers, but it couldn't hurt to hear her out. It wasn't like I was too busy.

"Okay," I said with a sigh. "I'll meet Rosemary."

Denise closed the coffeeshop with impressive speed and less than impressive cleanliness then led me north. Five blocks through the driving rain felt like fifty, and with every step I regretted my rash decision to follow Denise. A cup of tea made with my new kettle and my feet tucked up on my cozy couch was far more appealing than slogging through this deluge, raincoat or no.

Finally, Denise opened the gate to a small bungalow on a street densely populated with houses in various states of disrepair. This little cottage needed work—even in the darkness, copious moss was evident on the roof—but the grass was carefully mowed, and the door had a fresh coat of red paint.

Denise knocked three times in rapid succession, then followed it with two more knocks after a pause. I raised an eyebrow but said nothing. Coded knocks? Would Denise murmur a password to the inhabitant next and give her a secret handshake?

The knock must have been enough of an assurance, for the door swung open wide. To my surprise, the head hairdresser from Cut Right stood silhouetted against a warm glow from the living room beyond. It was incredibly inviting to my bedraggled self.

"Denise," the hairdresser said with a frown. Her eyes

flicked to me. "It's late. Is everything okay?"

"No, it's not. Rosemary, this is—" Denise turned to me. "I'm sorry, I forgot to ask your name."

"It's Morgan," I said, unwilling to give them more than that. I was still debating whether to turn tail and head for home. All my reasons for not touching a secret society with a ten-foot barge pole were flashing neon signs in my face.

"Morgan, this is Rosemary. Morgan just saved me from an attacker. She's the same woman who helped Amanda the other night. She has abilities."

Rosemary visibly relaxed.

"Morgan. Thank you so much for saving my sisters. I am the head of our sisterhood." Denise jolted at the revelation of the "sisterhood", but Rosemary smiled serenely then stepped back and waved us into the house. "Where are my manners? Please, come in and make yourselves comfortable. I'll put the kettle on."

If Rosemary were willing to serve tea, I could pretend to listen for a few minutes. Denise and I peeled off our raincoats and hung them on hooks in the entryway, then Denise grabbed a strange stone embedded in a strap of oiled leather that hung on a hook beside the door. She grinned at me.

"Hold still."

I watched in fascination as she passed the stone over my pant legs and whispered unintelligible words. My legs warmed almost unbearably. With a sizzling sound, clouds of water puffed off the fabric and wafted into the air. I ran my hands over my now-cool thighs.

"They're dry," I said in wonder.

"Amulets are powerful tools. But you know all about that, don't you?"

I did, in fact, know about amulets. I had made it my life's work to learn about the elemental plane through studying the world's religions and traditions. Tokens of spiritual intent were rampant, and I had collected many in my travels and used some

58

in rituals.

But to use an amulet as a precise tool, that was something new. I didn't want to show all my cards, though, so I gave Denise an enigmatic look. She nodded.

"I thought so. Come in."

I settled in a large armchair covered with a woven blanket, and Denise wriggled into a corner of the couch like it was her accustomed spot. Rosemary emerged from the kitchen with a steaming pot of tea and a plate of digestive biscuits, and I had to hold my back straight to avoid melting into a puddle of relief.

After Rosemary passed me a fragrant cup of tea, she sat on the couch beside Denise with her own cup and gazed at me, her eyes in her round, full-lipped face bright and piercing.

"Thank you for coming, Morgan. This is all very strange to you, I'm sure. Maybe a little less strange than to some, since you have your own talents."

"Denise said something about amulets of power and a good cause? Consider me intrigued but wary."

"Of course." Rosemary took a sip of her tea and made a face. "Too hot. We are a sisterhood dedicated to the preservation of—well, it's confidential. All I can say is that protecting my sisters is vital. Most of us were raised to become the current sisters, and we have all taken vows of solidarity and commitment to the cause."

"Rosemary," Denise said in a scandalized tone. "Why are you telling Morgan about that? I know she saved Amanda and me, but we still don't know anything about her."

Rosemary looked discomfited, but after some hesitation, she waved away Denise's concerns.

"Morgan has as much to hide as we do, given the powers she's exhibited. Besides, she feels trustworthy, and I'm an excellent judge of character." Denise subsided into the couch with a disgruntled expression, and Rosemary turned to me again.

"Care to elaborate on the cause in question?" I asked.

Rosemary shook her head with a wry smile.

"I hope you will forgive me, but I'd like to know you better before I trust you with that information. Denise has a point, after all. Anyway, our cause isn't relevant to the job. Each sister—there are nine of us—wears a necklace."

She pulled out a large golden locket dangling from a fine chain. After Rosemary's glare, Denise extracted an identical locket from her shirt.

"Honestly," Rosemary continued. "The sisterhood sounds more grandiose than it is. No one has attacked a sister for decades, and although we train to protect the lockets, we mainly live normal lives. However, in the past week, three of our sisters have been attacked by men intent on stealing the necklaces. You saved Amanda and Denise, but our sister Wanda's locket was stolen. We should have been able to handle these men. We train in self-defense all the time." Rosemary scowled, and Denise looked affronted.

"I don't know about the others, but I did everything right. It was like the guy couldn't feel pain. Every time I hit him, he didn't react. It was so frustrating. My attacks should have worked."

"It's true," I said in Denise's defense when Rosemary looked skeptical. "I wondered if he were on drugs of some sort."

"Well, that might explain Denise, and Wanda had apparently been drinking which slowed her reactions, but I expect Amanda's attack was from her lackluster training." Rosemary scowled at the thought of her wayward sisters and took a sip of tea. "She needs to work harder. In any event, we are clearly being targeted, and we don't know why or even by whom. As the eldest of our nine sisters, I am doing my best to solve the mystery, but I could really use some more muscle."

"Why don't we ask the motherhood for help?" Denise interrupted. "We aren't alone in this."

Rosemary wrinkled her nose at the suggestion.

"There's no need to bother the motherhood," she said sharply. "If I don't prove that I can solve trifling problems like this, how can the motherhood trust that I'm worthy for the next step?" Rosemary put her cup down. Her face changed from hesitant to decided. "And how can I ignore the arrival of Morgan in our hour of need? It feels fated. She has something we don't, something that allowed her to take on these mysterious attackers."

She paused, as if to give me a chance to explain myself. I felt no such compulsion. Caelus was my secret to keep. Rosemary shrugged.

"Whatever your talents are," she continued. "I am grateful for them. They clearly work when our amulets and training don't. Please, wait here. I have something I want to try."

Rosemary rose from the couch and walked swiftly to the hallway. She appeared a moment later with a ring clasped in her hand then kneeled on the floor beside me.

"May I?" she said with her hand out. "This amulet detects purity of heart. If you have bad intentions toward me, your hand will glow green. Pure intentions, and it will glow golden."

Normally, I would decline being tested for no purpose. What was it to Rosemary if I were "pure of heart"? But the lure of visible magic overwhelmed any disdain I felt for the process.

"You may."

Rosemary nodded and gripped my palm with her cool fingers. The ring pressed into my skin. Rosemary chanted a verse in an unknown language under her breath.

My hands slowly lit up as if the setting sun touched their skin. Rosemary smiled and let go.

"We need help," she said. "As you saw, my sisters are being targeted by attackers that are more than their match. Your abilities might tip the scale in our favor. Since you have proved

61

yourself, I would be honored if you accepted the temporary role of sisterhood protector."

I had no idea what the role of sisterhood protector entailed, but the title had a nice ring to it.

"What would you expect me to do?" I said after a pause. "Roaming the streets isn't very efficient. I got lucky with Amanda and Denise."

"We can work out a strategy," Rosemary assured me. "So far, the attacks have centered around the row of shops where the sisterhood's headquarters are. If you patrol the area in the evenings—that's when the other attacks happened—that would be the most efficient. You would be present and offer protection at those times. If we can catch the culprit and make him talk, so much the better, but the necklaces and my sisters' safety come first."

"This sisterhood," I said slowly. "I'm not in the market to join any secret society right now." Or ever. Once in a lifetime was enough to teach me the drawbacks.

Rosemary shook her head vigorously as soon as I finished speaking.

"No, no, I would never expect you to, and we don't often recruit. This is strictly a contractor position. We have a fund, and I can offer you a competitive per diem pay rate. Give me a minute to write a contract."

Rosemary took a piece of paper off the side table, wrote intently for a few minutes, then handed it to me along with a pen. I looked over the document, impressed. She was a woman after my own heart. The contract was meticulously drafted, despite its quick composition. I read it through, crossed out the pay—which was handsome, but I couldn't pass up an opportunity to negotiate—and wrote a new number. Rosemary took the paper and narrowed her eyes at the amount. She wrote a counteroffer and showed it to me.

"That will do," I said and signed the contract.

Rosemary smiled and Denise looked sidelong at her eldest

sister.

"I guess you're in the fold now," she said to me. "We aren't allowed to tell just anyone about our sisterhood." She sighed. "I have to admit, I'll breathe easier now that someone else has our backs. I've always felt confident in my abilities, but I had no game against this man tonight."

"Leave me your contact information, and I'll send you the details and a copy of the contract," Rosemary said. "Thank you for agreeing to work for us, Morgan. We'll all feel better under your protection. Just one more proviso: please keep the sisterhood a secret. We work hard to slip under the radar."

"Of course." If anyone understood, it was me. And it wasn't as if I knew anything tangible. I had no idea why these women had banded together, but I was curious to find out more.

I left a few minutes later—my tea needed finishing, after all—and strolled back to my condo, a mixture of anxiety and elation twisting in my gut. Caelus' presence didn't help, and I recited the spell under my breath to make sure he stayed put.

This was an opportunity, the opportunity I had been waiting for. It would be hard work, but I was no stranger to that. Following nine women and fending off predators would keep me busy, and learning how to use my new abilities would eat up whatever time was left.

But it wasn't as if I had other obligations. A little volunteering on the side and quality time with my kettle and couch were all that currently occupied my time. This was a purpose-built challenge gift-wrapped for me, and I wasn't going to waste it. Instead of random vigilante justice, I would focus on protecting vulnerable women.

As the young folks said, I was ready to kick some ass.

CHAPTER VIII

The next morning, while I sipped coffee made with my newly purchased French press, a message pinged on my phone. It was a text from Rosemary containing pictures of all nine women in the sisterhood along with their names and their daily schedules. I glanced through the images, noting their youth. No one was over twenty-five, and some were as young as seventeen. Indeed, the youngest two went to a nearby private school where they played on the tennis team, along with another member who was the coach.

I idly wondered how many secret societies were hidden in plain sight around the city, then I took a piece of paper and pen and planned my week. First up was some training—I had to figure out how to use my powers better if I were basing my employment off them—then I would visit each woman at work. Tonight, I would patrol the shop row as some of the sisters traveled home in the dark of an early December drizzle.

A thrill chased over my skin at the prospect of catching a thug in the act. These women were being targeted, so it stood to reason that another attack would happen soon. I hoped I would be there to stop it. I wanted to be the one to dish out retribution. After too many humiliating years under Peter's thumb, being on the powerful end of the stick would be sweet indeed.

I shook my head at the intrusive memory, foreign after so many years. Why was I so fixated on my past lately?

Rosemary was clear that I was the brawn, and that she would handle the mystery of motive, but I had brains of my own to draw conclusions with. These men had somehow discovered that the sisters' necklaces were important, and I would have to discuss this mystery with Rosemary. Maybe a jilted lover wanted to disturb the sisters' mission.

I texted Rosemary, telling her to give my phone number to

the sisters in case of trouble. After that message had sent, I added another one, asking for names and pictures of any current or previous partners of the sisters.

It was time to get a handle on my borrowed powers. I slipped on my raincoat, although the weather looked less rainy than blustery today, and locked my condo door behind me. At the elevator, a woman in her mid-thirties holding a toddler by the hand exited. She smiled at me.

"You must be the new neighbor. Did Doug find the paint for you?"

I blinked in surprise.

"Yes, he did."

"He's such a lovely man. So thoughtful." The woman turned to her protesting son and said, "Hush, Will. We'll have some fish crackers once we're inside."

The toddler pulled his mother to their door, and I entered the open elevator with misgiving. I had been too hard on Doug earlier.

A wash of fear and loathing swept over me at the memory of Doug. Visions of his potential motives scuttled through my mind, each more repulsive than the last. I swallowed hard. Why was I reacting to his friendly overtures so badly?

Memories of my ex-husband swam to the forefront, and my teeth gritted. Was I having a relapse of ambivalence toward men because of my previous trauma under Peter's thumb? I thought I had vanquished those demons years ago. Had the strain of switching to a new body stirred up old emotions?

The elevator door opened with a ping and I stepped out, determined to put my traitorous thoughts aside. I had more control over myself than this.

With my hood up against the wind, I aimed my steps to a park two blocks away from the main strip. It was little more than a patch of grass and a swing set, but it was empty on this stormy weekday. I lifted my hands in preparation and pondered my first move.

My willpower drew out Caelus' silver strands until my vision blossomed with the threads of the world. The fragile beauty of gently waving strands took my breath away. My fingers caressed silver that ran past me in a rushing river. The threads were cool and smooth, and I marveled that I'd never felt them before.

My eyes narrowed, and my fingers pinched a few threads. I twitched my hand. Instantly, a cluster of dried maple leaves swirled into the air on a gust of threads and twisted in a tiny tornado.

My smile threatened to split my face wide. I made the tornado larger until it towered over me, then I pushed it forward with a tweak of my fingers. It traveled around the swing set until my laugh of exultation broke my concentration, and the tornado disintegrated into a drifting pile of dead leaves.

What else could I do? My imagination felt like the only real limit. What could I do to gain the upper hand in a fight? My new role was as a security guard, after all.

I gathered the nearest wind threads and directed them to a branch on the ground the length of my arm. With a drunken twirl, it rose and wobbled like a helicopter uncertain where to fly next. With a thought and a twitch, I sent the branch careening into the trunk of its parent tree. It crashed with a cracking thud and dropped into pieces on the ground.

I must have used more energy and concentration than I had expected, because I was startled when the silver knot at my stomach burst outward and flowed over my body in a metallic stream. Quicker than I could react, the strands formed a human torso from the threads on my arm.

Caelus glowered at me, his head still resembling the man who had tried to help me on my first day in this new body.

"Do you not see the hypocrisy of this?" he said without preamble. "I have examined your memories in detail, and you were recently possessed by an earth elemental, except that you were the one suppressed. This time, you are subjugating me, and I've had enough. Release me at once, or I will take over by force. The pain will be immense."

I pushed aside Caelus' comment about hypocrisy. It was either him or me controlling this body. Never again would I submit myself to someone else's whims.

"I would be more frightened, except that your last takeover ended with me on top. Do your worst, Caelus. I'm ready for you."

His face contorted in a grimace of rage and concentration before he dissolved into my body, but I was ready for him. I chanted the modified spell again, tucking extra intent into my words and pouring all my disgust for my previous incarceration into the spell.

He put up a fight—pinpricks of pain lanced my skin until I wanted to scream—but it was only a matter of a minute before he twisted into his silver knot at my stomach once more. I breathed heavily for another minute, testing my defenses to make sure they were sound, then I straightened my hood. That was enough practice for today. The sisterhood awaited my help.

I walked three blocks to Cut Right and circled the area to assess the building. The salon was in the middle of a row of connected shops, with the storefronts facing Cormorant Drive and an alley along the back where cars and dumpsters were parked. Each store had an alley door, and there were plenty of places to hide in the cluttered back. This section would bear extra watching. I would recommend to Rosemary that her sisters use the front door when they could.

There wasn't much else to see from the outside, so I entered the salon and a chime sounded. The scent of perfumed shampoo and dry heat from hairdryers hit me in the face like a sachet of hot potpourri. The shop was quiet at this early hour, and only two customers were seated before the long mirror. Rosemary stood at the counter sorting paperwork, but she looked up at my entrance. Her eyes brightened.

"Morgan, good to see you. Please, come meet the others."

"I know them from pictures, but it will be nice to connect in person."

I followed Rosemary to the hairdresser who had cut my own locks a few days before. She was trimming the bangs of a child whose mother sat in the waiting area. She looked up and her eyes raked over my hair.

"That looks like my handiwork," she said with a smile. "Still working for you?"

"Great, thanks."

"Joy," Rosemary said firmly before the other woman could derail the conversation. "This is Morgan. She'll be helping us with security at night. Morgan, this is Joy."

Joy touched her chest with an absentminded gesture. A long gold chain plunged below the neckline of her fire-engine red shirt.

"Thank you so much for taking this on, Morgan. We've been so worried. After Amanda, then Wanda and Denise, we've been wondering who will be next."

"That's enough, Joy," Rosemary said with a forced smile. "We'll leave you to your customer. Mindy doesn't want to hear our boring adult talk, does she?"

The little girl stared at us with wide eyes. Joy rested her hands on the girl's shoulders.

"Of course not. And we're almost done! You're looking so pretty with your beautifully trimmed hair."

Rosemary took my elbow and guided me away from Joy toward the teenager straightening conditioner bottles on a shelf. Her brown hair was tied back in a messy bun, and delicate features in her narrow, pale face were pinched with distaste. She turned at our approach, and my eyes flickered to the necklace she wore exposed on her chest. The locket was

68

identical to Rosemary's.

"Miranda, meet Morgan," Rosemary said. She beckoned to the last woman who was trimming the top fuzz on an elderly man's head. Her straight black hair with orange-tinted highlights gleamed under the salon's lights, and heavy black brows dominated her dusky complexion. "Shu, you too. She'll just be a moment, Mr. Pascal."

Shu looked disgruntled but patted Mr. Pascal's shoulder and sidled over.

"Nice to meet you, Morgan," Shu said quickly. To Rosemary she said in a hiss, "I need to get back to my customer. Just because you only trust me to do the old men's cuts doesn't mean I shouldn't treat them right."

"Prove yourself worthy of the difficult cuts, and maybe I'll consider allowing you more leeway. Until then, back to Mr. Pascal with you."

Shu flounced back to her client and aggressively snipped his sideburns. The old man looked alarmed but didn't say anything. Shu's locket swung with her motions. Rosemary shook her head and turned to me.

"If she didn't cut unevenly half the time, I would let her take on more. She can manage shampooing and basic trims, but that's it." To the teenager, she said, "Thank you, Miranda." Miranda sullenly went back to her task, and Rosemary led me to the door. "Did you figure out a plan?"

"I'll focus on end-of-day travel, when it's dark out," I said. "It's easy for thugs to hide in the darkness, and it's when the others were attacked. When Cut Right closes, I'll hang around until you all leave, and same for the coffeeshop. When the sisters do their evening training in this building, I'll patrol the area as well. I have everyone's hours. Will that suffice?"

Rosemary nodded, her face relaxing with her relief. She might have antagonistic relations with her fellow hairdressers, but it was clear that she cared about the safety of her sisters.

"Thank you, Morgan. I will sleep easier knowing that

someone competent is watching over us."

Rosemary leaned over to rub at a fingerprint on the window with a frown. A wispy hair drifted toward me, and I took the opportunity to pull on Caelus' threads and flick air strands. The hair floated in the opposite direction, and I suppressed a smile.

The world through Caelus' eyes was enlightening. Rosemary's peach-colored strands swirled around her calmly, and silver air threads waved above her. Shu, surrounded by jagged tomato red strands that mimicked her annoyed expression, walked with Mr. Pascal to the counter to collect payment. She pushed a hand into her pocket and mouthed a few words when the elderly man reached for his wallet.

Multicolored strands flowed from her pocket to Mr. Pascal, where they twisted around his mossy green threads. He froze for a moment then pulled out a few bills.

"Keep the change, dear," he said in a wheezy voice.

Shu put a hand on her chest.

"Mr. Pascal, you're too generous. Thank you so much."

Mr. Pascal turned to go, and Shu's mouth twisted in a satisfied smile. I frowned. Had Shu done something to the elderly man to make him give her a larger tip? What was in her pocket?

I didn't have any answers, but as I held the door open for Mr. Pascal and followed him out, I concluded that Shu bore watching.

I was at loose ends until my security duties that evening, so I dropped by the women's center where Greta gave me pamphlets to fold. It was brainless work, but it was for a good cause and I could ponder my new situation while I did it. Questions were piling up, and I needed answers to do my job properly. Why was someone targeting this sisterhood? To answer that, I needed to know more about it, but Rosemary wasn't talking. I debated approaching another sister, perhaps Amanda or Denise since they owed me, but it could wait a little. If I gave Rosemary a day or two to prove myself, maybe she would reveal more of her own accord.

At closing time, I watched the back of Cut Right and the coffeeshop. No one was accosted, and I found myself both relieved and disappointed.

To amuse myself during my vigil, I played with air currents. I was becoming more dexterous with every practice session, and my darts of air could shoot a dead leaf off a tree with precision. It was tiring, though. Fiddling with my new abilities took energy.

The next morning, my body craved something, and I had a shrewd idea what it was. When I walked by Upper Crust on my way to the coffeeshop, my feet practically dragged my body there. With anticipation, I flung the door open and scanned the glass cabinet for lemon tarts. When I saw them, their golden goodness screamed at me to consume them.

How could I say no?

"How many tarts today?" The girl at the counter said with a mirthful smile. Apparently, I was here often enough to be a regular.

"Three will do," I said. "On a napkin is fine. They won't last long."

While she gathered my golden treasures, I looked into the kitchen beyond. I was surprised by the disappointment that flooded my chest at its emptiness.

"No Jerome today?" I asked casually.

The girl shook her head and accepted my money.

"He often takes his break now. Bread's rising, you see."

I nodded and retreated with my tarts of glory. No point in sitting while I scarfed them down. I had things to do, and no one would join me at my table today. Not that I needed company.

The tarts disappeared too quickly, but they called from my

stomach for a drink to follow them. I complied. After all, the coffeeshop was only a few blocks away, and I wanted to check in with the other sisters. Two birds, one stone.

Sacred Grounds, the coffeeshop where Amanda and Denise worked, was in the same row of shops as the salon, but at the end. A glass door opened at the corner of a busy intersection and invited me in. A scent of ground coffee beans wafted into my nose, and I breathed deeply.

Morning rush was in full swing, and the two young women behind the counter looked harried. I joined the line and studied them both. Amanda worked the till, necklace swinging from her quick movements. Her pale blue eyes gleamed with bright interest as she spoke with customers. Denise worked the espresso machine. Dozens of narrow black braids were pulled into a ponytail, and her coffee-colored hands slapped drinks on the counter with brisk efficiency.

When it was my turn, I looked into Amanda's eyes.

"Hello, Amanda," I said quietly. "My name is Morgan. Rosemary hired me."

Amanda's eyes grew as round as coins and her faint ginger eyebrows rose.

"Oh! So good to see you again. It's such a relief to know you're helping. I don't know what you said to Rosemary to convince her to tell you everything, but I, for one, approve." She glanced at Denise then back at me. "What would you like? On the house, of course."

I was about to deny her offer, then I remembered that my funds weren't limitless these days. That would take getting used to.

"Thank you," I said with a gracious smile. "Large dark roast, please."

I moved to the side to wait for my coffee. Amanda whispered something to Denise, who glanced at me. When I met her gaze, she smiled and nodded, although concern still shadowed her face. Rosemary's decision to bring a near-stranger into the fold clearly did not meet with unanimous approval. I watched them both for a minute, but when Denise handed me my cup, I retreated from the shop.

The day passed. I shopped for more necessities and watched the shops at closing time. I texted Rosemary to recommend that the sisters travel in pairs when they could, and to avoid dark alleys and the typical places where men might prey on unsuspecting women. I didn't want them to take any chances, even if I were watching.

Late in the afternoon on the next day, I walked to the high school and found a park bench across from the tennis court to identify the last three sisters from a distance. After a day or two of patrolling and watching in uncomfortable, cold, wet places, I had devised a system. From my new backpack— never an accessory I had embraced before now, but Morgan suited one—I pulled out a towel, with which I wiped down the damp bench, a foam square to give comfort and protection against the cold, and a thermos filled with piping hot tea. Rosemary never said I had to endure my vigils in discomfort. I might have looked like a woman in the flush of youth, but I had lived long enough to understand the joy of creature comforts.

I sat with a sigh, then my back straightened. I had almost forgotten the pièce de résistance. Carefully, I extracted a small box from the bottom of my backpack. When the lid opened, I breathed in the heady scent of citrus and my face relaxed in contentment.

I chewed my tart and sipped scalding tea while I watched the tennis team practice. We had a rare break in our December rains, and the team was out in full swing. Yellow balls lobbed through the air, and the sound of soft grunts drifted in my direction. Six girls and a coach practiced on the courts today. Four played doubles and the other pair volleyed on the other court. The coach was a sister, Wanda, but as she had already lost her necklace, Rosemary was certain she wouldn't be targeted. Wanda walked between the players, shouting encouragement and criticism in equal measure.

My two charges were easy to spot. One was tall and willowy with raven hair swept up in an effortless ponytail that swayed down her back in a silky rope. That was Jasmine, her Persian descent clear from her petite, dark-eyed features. The usual golden chain hung around her neck.

She was paired with Starr, the youngest member of the sisterhood, who was easily identifiable by her faded green hair with brown roots whose chin-length wisps were pulled back with clips. Compared to the put-together Jasmine, Starr looked less chic and more just-climbed-out-of-bed. Her face was red as she narrowed her eyes in concentration to whack the ball over the net. It sailed over her opponents' heads, clearly out of bounds.

"Come on, Starr!" Jasmine shouted in exasperation. "You do remember that we're supposed to keep the ball in the court, yes? The main point of tennis?"

Starr flushed even redder. Wanda looked over with a frown. She put hands on her short but muscled frame, a visor shading her narrowed eyes and pursed lips.

"Your aim has been off this whole session, Starr. Stay behind for ten minutes of extra practice at the rebound wall today."

Starr glowered but nodded. My heart squeezed for Starr's humiliation. It was never easy to be publicly criticized. Peter had always kept his comments behind closed doors. While it had made it harder to convince others of his duplicity, the lack of social embarrassment had been a silver lining.

The girls practiced for over an hour. Despite the cold and damp, I had nowhere better to be, so I pulled on Caelus' threads to practice my own skills. Few people were around—the weather was too brisk for lingering along this side street—so I sent acorns zooming toward a knot on a nearby tree for target practice. By the time Wanda shouted to quit for the day,

I was at ninety percent accuracy and very proud of myself despite the energy drain.

Caelus stirred, more of a grumpy feeling in my stomach than anything, so I recited the spell quietly and he settled. I turned my gaze toward the tennis team. Wanda had her hand in her pocket and muttered to herself as the girls collected tennis balls into a large basket. I wouldn't have noticed except my thread-vision was active since I had been practicing my powers. The woman's greenish-yellow strands swirled with multicolored threads and streamed toward the adjacent school.

Moments later, a man hurried out with a mug clutched in his hand and a towel in the other. Wanda stopped rubbing her pocket and smiled at him. He thrust the items at her with a manic grin, and she accepted them graciously before he marched back to the school building.

That was curious. What sort of amulet did Wanda have? Did it summon that man? Could she force him to do her bidding, or did it simply alert him to the end of practice?

The others all left, Jasmine hopping into a Porsche driven by what must have been her boyfriend, but Starr stayed with the basket of balls, a glum look on her face. She volleyed them toward the rebound wall in a lackluster cycle.

I hadn't caught Jasmine before she left, but now that Starr was alone, I could pop over and introduce myself. I swiftly packed my foam square and thermos into my backpack and strode toward the tennis court. Starr's face was set in an expression of bored resignation as she hit her ball again and again.

"Starr," I called.

Starr whipped her head around and gazed at me with suspicion.

"Who are you?"

"My name is Morgan," I said, stopping on the other side of the chain link fence. "I'm helping Rosemary with protecting your necklaces."

Starr's hand flew to her neck, where a gold chain was tucked underneath her exercise top.

"Yeah, Rosemary told us about you. That's great you're giving us a hand."

She gave me a small smile that didn't quite reach her eyes. I had the sense that life wasn't shaping up the way she hoped it would, and I sympathized. It was tough being a teenager. I could remember my own struggles, although they were many years ago.

Starr looked at me with an expectant expression when I didn't immediately reply.

"Do you need help with something?"

"No, no," I said. "I just wanted to say hello, give you a face for the name in case you see me prowling around your headquarters. I'll let you get back to your practicing."

I nodded my adieu and Starr gave a half-hearted wave.

I walked across the street, then a ping made me check my phone. It was Anna with a time to meet on Thursday, and I gladly responded then looked at my watch. I had enough time to warm up in a store before Sacred Grounds closed and I was due to patrol the shop row.

I wondered if an attacker would show up tonight. Maybe the thugs would back off now that I was on the job. I pulled a mean-looking face then laughed. This doe-eyed look wouldn't be taken seriously by any real crook. Maybe I should consider a studded leather jacket and some boots that meant business instead of my skinny jeans and work-appropriate blouse.

One change at a time. It was hard revamping myself. I had to work hard to fight my old biases and natural inclinations. March might be dead, but Morgan was a slowly evolving creature. I would emerge from my cocoon one day, fully formed, but that day was not today.

Motion caught my attention. A boy sauntered across the tennis court toward Starr. He was tall and lanky with the underfed look of a teenage boy. His dark hair flopped over his

76

forehead in a way that teen girls would love. The only desire I felt was the impulse to grab a pair of scissors. When Starr finally noticed the boy, she gave a shriek of fright then laughed and lightly pushed his shoulder. He said something that I couldn't hear, and she giggled again.

A brilliant thought popped into my mind. Could I use the air to make their voices louder? I quickly twisted threads around me to create a vacuum. Air flowed into the empty space, bringing with it sounds from a distance. I tweaked strands until voices spoke in my ear. I leaned forward in my eagerness.

"Don't look at me, Trent, I'm all sweaty," Starr said.

"Yeah, it's called exercise." Trent chuckled. "You look good."

He shifted his feet and looked down, and I recalled the awkwardness of being a teenager. These two must have started dating recently enough that they weren't entirely comfortable with each other yet.

"You'll look good cleaned up, anyway," he said, and Starr flushed.

I frowned. That comment was unnecessary. Weren't these two dating? Even Peter hadn't pulled out those sort of comments until we were already a firm couple.

"Jasmine was a bitch again today," Starr said. Her tone was bitter toward her sister-in-secrets, and I wondered again at the dynamic of this sisterhood. "She's so mean."

"Just quit the tennis team," Trent said. "Then you wouldn't have to deal with her. You're always complaining about it, anyway. Do you even like tennis?"

"I can't drop it," Starr said quickly. "I made a promise—" She swallowed. "A promise to the school. They could have accepted someone else at tryouts, but they chose me. It's my duty to play."

"Duty?" Trent scoffed and kicked a ball against the rebound wall. "Duty is just a word that adults use to keep us in line.

Screw the man. You don't owe anyone anything. Do what you want to do. Hell, do what you think is right. What if you had a duty to Hitler? Would you follow it?"

I shook my head at Trent's youthful bravado born of inexperience and testosterone, but Starr was listening hard. Her pale pink strands writhed in what must be her agitation, and her eyes raked Trent's face, searching for truth.

"Yeah," she said slowly. "I think you're right."

"Of course I am." Trent picked up two errant tennis balls and tossed them to Starr who caught them with a faraway look. "Do what I tell you, and everything will make sense. You know I'm the only one who doesn't keep you in the dark and feed you crap. I'll lay it out straight, every time. I'm the only one you can really trust. Come on." He slung an arm around her. "I'll walk you to the bus."

I waited until Starr and Trent had disappeared before I pulled my hood over my head and pointed my feet toward Sacred Grounds. My uneasy feeling intensified when I reflected on Trent's words. He was establishing himself as Starr's sole authority. It was probably all innocent, but I couldn't help remember similar words spoken to me in my younger years. I hoped Starr could sort out what she believed for herself.

The sky was almost completely dark now, so close to the solstice, and I was thankful for the orange streetlights. I had too much to think about to watch my feet.

I couldn't do this job forever. But how could I solve the mystery of the unknown attackers if I had no information?

CHAPTER IX

Tuesday and Wednesday passed in my new routine. I whiled away the days reading and volunteering at the women's center, then in the evenings I watched the sisters leave the row of shops after work and training without molestation. On Thursday morning, ready for a change, I strode briskly to Sacred Grounds to meet my closest friend.

Anna sat with two coffees on the table next to a window. She carefully peered at every person who walked by, including me, but she didn't react to my presence. My mouth twitched in mirth. I really was Morgan now.

I sneaked by a slim figure in a green hoodie and slid into the seat opposite Anna. She jumped and narrowed her eyes at me.

"Can I help you?" she said with suspicion. My mouth twitched again.

"I don't know, Vivienne." I called her by the name she used many centuries ago, the first time we were friends. My memories were hazy at best, but it was a surefire way to convince Anna of my identity. "Can you?"

Anna's eyes filled with tears, then she leaped to her feet and embraced me.

"I can't believe you're really here," she forced out. She pushed me back and raked her eyes over my face. "It's incredible. You're really here, March."

"It's not March anymore," I reminded her. "I'm Morgan now."

Anna's eyes lit in a crafty smile.

"How fitting. Back to your roots."

"Indeed."

We resumed our seats, and Anna looked me up and down with appraisal.

"It's a big change," she said carefully.

I chuckled.

"You don't have to hold back to be polite. I have a perky young body again. I can't say I miss the old one overly. While I enjoy fresh looks, the lack of backache is my biggest thrill."

"Well, you look great." Anna took a sip of her coffee. "A new lease on life. Incredible. What are you doing now? Do you need money or anything?"

"Thanks for asking, but I took as much out of March's accounts as I could and transferred them into my secret Sweet Thing account. I'm siphoning off that currently. A contact in the government is setting me up with identification, so I should be set."

I debated telling Anna about my security job with the sisterhood, but that would open a huge can of worms that wouldn't be appropriate for a coffeeshop. I wasn't supposed to tell anyone about the sisterhood, for one, and I didn't want to mention Caelus right now. The next time I saw Anna, when we had more privacy, I would tell her. I could use her advice. She was almost as well-informed about the arcane as I was.

"I'm volunteering for Grandview Women's Center as well," I said. "It keeps me busy while I decide my next steps. But what about you? What happened while I was possessed? How did March die? I have no recollection of those weeks."

"It's so weird to talk about you in the third person," Anna muttered, then she cleared her throat. "The elemental had control of your body and your money, and she made herself a huge stone temple. She messed with people's minds to force them to worship her—it made her more powerful—but we managed to subdue her with some help from other elementals. Merry got the short end of the stick, though."

I held up my hand. Merry was the current name of Merlin, and I didn't want to hear a sob story about him.

"Spare me the Merlin news. I have no interest in it." I shook my head and leaned back, digesting the information. "A temple. Insane. I guess I'm glad to be out of my old body. The

80

elemental burned a lot of bridges."

"You could say that. It was a huge risk, planting that amulet on your old body so you could fight the possession. I had to draw your blood to activate the amulet. Check out my battle wound from the elemental's retaliation."

Anna held up her arm and drew back her sleeve to expose a large bandage of gauze. I winced.

"That looks big. I'm sorry you were hurt for my sake."

"It was worth it," Anna said with a sweet smile. "I guess your soul jumped into the nearest host. There were casualties at the temple after the battle. You were probably drawn to the closest body."

"I was lucky," I said, waving at my new body, and Anna grinned.

Another thought occurred to me. I leaned forward again, interested to indulge in some chitchat. It felt like forever since Anna and I had sat down for a proper chinwag.

"Who was with you when I called? Are you dating someone?"

To my surprise, Anna's cheeks colored, and she looked at her hands.

"Yes, but you're not going to like it."

"What are you talking about?" I reached over and squeezed her fingers. "If you're happy, I'm happy. Why, who is it?"

"His name's Wayne," she said with hesitation.

I searched my memory for people with that name. My eyebrows contracted.

"You don't mean Wayne Gibson? As in, Merry's friend and destroyer of our plans?" Merlin, Wayne, and their friends had foiled me more than once in my quest to gain elemental powers. They might have been right, but I would never admit that.

Anna nodded without looking at me.

"It's him. I lost my memory—well, I think Merry made me forget everything about you and the organization, but he's never admitted it—and then I met Wayne. He was so sweet, and we hit it off immediately. We really have this connection. I haven't felt this way about anyone else before." She finally looks at me, her gaze pleading. "Don't be mad."

I sigh. Anna was many things, but earnest was new for her. She was serious in her admiration for Wayne, and I didn't have the heart to chastise her.

"As long as you know what you're doing. That crowd always seems to get in our way, now and in the past. Stay wary." I stared into Anna's eyes. "Just don't tell them about me, okay? They don't need to know I'm alive. It wouldn't help anything. This is a fresh start for me, and I don't want March's baggage around my neck."

Anna nodded, but her brow furrowed.

"I don't like keeping secrets from Wayne," she said. "But I won't tell him or the others. That's your secret to share. Or not."

"Or not," I agreed. "This has been nice. When do you want to meet up again? What's your schedule like these days?"

Anna looked concerned and guilty.

"If I'm keeping you a secret, I'm not sure when I can slip away. I have a lot of shifts at the coffeeshop where I work, and I'm with Wayne the rest of the time. I'll call you later, okay? We'll work something out."

My heart constricted. Anna was being pulled in two directions, and I wasn't winning. My only friend was choosing her man over her companion of centuries, and it hurt. Was I doomed to be forever solitary? Briefly, I wished I could stand in a grove of trees instead of being a lone oak on a hill.

I shook off the feeling. I didn't like making Anna hide me from her loved ones, nor did I enjoy keeping secrets from her, but it was for the best. Hopefully, we could find a way to make things work.

82

I had finished my dinner of pasta carbonara with grilled asparagus and a glass of pinot gris—I was rediscovering the joy of cooking, one recipe at a time—and had my feet up on the couch with a cup of steaming tea when my phone rang.

I frowned. Who would be calling me? Very few people knew me, and fewer still had my phone number. I picked up the phone.

"Hello?"

"Morgan!" The woman's voice was breathless, laced with veins of fear. "Is this Morgan? It's Miranda. I'm being followed. Please, help me."

I swung my feet off the couch and pressed the phone to my cheek in my intensity. Miranda, the young hairdresser's assistant and a member of Rosemary's sisterhood, was in trouble. No one was supposed to be at the shop row at this time, and Rosemary had assumed that the sisters were safe from attackers otherwise. Miranda's breathless panic indicated it was a mistaken assumption.

"Where are you?" I infused authority into the words. The sooner I knew where she was, the sooner I could reach her. I cursed myself for not putting car ownership higher on my list of priorities.

"Sixth and Laurier, I think. Oh crap, he's almost on me. I thought I beat him off, but it's like he can't feel pain, I swear. Damn it, I have to run."

"I'm on my way." I leaped to the door and thrust my feet into boots. My hand grasped my coat, and I raced out the door and down the stairs. I couldn't wait for the elevator to trundle to my floor.

"Back off, weirdo," Miranda shouted through the speaker. "Stay away. No!"

There was a scream, a rustling, then a crash and silence. The line disconnected.

I cursed and pushed the phone into my pocket. I would have

to run. The intersection of Sixth and Laurier was only a few blocks away. As I burst out of my front door and started to sprint, I thanked my youthful body. March had been long past sprinting age.

I gathered a few startled looks from passersby, but there weren't many people out at this hour and in this weather. I ran faster, and my long strides were hampered by my skinny jeans. Maybe I had been too hasty in dismissing the saleswoman's recommendation of yoga pants. Two blocks to go, one block… a scuffling noise from behind a low apartment block alerted me to the struggle. I raced around a dumpster and stopped to assess.

My eyes raked over the scene. Miranda was curled into a fetal position with her hands protecting her neck or maybe her necklace. The man had his knee against her side and was pulling at her elbows. It must have hurt, given Miranda's whimpering and squeaks of distress. A gash across her arm trickled blood over her yellow coat.

The man paused for a moment and shook his head as if to clear it. His face turned my way. One of his eyes had swollen almost shut from a blow Miranda had managed to land. His visible eye was glassy and unfocused. How bad was the drug problem in this part of town? Or was something more sinister happening?

It didn't matter. He might have been under the influence of drugs or something else, but he had to take responsibility for his actions, and nothing gave him the right to attack someone. I pulled Caelus' powers from the knot at my stomach and into my arms. Like a veil lifted from my eyes, colors drifted across my vision and swayed in a breeze I couldn't feel. Miranda was wrapped in a tight ball of her mustard strands, and the man's dissolute amber threads twitched erratically.

The man stumbled to his feet and approached me with his hands outstretched. Miranda peeked out from her defensive posture and gasped in alarm for me. I raised my own hands. I was ready for this. The thug wouldn't know what hit him.

With my yank at the nearest air strands, a rush of wind blew past me and pummeled the thug in his stomach. He released his breath with a surprised oomph, and his eyes grew comically wide as he flew off his feet and against the back wall of the building.

I smiled. Justice was so satisfying, deep in my core. This was right. At that moment, I thanked my lucky stars for leading me to this time and place and giving me the opportunity to take care of my fellow woman in such a powerful way. The years of subjugation under Peter's thumb almost seemed worth it if they had led me to this moment.

Miranda unfolded herself from her position and scuttled behind me. The thug pushed off the ground and dived toward me. Too late, I raised my hands, and before I could summon Caelus' power, the man was too close. Through the rush of blood in my ears, Miranda's scream faintly reached me, but my focus was on keeping my balance.

I didn't have a hope. With crushing hands, the man gripped my upper arms and shoved me bodily into the metal dumpster. His breath was hot on my face as he slammed me again into the metal bin, and hot pain flared on my forearm. I slithered to the ground, no longer a threat, and the man turned to deal with Miranda, who had fallen to her knees and gasped for breath a few steps away.

No. This was not how this ended. My heart pumped fiercely in my chest and hot rage flooded my body. It was an odd feeling. As a calm, rational woman that had previously been accustomed to pandering to a dominating man, I had developed an iron will to control my emotions. This molten fire was unexpected, but not unwelcome. Maybe it was time to let my inner magma bubble over. Where had pandering ever got me?

New Morgan, new life. No regrets.

My hands rose to clench air strands in my fists while my eyes scanned the area. The thug was almost on Miranda, his grasping fingers reaching for the necklace. Her chest heaved for breath, and she wobbled to a defensive stance with her arms at the ready. A pile of bricks left over from some remodeling project sat discarded beside the dumpster. Perfect.

With a flick of my wrist, I sent the topmost brick flying. It soared in a high arc toward the thug's head—and missed him by a hair. The brick crashed against asphalt beyond and spilt into three pieces.

The thug's head snapped to look at the brick, and Miranda kicked him in the knee. He stumbled forward, and I didn't let him react further. With another flick, I sent the next brick spiraling.

This time, it made contact.

With a sickening thud, the brick smashed into the man's head. There was a moment of hesitation, then he slumped over and fell still.

With a rippling sensation in my gut, Caelus blossomed outward. His thread-filled torso towered over me with eyes filled with fury.

"You have no idea what you're doing," he roared with the voice of a gale. "Stealing my abilities and flinging them around like you think you know something. This body was hurt. What would we have done if it had died? It's so fragile, yet you rush into danger without a care!"

I didn't bother answering Caelus. Instead, I mustered my willpower and pushed his head into my arm. His outraged face was the last I saw of him before he retreated into his silver knot at the insistence of my chanting.

I sucked air into my lungs like it was going out of fashion. Caelus, while I didn't want to admit it, had a point. Today had been a close shave, too close for my liking. I needed to practice more and take more precautions. I might have jumped into this body by a miracle, but I couldn't count on that opportunity again. This was my one chance, and I needed to pair my new no-regrets attitude with a hint of my old caution.

Miranda crept closer to me. Her breath came in gasps, nearly hyperventilating with the aftermath of her shock and fear. She pressed a hand to her chest.

"Is he dead?" she whispered.

I sidled closer to the downed man and watched him for a moment.

"Still breathing. That's probably a good thing. Manslaughter would be a terrible way to end the day, even if he deserved it."

The man moaned, and my heart leaped in my throat. Miranda scrambled backward.

"What do we do, what do we do?" she hissed.

I put up a hand for her silence and bent to the thug's face.

"Give me a minute," I whispered. "I want to try something."

The man groaned again, and I grasped silver threads that emerged from his mouth at the sound. My fingers pulled gently but firmly outward. The man's chest heaved. His eyes fluttered, but he didn't regain full consciousness. For a whole minute, I pulled slowly at the strands and he twitched as if in a seizure.

Finally, his eyes closed, and his body relaxed into an unconscious state once more. I let go of the strands and they flowed into his nose and out again with steady breaths. I sat back on my heels and let my eyes wander over the man's amber strands.

"What did you do?" Miranda whispered.

I turned to look at her. Her brown hair was tousled, and mascara ringed her eyes from tears. She rubbed her chest again with a grimace. I gave her a warm smile. She looked like she needed one.

"Made sure he wouldn't wake up for a few minutes. Lack of oxygen tends to do that. Now, I want to fix his memory so he doesn't know what happened here or why he was after you. It's a bit of an experiment, I'm afraid, so no promises on how

87

well it will work. If he wakes up, I can bash him on the head with another brick."

Miranda didn't react to my attempt at lightening the mood, so I turned to my work. I had seen Merlin fiddle with the strands at other's heads before, erasing their memories or changing their moods. He had figured out how to do it by himself, so why couldn't I? A lot of this thread business was led by intuition and powered by intent, so I allowed my fingers to find the correct strands and simply concentrated on what I wanted.

I tied a knot here, twisted a strand there, and within a few minutes had arranged the man's threads to my satisfaction. I stood up, dusted off my hands, then gave the man a swift kick in the leg.

"What was that for?" Miranda said.

"I want to wake him up. See how my memory alteration worked."

The man groaned and rolled onto his back. His eyes opened and he blinked at the cloudy night sky.

"Well?" I said to him. "Who are you? Why did you attack this woman? What are you doing here?"

The man's bleary eyes rolled toward the sound of my voice, but he didn't get up.

"Mmph," he grunted. "Graffle bintogrr. Wobble tobble."

Miranda and I exchanged bewildered looks.

"A different language?" she said.

"No." I shook my head. "That's gobbledygook. He's completely addled. Either that brick to the head did him in, or my little experiment went wrong."

Or right, I added silently. I might not have achieved my specific goal of memory loss, but the overarching goal of stopping future attacks worked perfectly. The raging fire in my chest roared its approval, but the calmer, more rational side of me winced at the carnage, no matter how much the man might have deserved the treatment.

"I'll call an ambulance anonymously," I continued. "The authorities can handle him now. Come on, I'll walk with you. Where are you going this evening, anyway?"

We headed out of the alley, taking slow steps to accommodate Miranda's shaking legs.

"I was going to meet Starr at the movie theater. I left early to buy chocolate-covered almonds at the corner store, but I never made it there. That guy jumped me at the corner and dragged me to this alley. He almost got the necklace before you showed up." She turned a grateful face toward me. "I'm so glad you did."

"I'm glad I could be there, too. I guess we have to adjust my patrols if attackers will come after you anywhere. I wonder how he knew where to find you." I studied Miranda's halting gait and pale face. Her hand hadn't ceased rubbing her chest as if it pained her. "Are you okay? Are you in shock?"

"No. I have a heart defect." Miranda grimaced. "Born with it, but symptoms didn't show until I started training hard with the sisterhood. I'll be replaced soon—my cousin Sarah is almost old enough to join—but Rosemary was hoping I could hold out until then. She hasn't told the motherhood yet."

I offered my arm for support, and Miranda took it with a grateful look.

"Are you still going to the movie?" I asked.

"No," she said with a shudder. "I just want to go home. It's not far. I'll text Starr to stay home, too. Who knows who's out there, waiting for us? When I became a sister for the order, I never expected this. My mum was one in her day, and she never had anything strange happen to her."

"Okay, I'll walk you home. And the next time you want to wander the streets after dark, give me a call, okay? I don't mind accompanying you—that's what Rosemary pays me to do, after all—but I can't protect you if I don't know where you are."

Miranda nodded vigorously.

"I will, I promise."

We continued down a side street. Miranda's thumb skated over the screen of her phone, texting Starr, while my mind recounted the attack tonight. Despite the gash on my arm, which still oozed blood into my new shirt, the evening had been a qualified success. True, I hadn't reacted quickly enough when the thug had come for me, but that could be fixed by a more ruthless attack on my part in the beginning. I should have followed up the blast of wind with another one. The best students were the ones who learned from their mistakes, and I was determined to master these abilities to their fullest extent.

My thoughts wandered. What else could I do with my new powers? My pulse still flowed hot and thick in my veins at the treatment of Miranda by a forceful man. Annoyance and a heady sense of power directed my mind to a new target. What could I do to my ex-husband Peter?

My eyes widened. Was it too late for vengeance? I was supposed to have been past this by now. The therapist I had seen for years as March certainly praised my calm rationality toward the subject. I truly thought I had put the past behind me, only keeping my wedding ring as a reminder to stay alert. But, with the emotions of this new body and the emergence of Caelus' abilities, new vistas presented themselves.

It wasn't right that he had got off scot-free while I paid for the years of torment with scars that had never fully healed. Didn't they say revenge was a dish best served cold? In a flash of yearning, I longed to taste that sweet flavor.

I didn't want to take time away from my important work with the sisterhood. Tonight's adventure only cemented my determination to protect these women, and the desire felt too right to ignore. But not every second of the day was accounted for. There was plenty of time to carry out my half-formed plans when the women were at work.

Peter would never see me coming. How delicious.

It was late when I arrived home after seeing Miranda to her door. The shower beckoned, and after I cleaned my wound, I spent a few entertaining minutes teasing the steam to stay in the shower stall with air strands. Caelus remained in his knot, for which I was grateful. I was too tired for another confrontation. I only wanted to sleep and greet the morning refreshed and ready to tackle the day.

My sleep was calm and untroubled for the first part of the night, but it soon devolved into fuzzy dreams of ordinary things. I glimpsed my legs sliding into pants, walking down the hall, riding in the elevator. It was dull but had that unmistakable dreamlike quality of unreality. I watched sleepily as my body wandered dark streets near my condo. I had an urgent sense of searching, but I didn't know what for. Supposedly, dreams of being chased meant that the brain was anxious. I wondered dreams of searching meant to my subconscious.

I could see the threads of the world swaying around me, and pleasure coursed through my veins. The threads brought such an ethereal beauty to mundane objects. My eyes followed green tendrils of a tree by the sidewalk as they fluttered with my passing.

The sense of searching increased, as did a feeling of desperation. I needed to find something, but I didn't know where to look. I was lost, without guide or tether, in an unfamiliar world. I had a mission but no knowledge of how to complete it, and failure crept closer with every step I took.

The oddness of my thoughts jolted me out of my dreaming complacency. These weren't my feelings. This was my body in the waking world, but I had no control over it.

Caelus had taken over.

CHAPTER X

I forced a watchful calmness over my thoughts. It wouldn't do to alert Caelus of my intentions. If I had emotions that were too strong, he would undoubtedly feel them, even through his preoccupation with searching. From our previous conversation, I knew of his artifact search. No wonder he felt defeated, if his grand plan was to wander dark streets until he stumbled upon one.

Mentally, I shook my head, then I projected thoughts of calm wonder while I gathered my strength. My attack would need to be swift and precise. There would be no time for second chances. Once Caelus was alerted to my opposition, I would have no hope. I needed to take over the body on the first try.

Was this what Caelus felt all the time? Being a spectator in my own body was hideous. I could do nothing, say nothing, be nothing except what Caelus wanted to do, say, or be. The lack of control almost overwhelmed me until I remembered that Caelus would feel my emotion if I weren't careful. I exercised my strong will and pumped out feelings of complacency until my horror retreated.

I would simply have to do this right the first time. I couldn't be subject to another's whims and desires. Never again.

I quietly gathered my strength, rehearsed the words of the chant one last time, then struck. With all my might, I pushed outward from the tight knot that Caelus had squeezed me into. The body doubled over in pain, but I couldn't feel it yet. I shouted the chant in my head, forcing my intent into every syllable. My strands writhed and prodded whatever part of Caelus' silver threads I could reach.

His strands wriggled with pain and I pressed my advantage. Slowly, surely, silver retreated as my burgundy took over. When the body's mouth was mine again, I chanted aloud.

That was the clincher. With my words, the silver condensed into a ball at my stomach. I panted with exertion. My skin tingled with the aftermath of my attack, but a smile crept over my face. I had won again and learned a valuable lesson in the process.

I directed my feet to an all-night pharmacy on Cormorant Drive. It was a fair walk, but my objective was crucial and couldn't wait until morning. In the store, a sleepy clerk lifted her head at my entrance, but I strode past her to the sleep aid section. There, I grabbed the strongest sleeping pills I could buy over the counter. On a whim, I swiped a bottle of lavender pillow spray as well. I couldn't be too careful tonight. The clerk yawned when I approached the till.

"Is that everything?"

"If that doesn't work, I don't know what will."

The clerk gave me a tired smile and passed me the bag.

"Sweet dreams."

As long as they weren't about roaming the streets at night, I would take whatever dreams I could get. I couldn't afford to have Caelus snatch control of my body again. With the sleeping pills, hopefully my mind would be too dazed to respond to his takeover.

To be certain, I spent a few minutes at home preparing my bed. Salt in a protective circle on the floor, cocoa powder in piles at the corners to calm restless spirits, and a spoken spell to bind them together. Certain that I had done everything possible to prevent another nighttime wandering, I swallowed a pill, sprayed my pillow with lavender, and fell immediately into dreamless sleep.

Through the combination of sleeping pills, spells, and fatigue, Caelus left me alone for the rest of the night. Or maybe it was because of the lavender. It was a potent scent.

I slept late and woke groggy with a dry mouth from the drugs. Even a cold splash of water on my face didn't dispel the thick-headed pall that draped over me. I expected it to wear off in an hour or so, but it was a terrible way to start the morning.

No matter. The drugs accomplished what I meant them to, and Caelus was not currently the captain of this ship. The thought put a spring in my step, and I slipped on a blouse with three-quarter length sleeves and pair of skinny jeans that the clothing store attendant had insisted I buy. I swung my coat over my shoulder and sailed out of my condo door.

Doug was in his housecoat in the hall with a newspaper and a stack of envelopes in his hand. He brightened when he saw me.

"Good morning, neighbor," he said.

Impulsively, I smiled at him. My previous coldness toward him needed to be repaired. I pushed aside misgivings that boiled in my gut. It didn't hurt to be friendly. I could always summon Caelus' powers if needed.

"Good morning. My name is Morgan, by the way."

"Morgan." He rolled the name around in his mouth as if trying to commit it to memory, then he glanced at my arm and his brows contracted. "That looks like a nasty cut."

I looked at my arm. I'd forgotten about my wound from last night. It hadn't hurt until I looked at it, but now that it captured my attention, the damn thing throbbed and stung. Skin around the cut was red and infected. My shoulders slumped.

"Damn it. I don't have any antibiotic ointment. I'll have to stop at the pharmacy again."

"I have just the thing." Doug nodded vigorously. "Let me grab it. Hold on a sec."

"That's okay," I said, then my arm pulsed with pain. I grimaced. "The pharmacy isn't far."

"Not a problem at all," he said and disappeared into his suite. His voice filtered through the door as he wandered away.

94

"I won't be a minute. Where did I put the first aid kit?"

I debated sneaking away while Doug was occupied—who knew what he was getting in there—but I resisted the antisocial impulse when I remembered the paint he had left for me.

He returned with a package of gauze, a roll of tape, and a small tub of green gel.

"My mother always swore by aloe vera," he said with a sage nod. "Antiseptic, you know. Works a treat. Here, rub that on. Be generous."

He held out the open tub of aloe vera, and I gingerly dipped my fingers into the cool goo and smeared it over my wound. It stung like a thousand angry bees, but the coolness of the gel soothed the burning. I wondered if Doug noticed the thin white lines of my forearm scars. If he did, he said nothing. Deftly, he placed the gauze on top and wrapped tape around my arm.

"It's not pretty, but it will heal." He smiled broadly at me. "There you go, Morgan. You have yourself a good day."

With that, he retreated. I called out a hasty thank you before he closed the door of his suite. I was conflicted. Part of me was wary of Doug, but the rest insisted that he might truly care about his new neighbor without ulterior motivation. The wary part of me was hard to convince.

I shook my head. The mysteries of Doug would have to wait. I wanted to talk to Rosemary in person. I walked swiftly through the bracing December air to Cut Right, Rosemary's salon. Once inside, Shu pointed at my target, who folded an apron in the back.

"Miranda was attacked last night, and not near the shop row," I said quietly when Rosemary greeted me. "She's fine and kept her necklace."

"Yes, she called me." Rosemary's mouth twisted with worry. "I don't know why the attacker grabbed her so far away from headquarters. How did he know she would be there? Are we being followed?" She shook her head.

How did he know, indeed? Suspicion crept over me. These

men knew of the sisterhood to target their attacks, and they must be working together. But who was the insider? Was it a jilted lover, as I had speculated, or was it a sister herself?

I kept this observation to myself for now. Rosemary hadn't yet considered that one of her sisters was behind this, and I wanted more evidence before I touched that sticky subject.

"We need to be more proactive," I said instead. "Get your sisters to call me if they walk anywhere after dark. I don't mind accompanying them."

"Good idea," Rosemary said with a fervent nod. "I will."

"And more information about the lockets wouldn't hurt."

"Come on." Rosemary washed her hands at the back sink and waved me to follow her. "It's time I showed you more about the sisterhood."

I glanced around the salon, curious that Rosemary would mention her organization so casually where anyone could hear her, but the only customer currently nearby was ninety if she were a day and looked happily lost in her own world. Even Joy, who was curling her wispy locks, hadn't bothered engaging her in conversation. Instead, she chattered at Shu, who listened unenthusiastically.

I followed Rosemary out the back door. It led to a dimly lit hallway lined with entrances to other shops on one side and alley-facing doors on the other. Rosemary led me to the end of the hall, through a locked door, and down an echoing cement stairwell. At the bottom, there were three closed doors in a windowless hallway. Rosemary opened one directly ahead.

When she flicked on the light, a thoroughly modern gym space greeted my eyes. Bright track lighting illuminated a large central mat surrounded by treadmills, stationary bikes, free weights, and a wall of mirrors. Rosemary turned to me.

"Our mission is to protect the lockets," she said with a wave around the room. "Through any means necessary. For the most part, that means keeping it secret and living double lives. But, in case anyone should target us, we keep ourselves in a state of readiness. When I was younger, I trained with the eldest sister, and now I train my younger sisters to defend themselves and their necklaces." She gestured me to follow her out the door. "Come on, I'll show you what the lockets are all about."

Back in the hallway, Rosemary walked to a door beside the stairs. She swung it open and stepped into a long and narrow room, sparsely furnished with a loveseat and a waist-high bookcase. Someone had spread a cheap rug on the floor against cold seeping through the cement foundation, and a string of Christmas lights hung from nails in the wall, but it was still cheerless. It was a well-hidden hangout for the sisterhood, but I preferred the headquarters of my previous secret organization. It had been a spacious complex behind the cupcake shop Sweet Thing. Although, those treats hadn't compared to Jerome's lemon tarts.

The top shelf of the bookcase contained only one slim hardback book with a plain black cover whose corners were blunted from overuse. Lower shelves held an electric kettle, a box of teabags, and a stack of steamy romance novels. This must be where the sisters gathered during work breaks.

"Our amulet library is through there." Rosemary waved at a door near the other end. "We have all sorts. Forgetfulness amulets, amulets of persuasion, amulets for mundane tasks like the drying spell you saw at my house. But I wanted to show you the Book of Souls."

"There's a showstopper name," I said. "What content could possibly live up to that promise?"

Rosemary smiled.

"Oh, it delivers. It has the legend of the Leaf, Seed, and Blood."

"I hope you have more, because that wasn't much of an explanation."

Rosemary gestured toward the loveseat and took the book in her arms as one would pick up a delicate newborn baby. I accepted her invitation and sank onto the uncomfortable tweed loveseat. It was small enough to fit the narrow space, which was the only good thing I could say for it. Rosemary joined me and laid the book on her lap with reverence.

"This book contains the basis of our sisterhood," she said quietly then frowned. "It's only a photocopy of the real thing, of course. The elders keep the real version. There are more pages, too, that I haven't seen. When I progress to the motherhood, I will be allowed to read more. I can't wait for that day."

Rosemary shook her head and stroked the book's cover.

"The legend of the Leaf, Seed, and Blood took place thousands of years ago," she said in a hushed tone. Her fingers opened the worn cover with a delicate motion to expose an illustration on the frontispiece.

I leaned forward, intrigued. The high-quality photocopy depicted a colorfully painted tree, done in an illustrated manuscript style from the Middle Ages. Small creatures crouched in the branches, curled around the trunk, and perched on the topmost leaves. Birds flew above the tree, and worms intertwined with roots below the soil line. At the bottom of the illustration were almost illegible words.

"The Book of Souls." Rosemary looked pleased at my interest. "It's all in Latin, so I'll paraphrase the story for you as we go."

She took on a sonorous, weighted speech as if she were reciting a memorized tale. Maybe she was. This sisterhood took themselves more seriously that I had previously thought.

"Thousands of years ago," she said, turning the page to an illustration depicting a lion gazing at a woman in devotion. The woman's hand rested on the lion's mane. "Humans and beasts, plants and birds, everything was connected. The bird knew what the beast saw, the beast heard the plant's cry, the plant sensed the human's need. A beautiful harmony existed between all living creatures. When one hurt, they all wept, but when one rejoiced, the earth blossomed with joyful flowers and animals danced in the meadows."

I tried with all my might to keep a straight face through Rosemary's florid description of this glorious utopia, and instead listened to the kernels of truth hidden in the flowery language. Was this some Garden of Eden-esque vision from a different culture? The hushed cadence of Rosemary's voice revealed her veneration for the story.

Luckily, Rosemary flipped the page at that moment, and my lapse in willpower went unnoticed. I schooled my expression into neutral interest by the time she glanced at me again.

"Then, disaster struck." Rosemary pointed a finger at the next page.

Among the calligraphy of indecipherable medieval Latin, another illustration lurked. This one was not as rosy as the last. In it, four faces ranging from angry to downright malicious encircled a fifth which stared at the others in pious sadness. The faces had no bodies. Instead, they floated in clouds of curlicues. The surrounding four each had their own hue, of orange, gray, blue, and brown. The central face was surrounded by strings squiggle of a multitude of different colors. It reminded me strongly of the threads I saw when I used Caelus' powers, and my curiosity increased tenfold.

"The ability to communicate with all living things was wrought by the element of soul. The other four elementals—fire, air, water, and earth—grew jealous of their sister, for she was worshiped by all living creatures for her great gifts to them. 'Why should she be so revered?' they cried. 'Where is our due?' For her beneficence to living creatures, she was captured by the other elementals and locked away in a prison of their own devising."

Rosemary turned the page. The next illustration depicted the rainbow-hued face at the bottom of a box with the other faces crowing with laughter above her. Three objects floated at the top of the page.

"The keys to lock away the element of soul were three in number. The Leaf of the Maiden, the Seed of the Mother, and the Blood of the Elder." Rosemary turned to the next page, which depicted the same tree that was on the frontispiece, but this time multicolored threads surrounded it. "When all three keys are reunited once more, only then will the element of soul be released from her prison and all living creatures be connected in harmony once more."

When it was clear that Rosemary had finished her story, I cleared my throat.

"That's a fascinating tale," I said carefully. "I don't follow how it relates to the sisterhood."

"One of our necklaces contains the Leaf of the Maiden." Rosemary touched her own locket. "This key was found by the leader of our order decades ago and given to a faithful friend to protect. The sisterhood formed after the keeper of the Leaf was possessed by a demon and almost destroyed it in the grip of the demon's evil tendencies. Now, nine young women are entrusted with replicas of the necklaces, and no one knows who has the true Leaf. We occasionally trade the necklaces to make sure the secret is safe, and we each guard our necklace with our lives. It's a strange system, but our leader insists on it. Maybe one day, when she passes, we will reevaluate our security measures." Rosemary drew herself up. "We are proud and honored to be the protectors of the Leaf, and it is our duty to keep it safe until it can be reunited with the other two keys."

"Where was the Leaf found?"

I was beside myself with curiosity. Where did one find magical objects? I had discovered and created many amulets myself, in my previous life as March, but how did others search? A squirming sensation in my gut alerted me to Caelus' interest in the topic, but I quelled the feeling with stern intention. I did wonder what he knew of this legend, seeing as it concerned elementals, and I wished he would be calm enough for a rational conversation. I couldn't relax my guard to talk to him without him attempting to take over my body. I especially wanted to know if he thought this Leaf was an artifact he sought.

"The founder of our order discovered it during an archaeological dig, almost seventy years ago. She had read the Book of Souls and recognized her find for what it really was."

"How close are you to releasing this soul elemental?"

"We've had the Leaf for decades, and the motherhood is close to finding the Seed, but the elderhood is still searching for the Blood." Rosemary sniffed. "It's ironic, given how much they ride us. They don't trust us to keep the Leaf safe, even though we've done so for ages. I think we've earned a little trust. Old women—you can never please them."

I bit my tongue—March had been far closer to elderhood than to motherhood, and a far cry from sisterhood—and asked another question.

"So, you believe you will bring this utopia to Earth, once all the keys are found."

Rosemary's eyes brightened at the thought.

"It will be amazing. Can you imagine? The Earth needs healing and communication more than ever. What if everyone could feel the joy of a soaring bird or a bounding deer? Even better, what if we could feel the pain of a felled tree, the cries of a lonely whale, or the agony of a fish in an oil slick? Wouldn't we fix our ways with that level of empathy? The world would change, and for the better. There's never been a more needful time."

"It sounds idyllic," I said, but inwardly I wondered what the drawbacks might be. Experience had taught me that nothing was ever simple, and everything had a dark side.

That was assuming this ancient legend held even a grain of truth. I continued, "I wonder who is trying to steal the Leaf. Is it someone who doesn't want this utopia?"

"Or someone who doesn't trust us to keep it safe," Rosemary said with a sneer. "What do you bet it's the Elders?

101

It would be just like them. Even the Mothers might think they should look after the Leaf, since they almost have the Seed. Yeah, keep them together. What do you bet?"

"It's definitely someone who knows the sisterhood well," I said. "Whoever is attacking knows too much."

"My sisters are above reproach," Rosemary said, her tone defensive. "They are all dedicated to the cause and have been trained since birth to take on their role."

"I don't doubt it," I said carefully, although I didn't share Rosemary's conviction. I would have to investigate the sisters quietly if Rosemary had unshakeable trust in them. "I was thinking of a close relative or romantic partner. Think about who else might know the details of your sisterhood."

"Yeah, I will." Rosemary nodded decisively then checked her phone and stood. "I need to get back, my next appointment will arrive in a minute. I hope that helped you understand the importance of our work, and how crucial it is that we don't lose any more necklaces." She scowled. "We need to solve this mystery before the motherhood and the elders find out. I'm too close—" She swallowed, and I wondered what she had been about to say. What held her back from calling the rest of her order for back-up? "I'll investigate further into who might be behind this. We need to recover the necklace that was lost."

I followed Rosemary out of the room and up the stairs, and she locked the stairwell behind me. We parted ways in the salon, and I exited the building through Cut Right's front door, pondering what Rosemary had told me. These women believed they followed an ancient prophesy that would manifest in a new world order.

I couldn't ignore Rosemary's tale, given both my long history of studying the arcane and the elemental currently residing in my body. My hand clenched involuntarily with my longing to examine the Book of Souls. As March, I had owned a whole library of spiritual treatises. What new information would Rosemary's book hold? And, if I could subdue Caelus

102

enough to answer my questions, what mysteries might I uncover?

I had nothing to do this morning, but a plan formed in my mind as I ordered coffee from Sacred Grounds. I was acting as security guard for these women, but my talents were wasted as simply brawn. Rosemary had told me she was investigating the motives of the attacking men, but there was no reason I couldn't poke around as well. Maybe an outsider's view would help. Rosemary's theory about the elders was interesting, but we needed facts. And I wasn't as convinced as she was that her sisters were innocent, although I couldn't imagine what one of them could be up to, nor how one could motivate men to attack on her behalf. I hoped that observing the sisters might bring me further clues.

I sipped my coffee as I walked around the corner to Sacred Grounds' back alley. This was the sisterhood's headquarters, and the site of three attacks to date. I patrolled here nightly, but were there any clues that I had missed?

I sauntered down the alley, unsure what I was looking for but scanning thoroughly despite my uncertainty. Chain-link fencing lined the back side, bordered by overgrown grass. The back of the building was pockmarked with a door for each storefront, and there were multiple dumpsters lining the alley. Short walls jutted out from each entrance to provide a single parking spot and a place for the dumpsters to rest. It was grubby, utilitarian, and utterly devoid of clues.

I peered at each location where Amanda, Denise, and Wanda were attacked, but other than a dumpster askew from my crash into it, nothing was amiss. I hadn't expected much, but hope was a difficult beast to suppress.

What was the common ground? Why had four different men attacked the sisterhood? As far as I knew, no one followed the sisters in their daily lives. The attackers were not people that the women knew, and the only commonality was that the thugs had tried to take the women's necklaces. Only someone who knew about the sisterhood and their mission would bother to steal the lockets. That suggested the men were working together or had a leader who directed them.

But to what purpose? Rosemary was convinced that the elders didn't trust the sisterhood to protect their artifact, but I wondered if the simpler solution was correct. It seemed more likely that a rejected lover of one of the women had enlisted the help of his friends to threaten her sisters and take away what she held dear. Maybe she had put the needs of the sisterhood over his, and he had reacted badly.

Or, as I was starting to consider more seriously, one of the sisters had mobilized some men she knew to attack her fellow secret-keepers. To what end, I didn't know, but that theory seemed more likely than a conspiracy involving other groups within their order.

I wasn't getting evidence either way at the sites of the crimes. There was one more to check, the street corner where I had rescued Miranda last night. I might as well be thorough, even if I didn't expect any clues to materialize where the other locations had been less than fruitful.

As expected, there was nothing to see at the site when I arrived. An old woman shuffled by with a walker, and I pressed against a nearby garage wall to give her space. When she had passed with a nod and a wheeze of breath, I stood straight and pondered my options.

Color flickered on my right, and I turned to look. A bird flew past, trailing gray streamers behind it, and landed in a tree that waved green strands from every branch.

Why was I seeing the threads of the world?

"Did you notice the threads at each location we visited?" Caelus' whispery voice was low and questioning. I was used to it being strident and furious, so I didn't react with immediate force.

I looked at his swaying torso and head made of silver strands that emerged from my left arm. His face was calm, pleasant even, and I relaxed somewhat. I would be ready to push him back the moment he tried to take over, but I was interested to have a civilized conversation with this strange being.

"What do you mean?"

"Look." He pointed his silver finger, and my eyes followed. Hanging from the edge of the garage, where the man might have waited for Miranda to pass, were two maroon strands as long as my forearm.

"Are those supposed to mean something to me?" I wasn't asking with sarcasm—I truly didn't know what Caelus was getting at—but he rolled his eyes at me.

"Touch one and we'll find out."

I reached out and gripped one strand between my finger and thumb. Caelus sent a few of his silver threads to wrap around the strand. It felt odd, different from touching other strands, but I didn't know what to make of it.

"What do you get from it?" I asked.

Caelus unraveled his strands and stared at the thread with narrowed eyes.

"It's from an amulet," he said at last. "It's been tampered with using human spells. I don't know what the amulet does, but its flavor is unmistakable. Human meddling leaves its own unpleasant aftertaste."

"You're saying that the attacker might have had an amulet with him?"

This bore thinking about. Amulets were rare, and the people who knew what they were even rarer. With the connection to the sisters, there was no way the amulet was a coincidence. The attacker must know about the sisterhood.

The men's immunity to pain sprang to mind. Could that have been caused by an amulet? If Rosemary had a whole room of amulets stashed in the basement of the shop row, it stood to reason that one could grant pain-reducing powers. I still didn't understand why these men were willing to sustain injuries for their unknown cause, but now I might have an explanation how they could.

"Either he had an amulet with him, or had one used on him recently. And the same is true of every location you have visited."

My head tilted back, and I whistled in reflection.

"Maybe Rosemary's theory about the elders isn't so far-fetched. They would have access to their own amulets, presumably. I wonder what it did to the men. Did it give them strength, or protection from pain, or something that would help in their attacks? Fascinating. I should phone Rosemary."

"At least it wasn't an artifact," Caelus said. "Amulet magic is easier to break. Artifacts were made with the help of an elemental and are far more lasting." He paused, and his face took on a too-innocent expression. "The Leaf that Rosemary spoke of must be an artifact. It sounds too powerful to be anything else. Also, she mentioned her amulet room in the basement. I wonder if there are any artifacts in there. It would be a good place to start looking."

"Your mission, of course." Caelus was sent here to find artifacts and destroy them to protect the balance of the world. His interest immediately put me on guard. I didn't want him to think that our little chat was an opportunity to take over the body and hunt artifacts, so I quelled his notion. "Rosemary locked up the place, remember? There's no way we're getting in there by ourselves, so you'd better sit tight and try to forget about artifacts."

As expected, Caelus puffed up and his expression grew stormy.

"You silly human," he spat. "You have no idea what you're interrupting with your invasion of this body that should have been mine. My mission is vital to the survival of this world, and you are thwarting me at every turn. No more, I say!"

"And that's my cue," I murmured and put my right hand on the top of his head. With some pressure and chanting, Caelus' rage-filled face grew smaller and more squished until he disappeared into the silver knot at my stomach. I sighed with a twinge of guilt. "It was a good chat, Caelus. If we could keep the name-calling and hostile takeovers to a minimum next time, I might let you out more often."

I was alone again, and it wasn't a great feeling. As precarious as our situation was, Caelus was a now-familiar face. He was always with me, and it wasn't terrible. Of course, the fear that he would take over again mostly overrode any soft feelings I had toward him, but I didn't hate his company when he wasn't railing at me.

I wished he weren't so hellbent on pushing me out of the way to focus on his mission. I would love to pick his brain about using the abilities that I borrowed. I had developed a lot of control already, but if I could learn from the source, how much more could I accomplish? I was only scratching the surface of what was possible, and already I was helping women in need in highly tangible ways. Where would Miranda be today if I hadn't come to the rescue with the wind at my back?

But with the way Caelus reacted every time he was free from his knot, it wasn't worth the risk. I couldn't lose control, not like the other night. I needed to be in the driver's seat, and until Caelus accepted that, it was too dangerous to allow him out.

I would have to start using his thread-vision more frequently, though. Caelus' hint about the strands at each attack location was fascinating. What amulet was being used, and why? Unfortunately, the clue came with more questions than answers, but any information was better than none. I dashed off a text to Rosemary detailing our find, then I tucked my phone in my pocket.

What next? I had hours until my next assignment. Anna was busy, my investigations were on hold until further evidence presented itself, and I had nowhere to be and nothing to do. What would Morgan do with spare time? I amused myself with imagining hobbies for my new existence—as March, I had practiced tai chi in the few moments that I hadn't been busy—but I swept the notion away. I wanted something productive, something of use, something that I really wanted.

Peter had always laughed mockingly at my tai chi. My gut clenched, but my brain spun in dizzying thought. Maybe there was something I could do today, something that I really wanted.

Blood pounded in my ears as I ran through a plan in my head. Tomorrow was Saturday. Chances were that he would be at home. I knew his address—*know thine enemies* was a sensible motto—I knew what I wanted, and I was ready. I brushed aside the rational voice that squawked in fear and disapproval, and molten anger flooded my body to replace it. I thought I had moved on from the trauma of my younger years, but maybe I hadn't. Maybe I had given up on anger too soon. Maybe there was something I could do to correct the past.

Tomorrow was the day I exacted revenge on my former tormentor.

CHAPTER XI

Preparation was key to a successful campaign. I took the bus to a mall, where I bought an oversized black hooded sweatshirt and a large pair of sunglasses. A balaclava in the winter gear section caught my eye, but I wanted to be unrecognizable, not excessively suspicious.

I spent the rest of the afternoon at the women's center. In the evening, I patrolled the shop row and counted each sister. Most departed in pairs or walked swiftly to a nearby car. Once they were all accounted for, I walked home and meticulously planned my morning. Nothing could go wrong. I wouldn't let it. When I had my mind set on something, little could stand in my way.

In the morning, I dressed for my mission and caught the Skytrain, the Seabus over Burrard Inlet, and one last bus into the hills, which finally took me within walking distance of Peter's house in West Vancouver. I was quite proud of myself for figuring out transit. Maybe I would cut it as a frugal twenty-something Vancouverite yet.

Multiple times during the journey I had misgivings about my mission, but then a molten core of rage pulsed inside me. I hadn't realized it had sat there, undisturbed, for so many years. I honestly thought I had exorcised that ghost ages ago and relegated Peter to a back closet of my memories.

The thing was, I had never felt as powerful as March as I did as Morgan. Morgan didn't have to think about propriety, finances, reputation, or social standing. Morgan could do whatever the hell she wanted, and now that she was unleashed, the coals that I had unwittingly kept glowing all my life had been stoked to a roaring inferno. I could confront Peter now and know I would win. The feeling was both frightening and empowering.

Navigating to Peter's house took me a solid fifteen minutes

huffing up from the main road. This was not a neighborhood whose residents frequently took the bus. The steep hillside gave me glimpses of ocean between houses. Peter's square, modern-looking dwelling boasted a large balcony off the second level, and I could imagine the expansive view. Impeccably manicured bushes and lawns covered rock terraces, interrupted by a well-maintained driveway of paving stones.

Peter's high-end Lexus sedan was visible through the garage door's frosted glass, but the other side of the two-car garage was empty. Good. His wife wasn't home. That would make things easier. I pitied the woman and wondered if she longed to escape the way I had. She had been married to him for ten years, now. They might even have a child, although my therapist had warned me against looking too deeply into their lives when they had married. At the time, I had agreed with her sound advice.

No matter. Peter was home, alone, and I could exact my revenge in peace. Peter was a wealthy man, and I was now far from it. Today, I could kill two birds with one well-aimed stone by draining his bank accounts. I knew an unsavory contact who could hack into Peter's accounts. If I gave him the passwords, it would be child's play for him. Peter guarded his wealth jealously, and removing that source of pride would hit him hardest and hurt him the most.

Peter had a terrible memory, and I could almost guarantee that he would have a list of passwords within easy reach of his computer at home. All I had to do was slip into his house, snatch the list, and skip back to my hacker contact. By this time tomorrow, I would be flush and Peter crushed. My lips curved in a satisfied smile as I imagined him explaining their new poverty to his current wife.

I flitted to the side of the house and hid from prying eyes behind established viburnum shrubs liberally planted in the yard. They were overdone, and I wondered who he had hired to do his landscaping. I certainly wouldn't be requesting their services.

Then I recalled that I now lived in a condo, and landscaping was not something I needed to worry about. New life, new me.

French doors led to a large office on the side of the house. No one was inside. I touched the handle, not expecting it to open, but it was miraculously unlocked. I opened it only far enough for my youthful body to slip inside.

A wide desk was covered with papers. A miniature statue of Cambodia's Prang temple sat as a paperweight on a precarious pile, and a half-eaten apple moldered nearby. I wrinkled my nose. Peter hadn't been the tidy one in our relationship. He hadn't needed to be. He'd had me to clean up his messes.

A torn piece of newspaper with a large image caught my eye, mostly because it was a picture of my old self. March wore a strange tunic and skirt with a ridiculous feathered headdress and stood before a huge stone temple. The text of the article was torn away, but red pen circled the image and words said:

Her breakdown my fault??

I stared at the newspaper, unsure how to interpret the words under the picture of my possessed body. I put the paper down next to a sharp letter opener and rustled in the mess on the desk, but another document on top caught my attention. It was a worksheet from an anger management course, partly filled out. My jaw dropped, and I snatched the paper off the desk. Under it were others, some completed with check marks on them.

My eyes raked the desk for more. A book called *Taming Your Inner Beast* was thick with sticky notes, and a calendar showed weekly meetings with a support group. A leather-bound notebook—always the spender on himself, Peter was—sprawled on the far corner, pages down and spine splayed. I gingerly picked it up and skimmed the words scrawled in Peter's near-illegible cursive.

Tara says I need to forgive myself before anyone else can, but I don't expect anyone else to, so what's the point of forgiving myself? I wish they would invent a time machine so I could go back and shake the old me. I don't know how I did it, what I put March through. Forgiveness isn't an option, certainly not by her anymore. She's dead, and there goes any chance of absolution from her. But I can do better for others, even if there's no hope for me.

My hands shook. What the hell was this? Peter writing a journal about his feelings? I would be more likely to believe in unicorns than Peter feeling remorse.

I threw the journal down in disgust and flipped through more papers, searching for evidence of his despicable nature. My overactive body pulsed with anger. I knew he was a scheming, manipulative bastard. Why wasn't the evidence here? He was so good at hiding behind a mask of charm. Whatever game Peter had started, I wouldn't play along. The rage in me declared that his evil was too strong to be denied, and today I would get my vengeance.

He was a vain man, excessively proud of his polished charm and well-proportioned features. Maybe I should disfigure him.

I snatched up the metal letter opener with its deadly point and wrapped my fingers around the handle. In theory, scarring his face would be sweet vengeance indeed, but the thought of deliberately drawing blood and inflicting slow pain made my calmer side squeamish.

But it was Peter. Maybe it would be worth putting on my big girl pants for that. My rational voice screamed its disapproval, but it was muted by the overwhelming focus of my mission. Taking away his money wasn't enough. I needed to hurt him more than that.

I tiptoed to the hall and stopped to listen. The house was quiet, but not an empty quiet. Someone was in the next room, and my instincts were confirmed when a rustle of paper and a soft throat-clearing emerged from the doorway.

I knew that sound intimately, although I hadn't heard it in years. My heart pounded with fear and rage in equal measure. It was time to make him feel as unstable and afraid as I had used to feel.

A pattering of feet poured ice on my hot anger. I darted around the staircase and flattened myself against the wall. I held my breath, afraid to make a sound. Peter wasn't alone.

"Daddy!" The voice of a small girl echoed through the hallway. "We're home. Mummy has groceries in the car she wants help with."

"Hi, sweets." My shoulders shuddered at Peter's deep voice. "How was ballet class?"

"So fun! We did pirouettes today. They're like spins on one foot. See? Like this."

There was a thump, and Peter laughed.

"Looking good. Maybe some more practice and you'll get it."

The little girl prattled on about her class, and two sets of footsteps walked to a side door that must have led to the garage. When the door clicked shut behind them, I fled my hiding spot and burst out of the office's French doors.

I passed a slight figure in a green hoodie like mine on the sidewalk and didn't stop running until Peter's house was a block away. When I felt safe, I shoved the letter opener in my backpack then put my hands on my thighs and just breathed.

That child clearly loved her father. How could Peter have hoodwinked his own daughter into believing he was worthy of love? I could detect no signs of tension, manipulation, or eagerness to please in their interaction. Maybe he kept it bottled up for his wife? I didn't believe for one second that he was truly changed.

I sighed. At least the child was okay. I wondered what my life would have been like with kids. I had been incredibly careful with birth control when we were together. I hadn't been able to fathom bringing another person under the umbrella of

Peter's influence, so I had never tried. I hoped his child was happy, although I couldn't imagine how.

I didn't know what to feel about Peter. Rekindled memories of torment, resentment, anger, and fear couldn't be doused in one afternoon. Just because he was trying now didn't erase what had happened in the past. That shared history had shaped me into the woman I was today. I was grateful to the universe for making me strong and resilient from that experience, but gratitude was nowhere near the list of feelings for Peter. The burning fury inside me said that he needed to pay for his sins, and trying now was too little, too late.

But if I hurt him, I would hurt his little daughter, and my calmer side knew that was unconscionable. I felt a fierce drive to protect that little girl, the same I felt for any girl or woman in need. I couldn't be the one to make her life harder. The world would do that soon enough.

The bus ride back to Cormorant Drive was long and wet. My eyes gazed past rivulets of water that streamed down the steamy window, and I cradled my bandaged arm when it started to sting. My rage drained away, leaving me confused by my reaction this morning. Passengers boarded and disembarked without my notice, and I only shook myself out of my thoughtful trance when the Skytrain loomed above the road, signifying my stop.

I walked slowly up the road with my hands in my pockets and my hood covering my hair. I was hungry, but lunch didn't sound appetizing. I wanted something comfortable, something that soothed. As March, I would have reached for a cup of tea and biscotti, but even that snack failed to grab my attention.

My thoughts turned to Upper Crust. *Lemon tarts*. My stomach growled its approval and I picked up my pace. It was strange that this body adored citrus desserts as strongly as

March had good wine. Tarts were harmless enough, so I didn't mind indulging the craving.

The bakery was warm and smelled heavenly. The heartiness of crusty bread, the light hint of sweet pastries, and the rich aroma of coffee floated into my nose and almost made me swoon with delight.

I didn't, of course. I wasn't that kind of woman, and my body was always under my control. But I could imagine a different person melting into a puddle of pleasure on the floor of this toasty bakery. I would almost feel sympathetic toward such a person.

Jerome was exiting the kitchen area as I stood in line. He had his raincoat on, a simple black shell, and his eyes had dark circles under them. I wondered about his life outside this bakery. What interrupted his sleep?

His face brightened when he spotted me.

"Morgan, hi. I didn't see you buy your daily lemon tarts this morning and I got worried." He smiled to show that he was joking.

I chuckled.

"I guess I'm predictable. I'm not sure what that says about me."

"That you know what you want. Nothing wrong with that." He glanced outside. "Are you rushing off after? I could buy you a coffee to go with those tarts."

I wavered. After my failure at Peter's house, company of the male persuasion felt like it shouldn't appeal. But Jerome's earnest face made me reconsider. I still didn't know his motives toward me, but maybe it was worth the risk. Anna wasn't willing to visit me, and it wasn't like I had people clamoring to enjoy my company. I could use a friendly distraction after the scene at Peter's house.

"It's just coffee," he said, as if reading my thoughts. "I could use a cup myself. It was a long morning."

"Thanks. That sounds great."

We sat against the window at a table for two with steaming coffees before us and a plate of lemon tarts. I pushed the plate toward Jerome, but he only laughed and shook his head.

"There's no way I'm getting between you and your tarts. Besides, after making pastries all morning, I lose my appetite for sweet things. I think I'll grab a burger for dinner tonight."

"You said it was a long morning." I picked up a tart and took a dainty bite when all I wanted to do was shove it into my mouth as quickly as possible and feel the citrus burst on my tongue.

Wait, why was I standing on ceremony? *No regrets.* I pushed the rest in and chewed in satisfaction. Jerome unsuccessfully hid his smile.

"Yeah, it was. I start at five in the morning to make sure the bread is ready for opening."

"That's early." March had been an early riser—the hormone shifts of menopause could be thanked for that development—but this new body appreciated a long, lazy morning.

"It's not so bad, but I come early to work on my own things. My kitchen isn't great at home." He cleared his throat and shifted in his seat, clearly uncomfortable with the direction of our conversation. "So, what do you do when you're not buying pastries?"

I was curious, but I let him change the subject.

"I work as private security for an organization." The explanation was specific enough to be true, but vague enough that no details of the sisterhood could escape.

Jerome looked politely confused.

"No offense meant, but most security types have a different build. Do you have special skills? Black belt in ju-jitsu?"

I laughed.

"Something like that."

I reached for another tart, careful to keep my sleeve over the bandage on my arm. He had been sweetly concerned the last time he saw me with an injury. What he didn't know wouldn't hurt him, and lying took more energy that I had right now.

Also, the new, suspicious side of me believed that he didn't need to know more about me than I wanted him to. He seemed genuine, but I wouldn't allow myself the sin of naïvety.

Motion outside drew my attention. In the car parked directly outside our window, a man in a ballcap gesticulated with wild arms. A woman sat in the passenger's seat, making herself as small as possible and averting her eyes from the shouting man. My heart squeezed at her posture, which was clear to anyone with experience that she wanted to avoid provoking the man into further violence against her.

I was on the verge of standing to intervene when the man opened the car door, leaped out, and slammed it shut. He stomped out of sight, and the woman in the car slumped in her seat with relief.

I unclenched the fist I hadn't realized I had made and forced myself to take a sip of coffee. Jerome glanced between me and the car.

"Looks like he's gone," he said quietly. I nodded stiffly, and he rubbed his neck with a sigh. "That's tough to see."

Jerome's rubbing exposed the dark blue lines of a tattoo on his neck. He was wearing a fully buttoned polo shirt again. It was an odd style for someone his age, and now I wondered if it were because he was trying to hide tattoos. My mind wandered as I imagined what lines crawled over his broad chest. I clamped down on the squirming in my gut with a stern talking-to. The hormones in this body were unruly.

"Have you tried lime tarts? Or orange?" I deliberately brought the conversation to a lighter place.

"Is that a request?" Jerome's eyes brightened and he leaned forward. "What about grapefruit?"

"I tried a pomelo once on holiday," I said, humoring his interest. "Like a grapefruit's mellow cousin. Delicious."

Until our coffees were finished, we spoke of inconsequential things. His enjoyment was always in earnest, and his genuine nature shone through with every word. I was drawn to him and had to remind myself to stay guarded.

But it filled something in my soul to chat lightly and easily with someone. As March, I had been too highly regarded with a reputation to uphold, and engaging in light, enjoyable conversation had been a rarity. Jerome was almost as easy to speak with as Anna.

"I'd better be going," he said eventually. "I'm about to lay my head down on the table and fall asleep. I'm sure I'll see you soon, though."

"Thanks for the coffee," I said when he stood. "And I'll be back for tomorrow's tarts, I'm sure."

It wasn't until after Jerome had left that I realized he hadn't asked for my phone number, hadn't pushed for anything, and had been the one to leave at the end instead of me.

Had I met a gentleman? Jerome was doing his best impression of one.

I wandered out of the bakery, pleasantly full of coffee, tarts, and conversation. Somehow, it was almost midafternoon, and I wanted to watch Starr, Jasmine, and Wanda leave their school. Watching the sisters might give me some hints about who the insider was.

It was the first clear afternoon in days, and I raised my face to the sun. It was low in the sky, so close to the winter solstice. At the thought, a fuzzy memory flashed through my mind of flickering vigil fires and the taste of strong wine from a long-ago solstice celebration. I closed my eyes and smiled. I had been Morgan once, and now I was again, but new and improved and ready to take on the world.

My phone's ringer tinkled from my pocket. I slid it out and frowned at the caller. It was Miranda—I had added the sisters to my phone contacts when Rosemary had given them to me, just in case—but why was she calling me? A sinking feeling settled in my gut.

"Hello?"

"Morgan?" A woman's voice whispered. "It's Miranda again. I think I'm being followed."

CHAPTER XII

Miranda's voice was laced with fear. I stiffened, ready to run wherever she needed me. Purpose filled my veins. Well, purpose or adrenaline. They felt similar today.

"Where are you?" I said. "Give me a location and I'll be right there."

"Garry and Twelfth, a block away from Cut Right. I went for a short walk during my break. I didn't think it would be a big deal, middle of the day and all, but I was wrong. Rosemary said it was okay, but she thought I was going with Shu, and Shu bailed at the last minute. I don't know, maybe he isn't following me. Let me turn the corner and see."

I cut through Miranda's nervous babbling, so unlike her usual composure.

"I'm only a minute away. Keep walking and talking, okay?"

"I can do that," she said a little louder. "My ex-boyfriend said he could hardly hear himself think around me. What a jerk, right? It's not like I talk that much. He should have met Joy. But then my sisters would have known about him, and they're all such busybodies. Good thing I ditched him. What a waste of space. I left an amulet in his apartment." She giggled, made shriller from nerves. "He'll have a hard time with future girlfriends. Well, maybe not such a hard time, if you get my drift."

I tuned out her incessant talk, feeling some solidarity for the ex-boyfriend's former plight, and focused on jogging toward Miranda's location. It was a solid four blocks away, but I was helped by the good weather. No soggy leaves to slip on here, only firm pavement and a clear path. I leaped onto the boulevard when pedestrians got in my way.

"He's getting closer," Miranda scream-whispered into the phone. "I can't outrun him with my stupid heart problem, and he's got that glazed look. What if he doesn't feel any of my punches? What do I do?"

"I'm almost there," I panted. Damn these jeans. I needed better gear. "Walk faster."

I turned a corner around a house painted a lively spectrum of rainbow hues and heard Miranda's shriek in stereo from my phone and in person. The quiet street a block away from Cormorant was empty except for Miranda and her attacker, a burly man with a ballcap that looked oddly familiar. When he yanked Miranda by her forearm and she let loose with a mean side swing that slammed into the side of his head, his face turned my way.

It was the shouting man from the car that I had seen with Jerome. Now, however, his eyes were unfocused, and his face passively blank instead of contorted with anger. Why had he fought with the woman in the car, and what did he have to do with the sisterhood?

I didn't have time to ponder such questions when the man jerked Miranda forward and snatched at her neck. She shrieked and clutched her necklace, then her face squeezed in concentration, and she kicked her attacker in the leg.

It was almost a perfect shot. A finger-span higher and she would have taken out his knee. As it was, the shock of impact loosened his grip, and Miranda wrenched free. He grabbed at her.

"My turn." I forced the words from my overtaxed lungs and reached for Caelus' silver strands.

My first blast of wind merely blew the ballcap off his head, which in his glazed state he didn't even notice. I narrowed my eyes and tried again.

This time, a large rock from a nearby garden provided the perfect ammunition. It sailed through the air and smacked the thug in his shoulder. It must have been agony, for he howled and let go of Miranda again. Whatever this guy was on, it wasn't as potent as the previous attacker's drug of choice.

"Run!" I shouted at Miranda, but she ignored me and faced the thug again.

"I won't leave you alone," she said breathlessly. She winced and clutched at her chest.

I ignored her, although I appreciated the sentiment. There wasn't much Miranda could do, not in her condition, and not compared to the tricks I had up my sleeve. As long as she stayed out of my way, we would be fine.

The man lurched toward us. He was too close by the time I had assembled my next strike, and the blast of wind that smacked him in the face caught me, too. We tumbled onto the sidewalk together and my cheek scraped the pavement.

The thug wasted no time throwing himself on top of me and pinning me to the ground. He leered at me, the only emotion I had seen on his face since the episode in the car.

His expression, paired with my immobility under him, made me shrink inside until I felt as small as the woman who had been shackled to Peter. Then, white-hot rage melted that woman. How dare this imbecile overpower me? How dare I let myself feel out of control like that? That woman was my long-ago self, not today. I was March no longer. Today, I was Morgan.

I screamed in his face, a primal howl of furious rage without fear. He looked confused, so I kneed him in the groin and bit his wrist at my shoulder with all my force. He yelled with pain and his grip loosened enough for me to wriggle an arm free and grasp a handful of mauve strands that floated around the thug's head. I pulled hard.

The man yelled again, then he twitched and shook in a seizure that rolled him off me. I didn't let go of my white-knuckled grip on his strands. Once seized, I would never relinquish the upper hand.

It was time to practice my mind manipulation again. Sure, I had addled the last guy beyond speech, but practice made perfect. I twisted the man's threads together, following the intuition that pulsed in my fingertips, then I pulled harder. What did I care if he could never talk again? He had attacked Miranda, attacked me, shouted at that woman in the car. I wasn't prepared to strive for perfection with this miserable bastard.

Blood throbbed with a frantic rhythm in my ears. I wrenched at his head strands, grabbing great swaths and tying them in oversized knots that lacked any semblance of finesse. The man's eyes rolled, and he drooled. Then, with one huge twitch, his body fell still.

My chest heaved with panting breaths. My hands shook as I tied another knot, and I wasn't surprised when a gathering of silver strands on my arm signaled Caelus' arrival. I was weakened by my fight, both physically and emotionally, and Caelus had sensed his opportunity.

"Don't mess with me right now," I said when his features formed. "I can and will push you back down, but it will tax both of us."

"I know what you feel," he said quietly. "Because what you feel, I feel. I came to tell you about the signal. Look at the man."

I stared at the unconscious body at my knees. My breath quieted as the enormity of what I had done sunk in. He wasn't dead, but how far off was he? At least he seemed like a waste of skin, and I couldn't imagine anyone missing him. My rational, more sympathetic side railed against this pronouncement, but I pushed it down. The world was better off without a man like him. I straightened my back.

"What am I supposed to be looking for?"

Caelus gave a soft tsk.

"His threads. Are they all the same color?"

I had been too busy during the attack to notice, but the man's mauve strands were interspersed with maroon threads of a familiar hue.

"They're the same as from the other attack sites," I said.

"Good, that's confirmation that the men are working together."

"Touch one," Caelus commanded.

I reached out and gripped a strand between finger and thumb. It pulsed with something indefinable that tasted like a phantom strawberry on my tongue. I looked at Caelus in question.

"What is that?"

"It's the signal from an amulet. He's been worked on. From the signal, I would guess mind-control. He was forced to steal the necklace from Miranda."

I sat on my bottom, winded from the news. Mind-control. Was that a thing? I recalled the man's glazed look, and how it matched the others. I had assumed drugs, but had the attackers all been under the influence of something more sinister, more magical? I looked at Miranda, who stared at me in confusion and concern. I wondered if she could hear Caelus or whether she thought I was talking to myself.

"Is a mind-control amulet possible? Have you ever heard of one?"

Miranda nodded slowly, her eyes still questioning.

"Yeah, I have. I don't know if we have one, though. You'd have to ask Rosemary. She keeps an inventory."

"What would it do?"

"It would make someone very suggestible for a short time. Like, you'd touch them with the amulet and tell them what you wanted them to do, and they'd do it, no questions asked."

I shook my head. What a power. Who controlled it now?

"Wait," I said. "That means that a single person might be behind these attacks. Did you know this man, Miranda?"

"No." Her eyes were wide and honest. "I've never seen him before."

"Someone is influencing random men on the street to attack members of your sisterhood to steal the necklaces." I rubbed my forehead. "That means that this man was a victim as well. He was innocent."

124

I wanted to stop my brain from stringing together the logical conclusion, but it steamed right ahead. If this man were innocent, that meant that I had irrevocably damaged his mind without good cause. Yes, he had attacked me, and I needed to defend myself and Miranda, but I could have stopped when he was down. I had deliberately addled his mind because I felt he deserved it.

I had appointed myself judge, jury, and executioner, but I didn't have the information nor the right to be all three. My next thought struck me like a blow to the face.

Was I the bad guy here?

I had so easily fallen into the trap of considering myself a victim again that I hadn't considered the responsibilities of being the one in power. I'd seen enough abuse of that power from others, but I'd assumed that if I had the reins in a violent situation, that my actions would be just and true. I'd always valued the accuracy of my moral compass.

Had the power I'd been granted through Caelus corrupted me? I'd thought that I would be less susceptible to it, as a woman who had known power abuse in the past. Could power corrupt no matter the wielder?

"Who would do that?" Miranda whispered. She reached out the hand that wasn't rubbing her chest, and I hauled myself up with her help.

"Rosemary has a few theories." I touched my grazed cheek and winced. "But I don't know which is right. I wonder if these men were randomly chosen, or whether they had the propensity to violence and the mind-control amulet simply pushed them along." The man shouting in the car crossed my thoughts, and I turned away from his pale face on the sidewalk. I was glad that people in this neighborhood all seemed to be at work.

If the mastermind behind the attacks chose men who were already bad apples, I felt less guilty about messing with this one's mind. Miranda shook her head.

"From what I know about amulets, they are pretty strong. I think one could make even a saint do terrible things."

Damn. There went that theory. I swallowed bitter bile that threatened to creep up my throat. I felt dirty from my actions, like I'd been swimming in a crystal-clear lake whose water had suddenly turned to manure.

"You'd better get back to Cut Right," I said to Miranda. "I'll walk you there."

I waited until Rosemary finished with her customer before I pulled her to the back hallway behind the shops.

"Miranda was attacked," I said without preamble. "She called me, and I got there in time to fend him off."

"Did he get the necklace?" Rosemary said, her mouth a tight line.

"No, and Miranda's fine too." I was surprised that the necklace was the first thing Rosemary asked about, given her usual level of care toward her sisters.

"Yes, I saw her in the shop. She seemed fine." Rosemary drummed fingers on her arm. "The attacks are getting more frequent. Denise was accosted this morning."

"What? Why didn't she call me?"

"She dropped her phone when she took Starr to the mall on the weekend. She was waiting until payday to get a new one. She's so careful, and she always parks close to work, so I didn't think it would be an issue. Especially in the daytime." Rosemary's face held only chagrin. "My mistake for underestimating our opponents. Denise isn't hurt, and she gave the man a run for his money, but he pulled out an amulet which weakened her. He then easily took the necklace. We need to get it back."

"That's two missing now, right?"

Rosemary nodded, her face bleak.

126

"I can only hope that they aren't the ones containing the Leaf."

"It doesn't feel like a coincidence that Denise was attacked when she didn't have her phone. I wonder if our culprit knew that."

"Culprit? Just the one? All the attackers have been different men."

"They're all under mind-control, the work of an amulet." I scanned Rosemary's face for a reaction and was rewarded by her dawning understanding. "Tell me, do you have any amulets like that in your collection?"

"Yes," she said quietly. "And one's missing. I checked my inventory last night. All amulets are accounted for—my sisters and others in the order check them out when they want one, like a library system—except for that one. But no one knows about the sisterhood or the amulets except for my sisters and the rest of the order, who have all devoted their lives to the cause. If the elders really were behind these attacks, they wouldn't have needed to steal our amulets. They have powerful amulets of their own. I don't understand what happened."

"Maybe someone close to a sister found out," I said, although I wasn't sure I believed it. Too many signposts pointed to a sister being the mastermind behind the attacks. Still, I had to investigate every possibility. "Pillow talk. And they broke in or coerced one of your sisters to get the amulet for them. Did you get the list of your sisters' partners for me?"

"I can tell you what I know." Rosemary brought her hand up to count her fingers. "I'm not seeing anyone and haven't for a few months now. Joy bounces between lovers, but nothing is ever serious so I doubt there'd be bad blood or any secrets revealed. Miranda is too shy and mousy to go after men. Shu has lived with her partner Jolene for a year. Denise, Amanda, and Wanda keep their romances a secret from me." Rosemary sniffed her disapproval. "Jasmine dallies with various high school boys but likes to keep them guessing. Starr has never expressed interest in anyone."

Starr was clearly dating Trent, that boy I had seen with her, and Miranda had her own secrets, but I kept my observations to myself. Rosemary, while seemingly well-intentioned, didn't need to know every detail of her sisters' lives.

"No obvious leads," I said with disappointment. "Too bad."

"Tonight is training night," Rosemary announced. "We'll all be at headquarters until nine, so you don't need to patrol until then. Oh, unless you want to join us."

I tilted my head in thought. Although I had my air powers, I could use more defensive tactics. Tonight could also be an opportunity to learn more about the sisterhood and what they did.

"Sure," I said. "I'll be there."

Starr sent me a text, saying she was home sick and wouldn't be going to training. I ate dinner at my condo, then meandered to the row of shops.

Cut Right's door was still unlocked, although the lights were off. I slunk inside, hoping that the other women were nearby. When silence met my ears, I walked quietly forward to investigate.

The door to the stairwell, usually locked, was propped open with a spent bottle of shampoo wedged under the door. I grinned and walked down narrow stairs to the small hallway at the bottom. Female voices murmured from the workout room's open door above the beat of high-energy dance music. I stepped through.

"You made it," Rosemary called out. She waved at me from across the room, where she curled a free weight into her chest. Next to her on a blue floor mat, Denise nodded at me while she stretched her legs.

128

I waved back at Rosemary and looked around the rest of the brightly lit room. Amanda and Shu gathered my attention easily from the center of the floor. Amanda's ginger ponytail flew around her face as she dodged Shu's intended grapple, and Shu's eyes narrowed in concentration. They danced over the central black mat with swiftness that spoke of long hours of practice, but even I could tell that Shu was better versed in defense than was Amanda. When Shu pinned the other girl to the ground, my suspicions were confirmed.

Miranda smiled tentatively at me from a stationary bike when I looked her way, and I smiled in return. Jasmine was in her own world on the bike next to her, earbuds in her ears and eyes glued to her phone. In a corner, Wanda focused on smacking a bag with rhythmic punches that hung from the ceiling.

Joy beckoned to me, and I ambled her way. She was red-faced on a treadmill, but her exertions didn't prevent her from talking.

"Are you joining us today? We train a couple of times a week. Rosemary's strict with us, but it's good. We're really prepared. Not that it matters much for these attackers, but we can only do what we can control." Joy's face darkened briefly at the reminder of the duress her sisterhood was under, but bad moods clearly couldn't infect her for long. She grinned. "And now you're here! Pick whatever you want to work on."

"What are Shu and Amanda doing?" I asked.

"Advanced self-defense techniques. We don't follow one particular school of martial arts. The sisters have developed their own unique style, picking the most useful methods from lots of different disciplines. Female-focused, of course. Once I finish my treadmill set, I can show you a few moves, if you like."

"Thanks."

I gingerly climbed onto the treadmill beside Joy's and turned it on with the same care one might take when disabling a bomb. When the treadmill started to turn, I jolted then walked with jerky steps. I soon grew used to the motion and walked with deliberate strides while I watched the others.

Shu now sparred with Rosemary, and in my inexpert opinion, the two were evenly matched. Hands darted with snake-like speed, and their nimble movements up and down, around and over, were mesmerizing and filled me with longing to do the same.

With a start, I remembered that my youthful body could do anything the others did. And, under Joy's tutelage, I could learn how. I should consider training my body the way I was training myself to use the threads.

Joy was a patient teacher, even if she overexplained every move, and by the end of the evening, I had learned three basic self-defense techniques. Oddly, my body responded with precision to Joy's lesson, and I wondered if Fiorella had practiced some form of self-defense, or whether my past lives were surfacing with phantom muscle memory. I had vague recollections of being a Viking shield maiden.

The sisters seemed closer after their training session, as if it brought them together under a common goal that their daily lives missed, and I envied them their camaraderie.

After training, everyone got to their destinations without mishap, and I breathed a sigh of relief when I reentered my suite.

My late evening plans of relaxing to the music of Rodgers and Hammerstein and sipping a nice merlot were dashed when my phone rang.

"Hello?"

"Morgan! It's Shu. Help, I—"

There was a crashing scramble, then silence. I immediately redialed, my heart in my throat, but it rang until voicemail clicked in. I frantically dialed Rosemary's number.

"Rosemary, it's Morgan," I said when she answered. "Shu just called for help, but she got cut off. Where would she be if not at home?"

"Um," Rosemary stammered, clearly thinking hard. "Maybe she's walking her dog? She and Jolene usually go together, so I didn't think to warn her."

"Just tell me where," I said. With the phone clutched to my cheek, I ran to the door and pulled on a new pair of runners. With no car and women being attacked every day, it had seemed like a sensible purchase.

"Right. Shu and Jolene live at Thirteenth between Azalea and Pine. They usually go around the block. Wiggles has short legs."

"Got it."

I hung up, flung on my coat, and dashed to the stairwell. I was lucky—Shu lived only a few blocks from my condo—but the streets stretched like putty with my need to get to Shu quickly.

The skies were mercifully empty of clouds, and a crescent moon shone weakly in the dark spaces between streetlights. I raced to the corner of Magnolia Street under the shadow of the elevated Skytrain and swung to the right. A huddle of what looked like a pile of clothes lay on the sidewalk a block away, lit by a colorful display of holiday lights on the nearest house. A ball of white fluff, orange in the streetlights, yapped at its fallen owner.

I picked up speed and dashed to Shu's side. The dog growled at me.

"Back off, Wiggles," I said. "I'm trying to help Shu."

Maybe it was my use of the dog's name, but the animal calmed and watched me warily. I turned to Shu. Her normally tanned face was unnaturally pale, and her black hair was matted at the temple with blood. There was a deep gash in her scalp, and my stomach constricted. Was she even breathing?

I placed a hand on her stomach and was relieved by its faint rise. Shu was still alive, but that head wound looked terrible. I pulled out my phone to call the emergency line, then I paused. Merlin often healed himself and others from terrible injuries. It was one reason he was still alive after centuries on Earth. Now that I had similar powers, why couldn't I do the same?

But I couldn't do it alone. Shu deserved better than the mangled job I would manage on my own. With hesitation, I let go of the spell containing Caelus.

CHAPTER XIII

Caelus swirled out of his silver knot, and strands pooled on my arm before rising to form his now-familiar face and body.

"This is a surprise," he said. "Releasing me of your own volition? I'm almost too shocked to fight for supremacy."

"Please, not yet," I begged. "Help me save this woman's life first. Then we can talk, or fight, or whatever you had in mind."

Caelus gazed at me for a long moment before he nodded and looked at Shu. Now that Caelus was released, I could see the snarl of knots in Shu's tomato red strands above her injury. It looked even worse than the blood, and I winced in sympathy.

"She is gravely hurt, but not beyond our aid. Now that you can see the threads, simply unpick the knots."

"Is that it?" I wouldn't have released Caelus if I'd known it were that easy.

"Do it gently," he said with a stern glance. "If you break one, it could make her worse."

I swallowed and kneeled to my task. The red strands were cool and slippery to my touch, but the knots slid out with ease. Once or twice I had to wiggle them gently apart, but after ten minutes of work, the snarls were gone, and threads flowed freely over Shu's body. Her gash had healed over, and all that remained of the injury was dried blood in her hair.

"I will wait quietly until you are alone," Caelus said. "I promise not to take over if you promise not to contain me until we speak again."

"It's a deal," I said, and he melted into my arm and flowed over my body.

Because he wasn't contained, I kept my thread-vision. It was disorienting but fascinating as well. I shook my head to focus my thoughts on Shu instead of the distracting strands and patted Shu's cheek.

"Come on, Shu. Time to wake up."

Shu moaned, and her eyes flickered open. She glanced with confusion at my face, then with growing terror around her.

"What happened? Where is he?"

"Calm down. The man is gone. It's just me."

Instead of calming, Shu sat up and patted her neck frantically. Her face contorted with despair.

"It's gone. My necklace is gone. I failed my duty."

Wiggles yipped, and Shu scooped the animal up and buried her face in its soft fur.

"You were attacked," I said gently. "If I hadn't healed you, you would be on your way to the hospital or worse. You did all you could. The others will understand."

"It's too important to mess up." Shu gulped back a sob. "I failed. It doesn't matter how. I only hope I wasn't carrying the true Leaf. I don't understand what happened. I felt fine, then as soon as the man approached me, every part of my body was so heavy. Even moving my legs felt like I was swimming underwater."

That was worrisome. The mastermind was handing out amulets to her thugs. Whoever the mastermind was, he—or she—knew exactly how to defeat the sisters.

"Come on." I lifted Shu to her feet and tucked my arm around her torso. "Let's get you home. Why were you walking alone, anyway? Where is Jolene?"

"She gets migraines," Shu whispered. "I had to take Wiggles for a walk. It was just around the block. I'm easily the best fighter of my sisters, I thought I could handle it. I guess I was wrong."

Shu tried to suppress her tears, but a sob escaped her every now and again which she stifled in her dog's fur. I shook my head in confusion. This sisterhood took their duties seriously and believed with all their hearts in the dire outcome if they didn't play their part.

What truth was behind Rosemary's legend?

134

I waited until I was back in my condo before I invited Caelus out to play.

"Okay, Caelus." I settled against the couch and sighed deeply. "Come out for a chat."

Silver threads swirled down my arm and coalesced into Caelus' form. I rubbed my free hand through my hair.

"What do you actually want, Caelus?" I asked. "I'm tired of fighting, but I'm willing to do it as long as you keep trying to take over this body and shove me into a corner."

"What, like you're doing to me?" Caelus arched an eyebrow, and I shrugged.

"Touché. It's horrible, isn't it?" I felt a pang of sympathy for subjecting Caelus to that treatment for days, but I couldn't fully regret it. Autonomy was too important to me. "What's your goal? Can I help you without giving up control of the body?"

Caelus looked puzzled, like he had never given the notion any thought.

"My mission on this plane is to find and destroy artifacts, those objects created with elemental magic. They don't belong here because they disrupt the balance of the world. A tremendous upset recently shook my plane of existence, and we're still reeling from the aftereffects. My leaders feel that any contribution to imbalance, no matter how small, ought to be eliminated. Artifacts fall under that category."

"And how do you propose to find said artifacts?"

Caelus looked uncomfortable.

"My leaders didn't give me instructions. I was supposed to figure it out on my own."

"And a bang-up job you're doing," I said. At Caelus' glower, I relented. "Just teasing you. It's a tricky job, no doubt. I have some ideas, though. If you were willing to accept my

135

control of the body, I could help you complete your mission."

Caelus crossed his arms, his look calculating.

"But not full-time, I imagine. Your security duties take up much of your attention."

"Yes, they do, and I'm not going to give up my goals to devote this body entirely to yours. But I can compromise. It's stressful to maintain your containment spell, and I know how frustrating it is to be suppressed. If we share this body to further both our goals, would that be enough for you?"

Caelus stared at me. I waited with my breath held. Finally, he nodded.

"I am willing to try our new arrangement. If you promise to search for artifacts and refrain from binding me, I will not take away control of the body from you."

"And you'll help me use your powers more effectively." Negotiation was a hard-earned skill, and I couldn't resist getting a better deal out of any bargaining I entered.

"And that. It will be to both our benefits." Caelus' lip curled. "Your finesse leaves something to be desired, and you're only scratching the surface of my capabilities."

"Excellent." I stuck out my hand to him. "Shake on it?"

Caelus studied my outstretched hand, then extended his thread-formed fingers toward mine. I gripped the strands firmly, and their cool slipperiness was solid beneath my grasp. I smiled.

"How about that lesson?"

We practiced late into the night. There was little air movement in the condo and fewer air strands, but Caelus didn't see that as a detriment.

"We can work on your finer skills," he said. "If you can manipulate single threads successfully, you will have the control to master larger scale maneuverings. There is a thread floating toward you—grab that and see what happens."

I tightened my lips in concentration and squeezed the thread between my finger and thumb. It set off a tiny chain reaction that knocked my lamp onto the couch. Caelus nodded.

"Good. Set the lamp back up and we'll do it on purpose."

It took twenty minutes and countless attempts before Caelus was satisfied. We moved to toppling objects further away then manipulating the temperature of the air around me. When Caelus finally allowed me to stop, I flopped onto the couch in exhaustion, shivering after my last bout of frigid air. Caelus looked unruffled as always.

"So," he said casually. "About the artifacts. Where do we start looking?"

I stared at the ceiling in thought. When I didn't immediately respond, Caelus floated above my head.

"Well?"

"I'm thinking." I rubbed my face, forcing my tired brain to work harder. "I had amulets at my old organization, but I don't think any were artifacts like what you're looking for. They weren't that powerful."

"And Rosemary's secret library of magical objects," Caelus reminded me.

"Yes, we'll certainly check that out when we can. I'll figure out a way. There's also this necklace that the sisterhood is protecting. What do you think that is?"

"Given what they say it will do when reunited with its other two parts, it must be an artifact. No amulet would be that powerful. The necklaces appear like amulets—surrounded by only a few weak threads infused with minor charms of protection—but the truly powerful threads must be locked within the locket."

"I don't know how we'll get the necklace. I'm supposed to protect the sisters who hold it, not steal it from them. Maybe we can leave that artifact for later. We know the sisterhood is taking good care of it in the meantime."

Caelus looked glum.

"Now what?"

"Museums would be our next best bet." I sat up straight when a thought occurred to me. "The grail. It must be an artifact."

"What's the grail?"

"It's a cup—ancient Celtic workmanship, La Tène style, made at least two thousand years ago—that was clearly magical. I found it in a shipwreck during my tenure as leader of my secret organization. I couldn't see threads back then, but the cup's magic was so strong that those who were sensitive could feel the hum of power. And, when I touched it, memories of my past lives came back to me."

"It's definitely an artifact," Caelus said. His eyes glinted. "Where is it?"

I sat back, defeated.

"Merlin stole it from me. Of course." I took a deep breath. "Back when I was trying to open a door to the elemental world. More the fool me, because that's how I became possessed by the earth elemental in the first place."

"But then you wouldn't be here, sharing this body with your new elemental friend."

I looked at Caelus in surprise. He was grinning.

"Aren't you the lighthearted jokester? You're much more fun to be around when you're not fixated on taking control of our body."

"It's my nature," he said. "Air elementals can't hold onto a grudge for long. We leave that to the earth elementals. So, when can we get the grail? It sounds like our best lead."

I sighed.

"It will take careful planning. Merlin won't give it up without a fight. Let's focus on museums and protecting the sisterhood necklaces from being stolen for now. We don't want someone else to get the Leaf before we do."

Despite the late hour, I lay awake for ages. My mind churned with the revelations of the day. Caelus and I were at a truce, which allowed me to relax. I hadn't realized how tense I'd been until I let go of the containment spell. I didn't know if I could trust Caelus, but it felt like a worthwhile risk. I was reasonably certain I could escape any bonds he trapped me in, which was a comfort.

Our lesson had been exhilarating, and I was eager for more. Power was exciting, but honing that power into a razor-sharp edge that I could wield with precision and accuracy had been a dream of mine for so long. With the right training, no one could stand in my way.

My stomach turned every time I remembered the glazed look of the man I had addled beyond repair. I needed to control this power with far more finesse. I couldn't afford to act as judge, jury, and executioner if I didn't have all the information. With Caelus' knowledge behind my new tools, maybe I could release the attackers from their mind-control. I would practice that with Caelus tomorrow.

That settled, my mind wandered to the other pressing topic of my day. My failed plans for Peter burned in my gut, and in the soberness of reflection, I questioned my motives. Why had I burned with such fire to wreak vengeance on my ex-husband? I thought I had exorcised that ghost years ago. Did he still hold such sway over my emotions?

I explored my face with one hand in the darkness. Its features were growing familiar to me, but it was still a new body. Did it have more control over my mind than I knew? I had assumed it was a vessel that I had poured myself into, but there was no denying the very real changes it had wrought on me. My fascination with lemon tarts was one trivial example.

Tarts brought my mind to Jerome, and heat rose in my cheeks, another reaction that my mind had trouble controlling.

Was it so far-fetched that this body of mine had unresolved anger issues, and it was channeling those urges into thoughts of Peter?

My gut churned in response. It shouldn't matter what self-improvement classes he was taking or how much his daughter loved him. Peter was a master manipulator, and a leopard didn't change its spots. My tired brain churned with implausible plans to hurt Peter without affecting his innocent daughter.

Caelus gathered himself above my arm and peered at me.

"What are you doing?"

I shrugged. It was strange having a constant companion, but oddly I didn't mind. I was so used to being on my own and relying exclusively on myself that Caelus was an intriguing novelty. Truth be told, I liked the company.

"Planning justice for myself. My ex-husband is a piece of work, and I never got the chance to fully make him understand what a lowlife he is."

I pulled my pillow out from under my head and fluffed it vigorously. Caelus swayed with my motion until I replaced the pillow.

"Revenge, more like," he said. "I thought you were embracing your new life, not dwelling on your past."

"What if the past won't rest until I lay it to rest?"

Caelus stared at me for a long moment.

"Let the wind blow away your troubles," he said finally. "Let the stink of yesterday drift away with the breeze. Fresh scents are all around you if you let them in."

With that, Caelus retreated into our body. I fluffed my pillow again. Damn it. Were my words from my rational mind or my rage-fueled body? Thornier still, what if my emotions had always been simmering under the surface, buried by the calm perspective of age, but reawakened by the passions of this second youth? What I told Caelus wasn't wrong—Peter probably did deserve any punishment I could bring upon him—but before my body switch, I would have agreed whole-heartedly with Caelus's pronouncement. How could I tell the difference between my two sides?

Sleep was elusive for long after our talk.

I slept to an hour that had my inner March shaking her head, but I was still bleary from my late night. When I finally shuffled out the door after a quick tea and toast made from Jerome's superb sourdough, it was nearly time for my volunteering shift at the Center.

My heart warmed when the cozy little house emerged around a corner, but I was still a few minutes early and had time to kill. I hated feeling idle. I always wanted to be moving, doing, working toward a goal.

My friend Anna popped into my mind, and I leaned against a fence to call her. I didn't know what her work schedule was, but I could check. Maybe she was free for a coffee. I could use a friendly face to talk to. Not that I could tell her about the sisterhood, but I was used to keeping secrets. There were other things to discuss. Anna and I never needed an excuse to chat.

The phone rang three times before Anna picked it up.

"Hello?"

"It's me, Morgan," I said. "Don't you have me in your contacts yet?"

"Hi, Nancy," she said in a falsely cheery voice. A rustling sound told me she was walking to another room. "It's my day off. Is there trouble at the coffeeshop? Did you try calling the manager first?"

My brow wrinkled. What was Anna playing at?

CHAPTER XIV

"This is Morgan," I repeated. "Formerly known as March. Remember?"

"Of course, I remember," she whispered. "Wayne was in the room. I had to cover for you. No one is supposed to know."

"Right." I was relieved by her explanation, but a pang of disappointment twinged my stomach. It wasn't a comfortable feeling, making Anna sneak around for me. I pushed the guilt down.

"Do you have time for a visit? I could use a coffee right about now."

"Wayne and I were just leaving to drive to Whistler for the day," she said. "We won't be back until late. Another time?"

"Yes, another time."

I didn't have the energy to sound chipper as I repeated her words. I was acutely aware that Anna was my only friend. Now that she was difficult to get hold of, our connection tenuous at best, the weight of my solitude felt crushing.

"Coming," Anna shouted with the phone microphone covered. To me, she said, "Look, I have to go, or we'll never make it there. Take care of yourself, okay? We'll talk soon."

After we said our goodbyes, I hung up and stared at my phone. Anna was keeping me a secret at my request, I reminded myself sternly. She was doing what I asked and doing it well, as she always did.

But I couldn't deny the hurt I felt at her choosing Wayne and her new friends over me. Anna and I had been through a lot together. This must be a momentary blip in our long friendship. She would be back.

Until then, I needed to create my own life. A new body meant new everything. I had to stop clinging to my past and move forward. It was proving more difficult that I had anticipated.

Nevertheless, my call with Anna had eaten up my remaining time, so I entered the center's house, albeit with a little less gusto than before. Inside, Greta was alone behind the counter. She hummed as she typed numbers into a spreadsheet on her computer.

"Ah, Morgan." Greta greeted me with a smile. "I'm glad you could make it. You'll be helping in the computer room today. If anyone needs assistance, you can lend a hand. When you're not busy, you can fold these pamphlets."

She handed me a stack of photocopied papers which I accepted. My chat with Anna had reminded me of my old life and my donations to the center. I asked a question on impulse.

"I heard that a major donor for the center recently died. Is the center still being funded?"

"Well," Greta said. She put her hands on the desk as if ready to deliver big news. "You're correct, but it's not the full story. There has been a hiccup with her will, apparently, and funding has been frozen until the lawyers sort it out. We rely heavily on that source, so management was pulling their hair out, you can imagine. Word on the street is that the donor set up a trust fund for the center in perpetuity, which is a relief, but who knows when that money will be available?"

My heart sank at the news. I had half a mind to phone my attorney, but I knew that was a fruitless endeavor. He wouldn't discuss the accounts of a dead client with a random caller. I wondered what the hold-up was. It wasn't like I had any dependents able to dispute the contents of my will.

"But there's more," Greta said breathlessly. I had the feeling she'd had a quiet morning and was bursting to chat with someone. "There's talk of another donor stepping in to fill the gap, with big money, too. It's all words now, but if it comes to pass, it will tide us over and then some."

I blinked my astonishment, and gratitude filled my jaded heart. Someone else cared about this cause so dear to me.

My shift was slow, with only three women using the

computers and none needing my technical assistance, although one benefited from a hug. When my two hours were up, I gave Greta my stack of pamphlets and exited the center. The slow pace of my work there had allowed my brain to chew on other problems. It was time to fight back against whoever was targeting the sisterhood. I hated waiting for the next attack. Proactivity always paid off, in my experience.

After consulting my phone for the bus timetable, I managed to board the correct one to a nearby mall. The attendant behind the counter of a security store didn't blink when I described what I wanted. After a moment in the back room, he emerged with the equipment.

"This motion-sensing camera is battery operated and connected to your phone via Wi-Fi. It can alert you when there's motion, and you can watch the livestream video on your app. Or, just set it up to send still-photo text alerts. Mount it with this clip."

He put the camera on the counter then held out his hand for money, which I happily handed over. This device might be a game changer. I would hide the camera in the alley behind Cut Right and Sacred Grounds. It wasn't perfect, but it was a likely location for an attack.

"Receipt, please," I said to him. There was no need for job expenses to come out of my salary. Rosemary had a fund she could dip into.

It would soon be time to watch Rosemary and Miranda leave the salon for the day, but I could set up the camera while I waited. At the back of Cut Right, a corner of the roof gave me an unobtrusive place to tuck the device. I had to climb onto a dumpster to do it—praying that I wouldn't fall in—but I eventually set it up to my satisfaction.

Halfway down the main road, I jumped when my phone pinged. Had the camera started working already? Was someone being attacked right now? I was only a few blocks away. I could easily run there in minutes.

I opened my app with eager fingers. It took me a moment to figure out what I was seeing. Finally, it clicked. Rust-colored feathers of an unusually pigmented pigeon mocked me from the bottom of an otherwise empty video of the alley. My shoulders slumped, then I rallied. An attack-free zone was a good thing. And the pigeon, as frustrating as the winged rat was, had shown that my camera worked as advertised.

Still, maybe the video was overkill. I changed the settings to still-photos, unwilling to watch the preening rat-bird in real-time.

Sundays were long when one was alone. My mind conjured a vision of Anna skiing with Wayne, a joyful laugh trailing from her mouth. I banished the sadness in my heart and walked briskly to my condo. There was plenty of time for a solitary cup of tea at home.

The silence of my condo was too much to handle, and I escaped to the company of my phone like the typical millennial I appeared to be. I scanned the news, but my brain must have been thinking about my new body, because my fingers danced over the screen to find police reports. I scanned the missing persons report for last week, curious to read more about Fiorella.

The face that now greeted me in the mirror every morning appeared under my scrolling thumb. I stopped and centered the report on my screen.

Missing: Fiorella Provenza. Brown hair, medium height and build. Goes by the name of Fi. Last seen on coach bus from Hope to Vancouver on November 29th. If seen, please call her brother Valente.

The telephone number beat a steady rhythm on my retinas. The woman who used to occupy my body was named Fiorella. She'd had a life, a home, a family. Maybe she'd had plans and

145

ambitions, some reason to get up and go. Why had she gone to Vancouver? How had she ended up dead at the temple site?

I pushed my tea aside, no longer able to swallow the comforting drink. There was nothing I could have done differently, but I still felt sick at Fiorella's loss. She was dead, and no one was able to mourn her and put her to rest.

No one except me.

I stood suddenly and grabbed my coat from the closet. There wasn't much I could do in reparation for stealing Fiorella's already stolen body, but I could honor her.

Once on the street, I ducked into a corner store for a quick purchase. Then, I hopped on the nearest bus and wound my way to Trout Lake, a tiny patch of water in the middle of the city.

The park was sparsely populated on this blustery Sunday, the darkening sky a dismal slate gray. One lone runner passed me on the path, his shoulders hunched against the wind. I shivered and adjusted the hood on my jacket.

At the water's edge, which was boggy enough that I was thankful for my boots, I took the supplies out of my bag. With a few deft movements, I folded sheets of newspaper into a passable boat. My fingers struck a match and lit a short pillar candle. When enough wax had pooled below the wick, I dribbled some into the boat and stuck the candle in place. With a deep breath, I placed the boat in the water and gently pushed.

"Fiorella Provenza," I said aloud. A gust made the candle flicker and the boat drift away. "I never knew you, but I wish I had. Your life was cut short far before your time. It sounds like you left behind a brother who loves you, and I hope that he might find his own peace in the wake of your disappearance. I thank you for the gift of your body, and I promise to look after it the best I can. Rest in peace, Fiorella."

I watched the little boat drift into the lake in the dim light of a winter's gloom. The spectacle mirrored faint memories of past mourning from other lives I'd lived and left a taste of melancholy behind. When I left, the candle was a tiny pinprick of light on the steely gray water.

Caelus, to his credit, waited until I turned away from the lake before popping out of my arm.

"When are we going to look for artifacts?" he said without preamble. "I've been waiting for you to make good on your promise. We've been doing your errands all day without a thought toward artifact-hunting."

I sighed and tapped my fingers on my thigh, then I shrugged.

"Now."

"Now?" Caelus looked taken aback. "I didn't expect that answer. Good. How?"

"That's the better question." I strolled along the path toward the main road. With any luck, there would be a bus soon. I hadn't yet figured out the system to my satisfaction, but buses did seem frequent. Where each one went was a different mystery to solve. My mind rolled around possibilities. "It's worth looking at my old amulet collection. I assume none were artifacts made by an elemental, but it's a place to start."

"Where are they?"

"When I disbanded my secret organization, I shoved them all in a cardboard box and put the box in my basement. Packing was a rush job at the end. The amulets should still be there."

"What are we waiting for?" Caelus' strands quivered with anticipation. "Our first real lead. Onward!"

I suppressed a grin at his enthusiasm and strode to the bus stop. There was no reason I couldn't humor Caelus this afternoon. It wasn't as if I were run off my feet today.

It took a few tries—the Sunday schedule had minimal buses, and I overshot my intended stop and had to trek under overpasses and across multilane thoroughfares to fix my

147

mistake—but I eventually stood before my house on Marine Drive. Well, my former house. I had been less than two weeks in my new body, but already my past as March felt like a forgotten dream. Everything was familiar, but in a hazy, unreal fashion. I rubbed my arms to dispel the shiver that raced across my skin at my ease at shedding my old identity. I had thought that my identity was firm, unyielding, central to who I was, but I was more mutable than I could have imagined. Morgan fit me like a well-worn glove, maybe even better than March had.

I shook my head to drive away my introspection and tromped up the drive after the mangled wrought-iron gate yielded to my touch. The driveway was empty of cars—no one had yet descended to fight over my house, which frankly shocked me, since it was worth so much—and I strode to the mudroom entrance without hesitation. Once again, I let myself into the side door and slipped inside.

A faint waft of mustiness hit me with the smell of a house that hadn't been lived in nor had its windows opened in too long. I wrinkled my nose. It hardly even smelled like home, and I walked past the carefully chosen furniture and paintings without a second glance. March and her cares were so far removed from my current life.

"Where are the amulets?" Caelus said when he emerged from my arm.

"Basement," I said. "We're almost there."

I breezed through the kitchen—whose counters seemed obscenely expansive after my condo, although I couldn't find it in myself to long for them—and opened a door within a walk-in pantry. The stairs were bare wood and descended into the darkness of the unfinished basement. I flicked on the light switch with familiar ease and trod gently to the bottom.

"Ugh, it's like a hole," Caelus said with distaste. "I much prefer your current dwelling, up in the sky."

"I didn't live down here," I said with amusement. "You're right, it's a hole in the ground. But a useful one to store old bits of rubbish that I don't need anymore."

"I hope your amulets aren't all rubbish." Caelus peered around. "Where are they?"

"Patience. You're worse than a dog who's smelled a squirrel. We're getting there."

A stack of boxes lined the far wall, leaning against the cement foundation like drunks after the pub closes. I frowned. Had the damp got to them? I shouldn't have left them down here. Maybe I should sort out what I wanted to keep and what I didn't.

I shook my head. No, those boxes weren't my problem anymore. March was dead, and I was simply pilfering through her old things for treasures. What happened to the rest wasn't my concern anymore.

The top box was from my office at the organization and had papers and lists with membership details. I wasn't in contact with any of these people anymore, save for Anna, and their names held no interest. The next few boxes had kitchen supplies and magazines from the communal area, and I shuffled them aside quickly.

The bottom box rattled and jingled when I slit the tape with my fingernail, and I smiled.

"Ready, Caelus?" I said. "Keep your eyes open for artifacts."

I opened the flaps with a flourish. Caelus peered in, his eyes eager. After a moment, his shoulders slumped.

"Nothing," he said in his whispery voice. "Just human-made amulets. We're back to square one."

I peeked in past his silvery strands. The box was a jumble of rings, necklaces, cups, and other odds and ends, more evidence for the rush I had been in when packing up my disbanded organization. Now that I could see with Caelus' vision, every item was wrapped in multicolored threads and pulsed gently. My mouth dropped open.

"I didn't realize what they look like with threads," I said.

"Pretty and powerful. No wonder they worked."

"Not like the amulets that Rosemary and the others sometimes use," Caelus said. "Those spells are tightly woven with purpose. These are simply clusters of power. Useful in the right circumstances, but not as effective as the directed amulets of the sisterhood."

"I'm sorry my amulets don't live up to your exacting standards."

He sniffed at my sarcastic tone.

"Don't blame me for the truth. Rosemary and her clan clearly know what they are doing. These were done by an amateur."

"Yes, yes, I gathered that already." I frowned at the pile of glowing items. "Should we take them anyway?"

"Might as well," Caelus said. "Maybe you could learn how to direct their energies into something useful."

I scooped the items into my backpack then crossed the basement to climb the stairs. I barely glanced at the house as I passed through it like a ghost.

Once on the street, I hiked to the nearest main road. A bus was in sight when I reached the traffic-filled thoroughfare, so I raced to the stop. I was barely breathing heavily when I arrived, and I smiled at my new body's fitness.

"Where are we going now?" Caelus said when I sank gratefully into an empty seat. No one could hear him except me.

"To the museum," I said. "With any luck, that 'Mysteries of the Dark Ages' exhibit is still showing. That's our next best bet."

I stared in dismay at the ticket counter of Vancouver's museum. A large sign behind the teller announced the new traveling exhibit coming next month—something about the history of fishing on the coast—and it mentioned nothing about the Dark Ages exhibit I hoped to see.

"When did Mysteries of the Dark Ages finish?" I asked the teller when it was my turn.

"A few weeks ago, but they finished dismantling it just yesterday." She looked at me sympathetically. "Did you miss it?"

"Unfortunately, yes." I drummed my fingers on the counter. "I suppose there's nothing to see anymore. It must all be tucked away in a back room, awaiting transport."

"That's right," she said. "All boxed up near the loading bay. But you're welcome to visit the rest of the museum since you're here."

I made my apologies to her hopeful face and retreated to the gift shop. Caelus emerged with a grumpy expression.

"Another opportunity lost," he said.

"Not quite yet," I whispered. I grabbed a ball cap with the museum's logo on it and placed it on the shop counter with a few bills. Once the assistant had rung my purchase through, I walked confidently outside and around the corner.

"What are you planning?" Caelus said.

"Whatever I can to get the job done." I pulled my hair into a ponytail and tucked the ballcap low on my forehead to shade my eyes.

The loading dock was hidden from the grand entrance and looked like most loading docks: excessive concrete, a semi-truck trailer pushed against a platform, and a slightly smelly dumpster in a corner. I wrinkled my nose, wondering why my life now involved far more dumpsters than necessary.

My heart leaped. I was luckier than I deserved, for the door leading inside was propped open with a wedge. Someone must have been unloading the trailer and forgotten to close the door after them.

"Terrible security," I muttered to Caelus as I slid inside and slunk down the dim hallway. "But I'm not complaining."

A door marked "storage" was my target, and I noiselessly turned the doorknob. The large room was stuffed with musty-smelling wooden crates, although not all lids were stapled down yet. I ran to the nearest crate and peered inside, Caelus' cheek beside mine.

"Nothing," he said at the sight of smaller boxes packed in cardboard pellets. "I would see errant threads this close to an artifact, even through boxes. Try the next one."

I raced from crate to crate, increasingly aware of time passing. Someone was bound to notice the open loading dock door, or finish their tea break, or arrive to staple the crate lids. We needed to check the crates quickly and get out of there.

"Did you finish—" A voice started, then the tone changed. "Hey, who are you?"

My head whipped around. An older man with a paunch and a clipboard stared at me. His murky yellow strands wiggled with his dismay.

"Just helping pack up," I said, pitching my voice low to remain less identifiable. I hoped my ball cap would hide my face in this dim light. "I'll get the truck."

I edged toward the door.

"You can't be in here," he said in a louder voice. "Did you take anything? You're going to have to come with me."

Instead of answering, I burst into a sprint. He dropped his clipboard and grabbed at my arm, but I dodged and whisked past him. Through the hallway and out the door with the man's cries for security drifting in my wake, I raced away from the museum. When a few blocks were between me and the building, I dropped the ball cap in a nearby garbage can and slowed to a walk, my breath coming in heaving pants.

"We found nothing," Caelus said after a moment of silent walking. "None of the items we saw were artifacts. Where are we going now?"

"Back home," I said with a sigh. "I'm sorry, Caelus. We'll have to think of another plan for finding your artifacts."

152

My photo collection had grown steadily over the afternoon and evening, and I was thoroughly sick of the rust-colored pigeon and tops of heads by nightfall.

"How many random people walk down this alley?" I muttered to myself over a late dinner of chanterelle and asiago risotto at my kitchen table. I had lit a candle for ambiance and to stave off the cold drizzle outside, but it flickered alone, reminding me of my solitude.

I had always liked my own company as March, but that was when I had been surrounded by other people. A few friends, plenty of acquaintances, and many colleagues filled my days, so that when I'd retreated to my own home, it had been with relief. Now, there was only Anna, and she was shaping up to be a poor friend to Morgan.

"I need to get a life," I said. It sounded more pathetic out loud, and I reached for my phone to turn on some music. Maybe that would drown out my melancholy thoughts.

The phone pinged in my hand.

"If it's that pigeon I'm going to shoot the damn bird," I growled then sighed and opened the text. I had to check, even if it was the rat-bird.

The still photo of a man crouched behind the dumpster piqued my interest. I peered at the photo. No one hid behind an oversized garbage bin in a dark alley with good intentions. It was almost time for Amanda to close the coffeeshop, and I was due to patrol. This time, I could practice my new skills.

"Ready, Caelus?" I said as I stood to leave. The answering swirl of silver strands around my middle made me smile. I forgot—I wasn't alone.

Rain splattered against my face despite my hood as I jogged to Sacred Grounds. I was getting heartily sick of this gloomy alley. Maybe this time I could get some answers from the man.

Did he know who controlled his mind?

"Caelus," I panted. "Can we remove the man's mind-control, do you think? I want some answers today."

Caelus shimmered out of my arm and swayed with my motion. He nodded at my question.

"Yes, we should be able to. Human-made amulets are never as strong as an elemental."

"Glad you're so modest, too," I said with a grin.

Caelus huffed and melted into my arm again.

The darkness of the drizzly December evening had swallowed any pedestrians into their homes. I was alone, my feet pounding the pavement, and I was thankful for it. I hadn't yet been confronted by a curious spectator about my unusual abilities, but I had been lucky so far. It was time to be more circumspect. The dark helped.

When I rounded the corner of the alley, my breath heaving in my lungs, the click of a door shot through the pattering of rain on the road and my own panting. When a familiar ginger-haired figure emerged from the coffeeshop's back door with a garbage bag in one hand, I shouted.

"Amanda! Get back inside."

A shadowy figure surged from behind the dumpster toward Amanda. She shrieked and backed away. Rosemary had admonished Amanda's lack of training, and apparently Amanda knew her own inadequacies. Wide eyes were the last thing I saw before the door slammed shut.

The man fell against the closed door and yanked at the handle, but Amanda must have locked it from inside. He growled. It was a deep, sinister noise, and the hairs on my neck stood up. With a slow, fluid motion, he turned to me.

In my haste to get Amanda to safety, I had run toward the man. Now, my feet were planted only steps away.

It was too close. Caelus' wind powers were ideal for long-range attacks, but I wasn't skilled enough to use them up close. The man advanced on me with his teeth bared. His eyes, when they glinted in the light of a distant streetlight, were glazed. I backed up and snatched as many air threads as I could reach. With a pitiful effort, I threw them at the man.

He barely flinched when a gust blasted his face. My foot caught on a wheel of the dumpster, then my back pressed against it. Damn. Nowhere to go. I tried to slide sideways to escape the man, but he merely chuckled and put a heavy hand on each forearm. I froze at the touch, my heart thundering in my chest but my brain devoid of useful thought.

"You're a lot of trouble," he slurred, sounding for all the world as if he were staggeringly drunk. "I should get rid of you right now. Save us all."

My frozen stance broke apart, and I kicked and scratched anything I could reach like a cornered rat. I might not be able to use my abilities right now, but I'd be damned if I went down without a fight. I had spent too many years giving in to do it now.

The man hardly reacted to my attempts, even when a well-placed knee met his groin. How strong was this mind-control? I was both awed and terrified. How could I snap him out of it?

"Caelus!" I screamed. "A little help, here!"

Caelus emerged, but his face was as frightened as mine.

"Without your arms, there isn't much we can do," he said. The man looked around for company, but Caelus was invisible to him. "We will need to practice this scenario later."

"How is there going to be a later if I don't get out of this?" I shrieked.

"Shut up," the man growled. "I'm done with you."

For a brief, wonderful moment, the man's hands left my arms, but my relief was misplaced. His fingers wrapped around my neck and squeezed with all their considerable force.

My hands scrabbled at his wrists but couldn't budge his strangling grip. Stars exploded in my eyes, and I panicked. Flashes of Peter doing the same thing tormented me, his hot breath on my cheek, a solitary tear running down his face even

155

as he squeezed the breath from my body.

Is this how my second chance would end? In a dark alley, full circle from what I had escaped all those years ago?

CHAPTER XV

My vision was tunneling when the man's fingers released my neck. I fell forward on my hands and knees, coughing and retching as blissfully cool air fought to enter my lungs. Grunts and thuds interrupted my heaving breaths, but when I collected enough of my senses to recognize what they were, I looked up.

A huge, dark figure held the man's shirt front and punched him in the face once, twice, three times. His expression was grim and resolute. No righteous rage crossed his features as he dealt out justice on my attacker.

When I remembered that the man was under the influence of an amulet, I croaked out my savior's name.

"Jerome. Stop."

His face whipped toward mine, and he dropped the man without a second look. He skidded to his knees next to me and gently touched my shoulder.

"Are you okay?" he asked then shook his head. "Of course you're not. What can I do?"

I coughed again.

"I'll be fine," I rasped out. "Just—I need to get closer to him. Help me?"

As gentle as if he carried a baby bird, Jerome carefully tucked a hand under my elbow and helped me up. I shuffled toward the man crumpled on the ground. He groaned.

His face was a bloody mess, and two white teeth smeared with dark blood lay on the ground near him. My stomach turned over at the carnage, but a small part of me rejoiced at his pain. My throat really hurt.

I could have died at his hand. Suddenly, his face wasn't bloody enough. I could addle him in the same way as the previous attacker. A few well-placed yanks at his head strands, and he would never strangle another woman again.

My eye caught the maroon strands of the mind-control

amulet, and I sighed inwardly. As much as I wanted to hurt him, he wasn't in his right mind. He was as much a victim as I was. I steeled my thoughts and kneeled next to his face.

"Okay, Caelus," I whispered. Even if I hadn't cared if Jerome heard me, I couldn't force words any louder through my ruined throat. "How do I stop the mind control and make him forget?"

Caelus emerged from my arm and gazed at the moaning man before us with a dispassionate eye.

"I'll direct your hands, if you'll let me," he said finally. "And pay attention so you can learn for next time."

I nodded my assent, and Caelus' form disappeared into my body again. Silver threads flowed over my hands like luminous gloves, and my fingers moved of their own accord. It was a disconcerting feeling, and I had to actively relax my arms to prevent fighting the sensation.

I watched closely as my fingers picked apart knots and twisted threads. The maroon amulet strands that Caelus had recognized earlier were easy to see even in the dark, since threads glowed with their own gentle light. Caelus shimmied them out from their tangles and dropped them on the ground without ceremony.

"What are you doing?" Jerome asked in a whisper.

"Give me a minute, then I'll explain," I said softly. My concentration was wholly focused on Caelus' movements. I wanted to learn exactly what he was doing, as I doubted this would be the last time I would need this skill.

It was tremendously complicated, but the more I watched, the more I understood the patterns of what Caelus was doing. When I guessed his next movements before he did them, a small smile lifted my cheeks. I was getting this. With practice, all of Caelus' abilities would be mine. Then I would be unstoppable.

My smile soured when my throat seized. In our next lesson, Caelus and I would focus on close-range combat. I couldn't be taken off guard like that again. Tonight had been too close. If Jerome hadn't been there...

Finally, Caelus lifted my hands and sent his silver strands back to my torso. He didn't fully retreat, and my vision remained filled with softly glowing threads. The man was still unconscious, so questioning him about the mastermind was out. I sat back and sighed, which sent a cough spasming through my body.

"He has an amulet in his pocket," Caelus said.

Threads spilled out from the man's right jacket pocket, and I reached in and pulled out a keychain. Threads swirled around it, and I was willing to bet the amulet could stop pain. Too bad I didn't know the activation words because my throat was killing me.

"I'm done," I whispered to Jerome after I slipped the keychain into my pocket. "Let's get out of here."

"Don't you want to call the cops?" Jerome glanced at the man on the ground then back at me. His voice was calm, but his sand-colored strands jumped around with frenetic energy. I wondered what it meant.

"No," I said. It was true. I had no way of explaining about the mind-control, and the man would get a much harsher sentence without that knowledge. "I have my reasons. Besides, he's been punished enough. I don't think his nose will ever be the same again."

Jerome gazed at the unconscious man, and guilt flashed across his face. I touched his shoulder and he twitched.

"Thank you for helping," I said quietly. "He would have strangled me if you hadn't been there."

Jerome nodded with a jerk, but his strands squirmed. He stood and gave me his hand to haul me up. We left without a backward glance at the man. I resolved to give the emergency line another anonymous call when I got home.

Before we exited the alley, Jerome picked up a white cardboard box. I glanced at it with interest.

159

"Taking home some of your handiwork?" I brightened. "I don't suppose you have a tart in there?"

Jerome laughed, and the sound broke our solemnity.

"Sorry, no. You'll have to come by the bakery tomorrow. But yes, there is baking in here."

I coughed again, and Caelus popped out of my arm.

"You can heal yourself, you know," he said with a casual air. I glared at him, and he continued. "If you find somewhere to sit, I can direct your hands again."

I gave a small nod and looked around for a suitable spot. The drizzle hadn't abated, and every surface was wet and unappealing. Half a block down, a covered bus stop lit with a softly glowing advertisement beckoned. It was late enough that the already limited Sunday buses were few and far between. I pointed at the dry bench inside.

"Can we sit for a minute? Breathing is hard right now."

"Of course."

Jerome steered me toward the bus stop, and I sank gratefully onto the bench. As before, Caelus took control of my hands and massaged the strands at my neck. I kept half my attention on his movements, but I reserved the rest for Jerome. His brow furrowed with confusion.

"You look like you have something on your mind," I said. I knew what was coming, and I liked to meet things head-on. "Spit it out."

"A few things." He clenched his fists then released them with effort. "Who was that guy? Why did he attack you? What did you do to him after? What are you doing to yourself now?" He took a deep breath and released it with a whoosh. "You don't have to answer any of those questions—you hardly know me, and you don't owe me anything—but that's what's on my mind right now."

I gazed at him steadily until he squirmed. It was sweet, and despite the trauma of the evening and my sore throat, my stomach grew warm at the sight. I sternly told my hormones to

160

settle down.

"You remember I told you that I have a private security job," I said finally.

He nodded but still looked puzzled.

"You don't have any gear," he said with a glance at my waist. "No taser, no nightstick, no knife."

"That's true. I'm getting there." Already my throat was feeling better thanks to Caelus' ministrations. I could feel his smugness at that thought. "I didn't know the man, but I knew he was there to attack one of my clients. I approached him, and things got out of hand. As for my weapons." I took a deep breath now that I was able to. I wish I'd had this healing ability as March. It would have saved me a few ibuprofen nights, that was certain. I looked Jerome squarely in his warm brown eyes, lit by the soft glow of a cellphone advertisement. "I have supernatural abilities. They're a recent development, and I'm still learning how to use them."

My hands finally dropped to my lap as Caelus finished his healing. I glanced at them then back to Jerome to gauge his reaction. His face held a mask of polite puzzlement, but wariness lurked underneath.

"I don't understand. What do you mean, supernatural?"

"I can make the wind do whatever I want," I said. I tightened my lips as I considered how best to explain, but there was nothing better than a demonstration. "Let me show you."

I raised my hands and yanked at the nearest air threads. A blast of wind buffeted our faces. Jerome's jaw dropped, then he snapped it shut.

"Coincidence," he said hoarsely.

I grinned.

"Maybe." I twitched air strands in rapid succession to drum out the beat of "Jingle Bells" on his face. "Or maybe not."

His breathing came short and fast. He glanced at my hands, my face, and my hands again.

"You're for real," he said. It wasn't a question.

"Indeed." I leaned against the glass wall, feeling drained. "Real as rain."

He leaned back to join me, and we were silent for a minute. He let out a long breath that was half a curse, half a sigh.

"I heard eating sugar helps with shock," he said eventually.

I turned my head to look at him.

"I'm willing to try."

He gave me a wobbly grin and pulled his bakery box onto his lap. With a reverence better suited to crown jewels, he lifted the lid and presented the box to me. His strands coiled tightly around his body. Was he nervous?

I looked in. Although slightly squashed from its rough drop in the alley, the half-cake was still gorgeous. Perfectly smooth fondant wrapped around the circumference and over the top in an unbroken layer of geometric patterns in black and white. A flowing wave of fondant on top softened the harsh lines. The cake inside was a vibrant red velvet that looked firm and moist. My mouth watered in anticipation.

"It's gorgeous," I breathed. I looked at his face and caught the end of a relieved look before he schooled his features into a façade of calm. "Did you make it?"

"Yeah." He took a folding knife out of his pocket and cut a slice. The knife was very sharp with a mahogany handle well-polished with use. I accepted the slice with eager fingers and brought it to my lips immediately.

It was as moist and flavorful as I had imagined, and I barely suppressed a moan of satisfaction. Jerome looked pleased with himself.

"Even the fondant is delicious," I said once I'd swallowed my first bite. "I've never eaten appetizing fondant before. The stuff on my wedding cake tasted like cardboard. Everyone peeled it off."

Jerome's features didn't change, but his strands jolted at my pronouncement.

"Are you married?" he asked offhand.

162

I shook my head vigorously.

"It didn't end well. It didn't really start well if I'm being honest. The middle was terrible too. Good riddance. Maybe the fondant was a sign I should have listened to."

I smiled to indicate that the topic wasn't a sore point, and Jerome laughed.

"Fortunetelling through baked goods. Maybe it's a new thing."

"Makes as much sense to me as cards or crystal balls." I believed that those items could help direct the mind to pick up signals—if not of the future, then at least of the past—but I didn't believe they worked without an accompanying amulet. With an amulet full of power nearby, even cakes could give guidance. "Wait, is the bakery getting into wedding cakes? I haven't seen them advertised."

"No." Jerome took a deep breath. "I am. Trying to, anyway."

I put up my hand.

"Hold that thought. I need to shove more of this delicious cake in my mouth." For effect, I closed my eyes while I chewed. "Mmm, so good. Sorry, you were saying?"

A smile tugged at his mouth. It looked good on him, softening the hard lines of his face.

"I want to get into wedding cakes." He shrugged in a defensive gesture. "I've never told anyone about that. In person, anyways. I have a website. My first client's wedding is coming up, and I'm perfecting my technique. She's not paying much, since it's my first cake, but I can take pictures for my website."

He pulled out his phone and flipped to his photo gallery. Through the overexposed image, I could make out the entirety of the black and white cake. It was a magnificent two-layer structure with striking patterns.

"It's gorgeous," I said, and the smile tugged at his mouth again. "But please tell me you will take better pictures for your

163

website. I can hardly see the cake in these."

His shoulders and strands drooped as one.

"I don't have any other camera. Just my phone." He squared his shoulders. "I'll try to set up better lighting next time."

"Where's your business card?" I held out my hand for one, but Jerome's jaw worked.

"I don't have one yet."

"What's your business plan? Have you approached the bank yet for a loan to get you started? Where do you bake these cakes, anyway?"

With every question I asked, Jerome grew paler and his strands twitchier.

"Bank? I hadn't thought about it. I don't think they would be interested. My credit—" He flushed. "Upper Crust allows me to use their kitchen after hours. That's where I came from tonight—I was working on the cake."

"And then you're up at five the next morning for work?" I glanced at his face and noticed the black circles under his eyes. "That's dedication."

He shrugged.

"It's the only way to get access to a proper kitchen with the right tools. My apartment isn't exactly up to code."

I looked at Jerome with new interest. He had ambition and dreams, that was certain, but he would fail without a good plan. Baking and business were different skill sets. To my business mind, it hurt to see someone floundering like Jerome clearly was. I wondered what advice I could give that he would benefit from most. I would have to think about that.

"I'd better let you get to bed," I said, standing. "Five o'clock isn't that far away."

"Can I walk you anywhere?" He suppressed a yawn on his last word, and I chuckled.

"I'm okay, thanks. Get some sleep."

"At least let me give you my phone number." He held out

his hand for my phone. "Then you can call if someone jumps you on the way home."

I passed my phone over, oddly grateful for his suggestion. It was strange, since I was the one with the security job, that the offer of protection would tickle me so much. But it meant that someone cared enough about my wellbeing to offer me a lifeline, and that felt good. My solitary existence had been grating on me, and it was nice to know someone was on my side.

Even if I hardly knew Jerome, I was grateful for his attention. The suspicious streak in my new body still wasn't entirely convinced that he didn't have some ulterior motive, but my objections were being worn away with every meeting. Jerome had yet to show me his bad side. I would be watchful, but in the meantime, I would enjoy the company of someone who seemed to genuinely care.

I returned to the front door of Sacred Grounds after I left Jerome and walked Amanda to her car. She was quiet and frowns wreathed her face.

"Are you okay?" I asked to break the silence.

"Besides almost being attacked by a crazy man who can't feel pain?" Amanda rubbed her forehead. "I'm sorry, I didn't mean to snap at you. You've been so helpful. I'm just annoyed at Rosemary."

"How so?" I asked when Amanda fell silent again.

"I don't know why she isn't taking this more seriously. She hired you, which is a good step—although there were some sisters who questioned letting a stranger know about our sisterhood, you can imagine—but she hasn't called the rest of the order for help."

"Why don't you?"

"It's not my place." Amanda shrugged. "The eldest sister is

the liaison to the rest of the order, and we are supposed to follow her leadership. I just don't understand why she's not calling for backup, or making us leave town for a while, or something. Especially since all of our training is useless against these psychos."

I was silent for a long while. Rosemary's actions confused me, too, and I wasn't sure what to say.

"Ask her about it," I finally offered. "Maybe she has a good reason. In the meantime, I'm happy to walk you home."

Once I waved goodbye to Amanda at her door, I stumbled to my condo to fall into bed with a grateful sigh. I slept in again and woke craving tea and lemon tarts in that order. As the kettle boiled, I decided that after my close call last night, I needed to follow every lead I could. Today, I would investigate.

Over my morning coffee, I wrote down my suspect list. I included every sister, then crossed off Amanda, Denise, Miranda, Shu, and Wanda. Unless the mastermind was particularly devious, it was a stretch to imagine she would make a thug attack herself for show. That left chatty Joy, downtrodden Starr, snotty Jasmine, and Rosemary herself. They would be worth watching.

The rest of the sisterhood's order was also a possibility, but I had no way of contacting them, so Rosemary would have to take the lead on that front. The only other options on my suspect list were close companions of the sisters. While I drained my coffee cup, a text arrived from Rosemary asking if I was okay after last night. I answered Rosemary's text with an affirmative and asked for contact information for Shu's girlfriend Jolene and Joy's most recent fling.

When I slipped on my boots at the front entryway, Rosemary called.

"Hi, Morgan," she said. The sound of women's voices chattered in the background, and someone turned on a hairdryer. "Joy says she went on a few dates recently with a man named Justin. He works at a bank downtown, but she says she never told him anything about the sisterhood and their breakup was mutual. Jolene works at a physiotherapy clinic on Oak Street, and Shu says she takes her lunch break at noon. Jolene knows about the sisterhood, and, obviously, Shu trusts her completely." Rosemary's pinched voice told me that she didn't trust anyone except her sisters. "I hope that helps."

It sounded like Joy's dalliance was a nonstarter, but I could visit Jolene today. Rosemary didn't know about Starr's boyfriend, so I would quietly meet with him as well to cover my bases. Someone with insider knowledge of the sisterhood was after those necklaces, and it only made sense to check with the partners, if only to rule them out.

A quick stop at Upper Crust earned me a small box of tarts and a swift smile from a harried-looking Jerome as he kneaded a huge ball of bread dough with powerful pushes of his hands. I left quickly to stop my eyes from lingering on the slide of bicep muscles under his polo shirt, today a cherry red.

My next stop was at Sacred Grounds. I leaned over the counter to chat to Amanda who was filling coffee orders. Now that Caelus and I had a truce, the multicolored threads that wrapped around her necklace were evident. They must be the protection spells that Rosemary mentioned. Amanda's eyes brightened when she spotted me.

"Morgan! Thank you so much for last night. It's wonderful that you're here now. I feel so much safer with you around."

"You're welcome." I watched her squirt flavored syrup into a mug. "Amanda, I'm looking into who might be doing this." I kept my words deliberately vague so the customers nearby who were waiting for their drinks didn't overhear. "That said, please tell me who you dated last. I need to explore all avenues, no matter how improbable."

Amanda shook her head, but a knowing smile crossed her lips. She poured hot milk into a metal jug and held it under the steamer.

"I promise he had nothing to do with this," she half-shouted over the screaming nozzle. "Denise, Miranda, and I borrow special tools." She waggled her eyebrows at me then turned off the steamer to whisper her next words. "They cause memory loss. He has no idea who I am. Makes things much less complicated."

I blinked at that. Amanda spoke with such nonchalance at wiping someone's memory. I could imagine dire situations that might call for such drastic action, but to uncomplicate a relationship? I wondered at Rosemary's grip on her sisters. Did she truly condone such behavior?

"Okay," I said. "Thanks for letting me know."

It was close to noon, so I hopped on a bus that meandered toward Jolene's clinic through a grid of tightly packed houses and occasional low-rise apartments. The sun was shining, although low in the sky at this time of year, and the city had hung festive wreaths on lampposts of the main drag. I took a deep breath and filled my lungs with crisp autumn air. Despite my near throttling last night, I felt light and full of hope. Maybe today I would figure out who was after the sisterhood.

My phone pinged and I glanced at the pigeon in her full feathered glory before shoving my phone back into my coat pocket. Beaky had better watch out. If I caught her red-taloned, feathers would fly.

A tiny woman with glossy black hair and huge dark eyes wandered out of the small clinic at five minutes after twelve. I took a gamble and approached her.

"Jolene? My name is Morgan. Your partner Shu knows me."

Jolene nodded swiftly. She reminded me of a bird, small with petite features and short, jerky motions.

"Hello, Morgan. Yes, Shu told me all about it. We share everything."

"Of course. Then you won't mind me asking what you think of the sisterhood."

168

"It's Shu's destiny," Jolene said quickly. Pride shone through her words. "I fully support her role. I only wish I could play a more active part, but they have no need of another sister. It's a lovely notion, these nine women protecting such a precious gift. I hope the rest of the order fulfills their parts soon. I'm looking forward to the new regime."

"Indeed." I studied Jolene, but either she was a highly accomplished liar, or she was genuine. Even her strands—I was learning how to interpret a person's true emotions from their threads' movements—swirled calmly. "Thank you for your time."

"I hope you find the culprit soon." Jolene's eyes were big in her tiny face. "I'm so worried for Shu."

"I hope so, too."

Jolene felt like a dead end, and the sisters' other partners wouldn't remember enough to attack anyone, but Starr's secret boyfriend was a possibility worth pursuing.

While I watched, Starr and Jasmine walked to the bus stop after school, Jasmine surrounded by a gaggle of girls who were as polished and put-together as she was. Starr trailed far behind, clearly not welcome in the group. When they stepped onto the bus without any suspicious behavior, I gave up on them to pursue my other quarry.

Trent dawdled down a sidewalk, the weak sun filtering onto him through leafless branches of soaring beeches overhead. He whistled as he walked, and everything from his slow pace to his softly drifting strands indicated his ease.

I walked quickly to catch up to him. He studiously ignored me in the fashion of most teenagers, but when I cleared my throat, he deigned to look my way.

"Yeah?"

"Hello, Trent," I said. "My name is Morgan. I know your girlfriend Starr."

His eyes narrowed and he looked me up and down.

"I thought she hadn't told her family about us." He sniffed.

"I don't know why. So, she finally let the cat out of the bag?"

"Not intentionally. But don't worry about that. Are you and she on good terms?"

"Uh, yeah," he said with disdain. "What's it to you?"

I sighed internally. Every time I wondered what it would have been like to have children, a teenager would remind me that not everything I had missed out on was worth pining over.

"I care about Starr's well-being," I said blandly. "But she has important duties to fulfill in her home life, and it's important that she doesn't forget it."

I carefully watched Trent's strands for signs that he knew what I was talking about. His chest swelled, but his strands didn't twitch with hidden knowledge.

"And her needs and wants don't matter? No wonder she likes hanging out with me. She's probably so burdened with expectations at home that she can hardly breathe. She needs freedom to act out her own free will! She's seventeen, she needs autonomy. Isn't it enough that the man breathes down our necks without family getting on their high horses too? It makes me sick."

I steeled my expression into a smile. I was aiming for conciliatory, but it likely came across as patronizing, because Trent's face darkened.

"You'll understand 'the man' one day," I said. "When you pay taxes and become him. Thank you for your time. Goodbye."

Trent opened his mouth to berate me more, but I spun on my heel and strode back along the sidewalk. He was full of righteous indignation, but I couldn't spot duplicity. He wore his heart on his sleeve, and I doubted he was the mastermind, despite his questionable influence over Starr. I hoped that Rosemary was having better luck with her investigation into the elders.

What avenue could I pursue now? Joy and Rosemary needed further investigation, but I wasn't sure how to approach

170

them. Maybe I could sneak into Rosemary's little bungalow while she was at work.

I nodded to myself. Rosemary was at the salon right now. I knew this, because I was due to patrol the shop row in a few hours at the end of her shift. Her house was only a few blocks away.

I strode purposefully westward, and my tight jeans restricted my longest strides. I needed to rethink my wardrobe, and soon.

Rosemary's house was even shabbier in the daylight, but bright curtains were bunched against the windowpanes and a hedgehog bristle brush invited visitors to clean their shoes before entering the front door. I walked confidently to the back—skulking would only advertise to the neighbors that I didn't belong—and tried the back doorknob that led to the kitchen.

It was locked, of course, so I summoned Caelus.

"Any ideas for getting into this house?" I said when he emerged from my arm. "I want to look for evidence that Rosemary is the mastermind."

"You could focus a jet of air that was strong enough to break the window," Caelus suggested.

"I was hoping to be less destructive." I rattled the doorknob again. "What about the lock? Could I jimmy it open somehow?"

"Maybe," he said. "I think so."

"What if I made a slender air blade, with serrations? Then I could wiggle it in the keyhole to unlock the door."

I fashioned a crude blade, and with Caelus' help, we created a jagged edge. I shoved it in the keyhole and wiggled it around for a minute.

"Why isn't it working?" Caelus said.

"Give me a minute," I said with gritted teeth. "I haven't done much breaking and entering before. Wait." The door clicked and a proud smile washed over my face. "I did it."

I swung the door open and entered the house cautiously. I assumed Rosemary didn't own a dog, otherwise my commotion would have alerted it to trespassers, but I walked into the kitchen with trepidation anyway.

The house was silent. Kitchen drawers yielded nothing except organized utensils and pots, and the bathroom had open shelving. The living room was similarly devoid of hiding places, which left Rosemary's bedroom.

Her neatly made bed with its quilted coverlet was as tidy as the rest of the house, but here, at last, I found something.

"Caelus, look," I hissed. "Look at all those threads."

"Quick," he said. "I need to check what they are."

I kneeled beside the night table, from whose partly opened drawer spilled a tangled mess of multicolored threads. When I yanked the drawer fully open, the threads trembled and jostled against each other.

Inside, a lidless cardboard shoebox contained at least twelve items, including expensive-looking rings, three bracelets, and a calligraphy pen. Each item had a ball of yarn-like threads ceaselessly weaving around it.

"Amulets or artifacts?" I asked Caelus.

His searching eyes dulled.

"Amulets." His strands drooped. "All amulets."

I stood and clapped my hands. After Caelus stopped swaying, he glared at me. I ignored his thunderous face.

"Then let's go to the source," I said. "Rosemary's amulet room. If she has any artifacts, they have to be there."

"But I thought you said it was locked," Caelus said, but his shoulders straightened.

"So was Rosemary's house, and we made quick work of that."

"We'll have to be sneaky," I warned Caelus as I strode

172

toward the shop row along Cormorant Drive. "I'm still not convinced that Rosemary isn't behind the attacks. She's a suspect, at the very least. We can't let her know that we're looking for her amulets."

"How are we getting in, then?"

"With a cunning plan, of course."

I entered Cut Right like I owned the place, and Rosemary smiled when she saw me.

"Morgan, good to see you."

"Hello, Rosemary." I walked to her side as she trimmed a woman's blond bangs, then I said in a stage whisper, "Would it be all right if I used the bathroom?"

"Of course," Rosemary said. "Through the back door. Get Shu to give you the key."

I nodded my thanks and asked Shu at the front counter for the key after she finished ringing up her client. When I exited the salon into the back hallway that connected all the shops, Caelus emerged.

"That was your cunning plan?" he said with a raised eyebrow. "Ask to go to the bathroom?"

"And did it work?" I raised my brow back at him. "Where are we now, and without suspicion, I might add?"

Caelus grumbled incoherently but gazed toward the stairwell intently.

"Over there," he said. "Try to unlock the stair door."

I shook my head slightly but didn't comment on his impatience. I knew that the lack of progress on his mission bothered him. His stronger emotions welled up from time to time, especially his fear that he would be brought back to his plane of existence without removing a single artifact from the physical world.

When I reached the locked door, I crafted another air key more easily than at Rosemary's house. Wiggling it in the keyhole was another matter.

"Hurry up," Caelus said.

"You think I'm not trying?" I panted. "It's not coming."

"Morgan?"

Rosemary's inquisitive voice traveled down the hall. I dropped my hands and the bathroom key jingled in my fingers.

"Hi, Rosemary. The bathroom door won't open." I waved helplessly at the stairwell door.

"That's because the bathroom is here."

She patted a door on her right with a clearly marked washroom symbol emblazoned on its surface. I heaved a sigh for Rosemary's benefit.

"Whoops. I could have sworn Shu said the last room on the right. I must have misheard."

"I'll wait for you." Rosemary said with a smile. "I need to use it after you."

I nodded, unlocked the door, and slipped inside. Once we were alone, Caelus growled.

"Now what?"

"We try again another day." I leaned against the wall, defeated. "Rosemary won't let us wander without a good reason."

"Do you think she's the mastermind?"

"I don't know."

The next day, I tossed my phone on the bed, dissatisfied with reading the news on a tiny screen. What I really felt like was a large coffee and a thick newspaper to read while I sipped.

No one was expecting me until my evening patrol, and my only other plans included a lesson with Caelus. I had plenty of time for a leisurely morning while I deliberated the next steps in my investigation.

At the corner store, I handed over a crisp five-dollar bill to the attendant. He chuckled when he handed back my change.

"Haven't seen someone your age buying a newspaper for

years. Feeling retro?"

I raised my eyebrow.

"Self-education should never be mocked."

The man nodded his head in penitence.

"No offence meant. Enjoy your day."

I was tired of visiting Sacred Grounds, despite their delicious brews, so I walked the extra two blocks to another local coffeehouse. Their coffee wasn't quite up to par, and their baked goods didn't hold a candle to Jerome's lemon tarts, but it wasn't a bad spot to relax in the morning. I sat at a window, spread my paper on the table, and soaked in the coffee bean-scented air.

On the local pages, my eye caught on the name "Grandview Women's Center". Why were they in the news? I read on.

In a surprise move, enigmatic financier Jordan Prang announced a massive lump-sum donation to multiple women's help centers around Greater Vancouver, including the Grandview Women's Center in East Vancouver and Gaia House in Richmond.

I sat back, stunned. The name "Jordan Prang" had my ex-husband written all over it.

CHAPTER XVI

Jordan Prang was clearly a pseudonym of Peter's. Jordan, the site of the ancient city of Petra, and Prang, a temple in Cambodia, were two locations that I had loved best of all our trips together. That he had known those details astonished me. Why would he choose that name? If I were still alive, I would assume it would be to taunt me. But, since Peter thought I was dead, the significance of his choice eluded me. For a kinder soul, it would be a tribute to my life, but Peter was not a kind soul.

I read further, desperate to make sense of this development. Not only was Peter pitching in funds until my estate was settled, but he had promised to double my trust fund, "in honor of a great benefactor". What a fraud. What game was he trying to pull? I would have said it was a publicity stunt if he had used his own name, but he was operating under a pseudonym.

I shook my head and turned the page, unsure what to think. Maybe he had grown and changed, the way my simmering hatred had mellowed and healed with age. My chest burned with indignation at this notion. Peter didn't deserve appreciation. No matter how much money he donated, it would never erase the past.

I breathed heavily at the conflicting emotions of my head and body and flipped through the next few pages without absorbing the content. When I finally slowed down, March's face stared back with a short paragraph underneath. I huffed a breath through my nose as I read my obituary, which was clearly written by my administrative assistant. While we were sociable acquaintances, we were nowhere near friends.

My heart squeezed. No one had cared enough about me to write a personal ode to my life. The only person who would have qualified was Anna, but she knew I wasn't dead. There was no one else.

That realization had never bothered me in the past, but now, torn from every link to my past life and thrown onto the stormy waters of anonymity, my lack of connection stood out starkly. What was the point of March's life, if no one even cared if I had died?

The center cared, I reminded myself. My funds allowed many women to find new lives for themselves away from their persecutors.

But as meaningful as that contribution was, it wasn't connection. I sat up straight. I wanted to do things differently this time around. By some miracle, I had been given another chance and the ability to meet my previous failings with an unflinching gaze. I could change. This time, I could be different.

I wasn't sure how to accomplish this, but the intent was there. Now, I only had to recognize opportunities when they arose. I shook out my paper with a brisk nod and stood. Today was another fresh start. Every day I was alive was a chance to remake myself into a new and better me.

New Morgan, new life. No regrets.

The mall was only a short bus ride away. I deposited my coins—finally putting in the correct change without asking the driver—and looked out of the window, full of determination. At the clothing store, the saleswoman recognized me and walked over.

"Back again?" she said with a smile. "What can I help you with today?"

"I need a pair of those exercise pants," I said. My attempt to hide my shame must have failed because the woman laughed kindly.

"I hate to say I told you so, but I did tell you so." Still

177

chuckling, she led me to a table of folded pants. "I'd recommend two pairs, so you always have one handy. Lots of colors to choose from. And don't forget a supportive top for exercising."

I sighed—March wouldn't have been seen dead in this sort of gear, even as a young woman—but I wasn't March anymore. No one expected the well-dressed businesswoman with nary a hair out of place. Morgan could be more rough-and-tumble.

Besides, I needed the flexibility. Chasing after the sisters and handling their thuggish attackers was not a job for delicate pantsuits or skinny jeans.

After minor deliberation with some gentle guidance from the saleswoman, I selected two pairs of black stretchy pants and a black top. As I walked to the till, my eye caught another exercise top. It was a deep, wine red that complemented my own threads, which made me smile.

"I'll take that one, too," I told the woman. "And cut the tags off, please. I'll wear them out."

Since my security job entailed far more running than I was used to, I decided to jog back to Cormorant Drive for practice. I was expecting to last a minute at the most—I had never been a runner in my previous life—but my new body surprised me. Clearly, Fiorella had been fit. I paced with effortless grace along the sidewalk dressed in my new gear and an exultant smile.

When I reached my local park, deserted except for a mother and her toddler on the playground, I dropped my bag and planted my hands on the ground. Push-ups were usually beyond me, but my toned biceps and the ease of my jog here made me optimistic. I pushed my body up and down repeatedly with a grin on my face. I would keep this up, I vowed to myself.

178

Caelus' abilities were one thing, but strength was another kind of power. Rosemary's training session had introduced me to that concept. I wanted to be as powerful as I possibly could.

When my arms wobbled from the strenuous exercise, I readied myself for a magic lesson. Caelus flowed out of my arm.

"I need a plan for close combat," I said when he emerged. "This body almost died last night, and I had no idea how to stop the attack once the man got too close. I can work on my physical strength, but I will be hard-pressed to match a typical man's muscle."

"I agree," Caelus said with a nod. "Last night was too close. My mission would have been aborted, and I likely would have been demoted to a lower level of elemental."

"I have no idea what that means, but I can't imagine it compares to the fact that I would be dead." I narrowed my eyes at him. "Dead for a human means completely gone, in case you didn't know."

"In a way," he agreed, which raised all sorts of questions about my past lives in my mind. He didn't give me time to ask them. "What can you do in close quarters? First, never forget that breath is crucial to a human. Removing air from an attacker's lungs would be effective."

I nodded slowly. Of course. Air was crucial to life. A cloud of silver threads pooled in front of my face with my exhalation, and I followed the motion with my eyes. With trepidation, I squeezed three strands between my fingers and pulled them away from my mouth. More followed their brethren.

Nothing happened for the first few seconds, then my chest constricted. I pulled harder and my diaphragm contracted involuntarily. My eyes widened and I tried to breathe in. No breath entered my lungs, and alarm creeped around the edges of my mind. I pushed it away—I had no patience for panic—and let go of the strands at my lips.

Instantly, air flowed into my lungs with a gasping heave. I

breathed deeply for a moment before a slow smile lifted my cheeks. That would be another indispensable tool in my arsenal, I could tell already.

"Exactly," Caelus said in a smug tone. "Now, try it again."

After I practiced removing air from my lungs to Caelus' satisfaction, we brainstormed the best ways to combat an aggressor who was too close, and I trialed as many tactics as I could without a target to practice on. Almost an hour passed while I spoke to myself, and the curious mother had taken her child home long before I finished.

Finally, I threw myself on a nearby bench, tired from my efforts but happy with the results. I felt a hundred times more prepared for anything an attacker might throw at me. Long range, close combat, even some defensive air bubbles Caelus and I had dreamed up, they all covered me like an invisible layer of armor. I felt like a tank ready to deploy my weaponry at the enemy.

"What are our next steps for finding an artifact?" Caelus said after I had caught my breath. I froze. After the attack last night, I had completely forgotten my promise to him.

"Let's ask Rosemary to show us the amulets," I said. "I assume she has nothing interesting, but better to check and rule it out. Then we can plan a trip to some out-of-town museums. Does that sound reasonable?"

Caelus nodded tightly. I sat up with a thought.

"Are you sure you can't tell which sister is wearing the artifact? That would save us a lot of effort. We could just protect the one necklace instead."

"We would have to open each locket to determine which was the real one, and I expect Rosemary would have objections."

"Yes, doubtless she would."

As far as I knew, the lockets hadn't been opened for decades. According to Rosemary, to the untrained eye, the contents all looked the same, so none of the sisters ever peeked. To Caelus, however, the difference would be clear in the threads.

"I'll try to figure something out," I promised Caelus. "At least we know the location of one artifact."

I ran back to my condo and showered before Starr and Jasmine finished school. I wanted to follow one of them home to watch for dubious behavior. At an inconspicuous distance to the bus stop where the two girls waited, I pulled up the hood of my raincoat and followed them onto the bus. They were in their own worlds, and I averted my face and dropped onto an empty seat.

Jasmine exited first, and I followed her discreetly. After two blocks, she swept toward an imposing two-level house with immaculately manicured shrubbery and disappeared through the front door.

My shoulders slumped. I hadn't expected any results from this watch, but my lack of progress was disheartening. I suspected that one of the sisters was the mastermind, but I had no way to prove it. Maybe I could follow Joy home next, and Starr the day after. As unlikely candidates as Joy and Starr were for evil schemes, they were two from a very small list. I couldn't afford to overlook any potential leads.

I hopped on a bus traveling in the opposite direction and followed my rumbling stomach to Upper Crust to satiate my citrus cravings while I waited for Cut Right's closing time.

The bakery's shelves were nearly empty at this late hour, and I scanned the glassed-in counter for my favorite treat. My eyes darted over three scones, four cookies, and one lonely croissant, but no bright yellow goodness leaped out like a ray of sunshine. My shoulders slumped.

"Are you Morgan?" the woman behind the counter said to me.

I looked up. She held a box in her hands with a quizzical expression on her face. I nodded, and she gave me the box.

"Jerome asked me to give you this if you came in," she said with a smile. "He's such a sweetie. I wish my boyfriend baked for me."

I took the box with a puzzled frown and slid open the lid. Inside were four tarts, but they didn't contain the dazzling yellow I was expecting. Instead, they were a pale pink, surrounded by familiar flaky pastry. Tucked between two of the tarts was a note. I flicked it open with one hand.

Not sure if pomelo is strong enough by itself. I'll try grapefruit next.

My mouth widened in a smile. Jerome had remembered our conversation about different tart flavors and had taken my flippant remark to heart.

I gazed at the tarts for a long moment, various organs in my chest wriggling strangely, then my shoulders shrugged. No point in letting a good tart go to waste. My fingers plucked one pastry out of the box, and I brought it to my mouth.

The flavor was delicate, as Jerome has warned me, but it brought back mostly happy memories of a trip to Thailand. I closed my eyes and savored the taste on my tongue.

The women of Cut Right had left their salon without mishap, and I was sitting at the window counter in a taqueria, licking salsa off my fingers after a meal of carnitas. It was another establishment whose door March would never have darkened. It was too bad, I thought while chasing an errant chunk of avocado around my plate with my last tortilla chip. So many years of being uptight, missing the flavor sensations of tacos.

My phone rang, and I checked the caller and answered.

"Hello, Rosemary."

"Morgan," she said by way of greeting. "Amanda left Sacred Grounds earlier than expected and was attacked at the end of the alley."

"What?" I sat up straight. "Where in the alley?"

"At the end closest to the coffeeshop, I think."

Breath forced through my pursed lips. That was one section that my camera couldn't see.

"Why on earth was she in the alley?" I said with exasperation. "No one should be using the back door these days."

"The man grabbed her as she walked by on the side road. She managed to stumble back to the coffeeshop where Denise was closing. She thought her car was close enough to risk walking by herself, expressly against my recommendations." Rosemary gave an aggrieved sigh. "This is exactly why I haven't asked the motherhood for help yet. If my own sisters won't listen to my leadership, what does that say about me? Anyway, her necklace was stolen. That makes three missing."

"And is Amanda okay?" Rosemary often missed what I considered to be the most important point.

"Amanda will have a black eye, but she's fine," Rosemary said impatiently. "She came over faint, just like Shu did, and I searched her and found a strength-draining amulet. Someone planted it on her and triggered it, but she has no idea who. I'm so done with all this. Who is stealing from my amulet inventory? And some of my strength amulets are gone with a note saying they were borrowed by the elders, but I wasn't informed of that, and I expect it's a lie. I guess that explains how the attackers managed to get the better of my trained sisters. We can't afford to lose any more of these necklaces, Morgan. I need to take more drastic action until this is resolved."

"What are you thinking?"

The sound of drumming fingers filtered through the speaker.

"I'll have to call on the motherhood for help," she said at last. "I hate to rely on them, and I especially don't want them to think I'm not ready to join their ranks after this debacle, but this has gone far enough. They have a safehouse that we can live in until this gets figured out."

"How long will that take to get to?" I asked.

"I'll rent a bus. I can call it in. It will take a few hours to get organized, though, and I don't want to lose another necklace."

"Can you simply gather the necklaces together and put them in a safe?" It seemed like a ridiculous requirement to spread them out among the women, especially if they were vulnerable to attack.

"No," she said shortly. "It's not permitted. They need to be separate for the safety of the artifact."

"Then we'll gather all the sisters together," I said. Rosemary's dismissal of my suggestion eased my suspicion that she was the mastermind. "Bring everyone to the rooms under Cut Right. You might need your amulets for protection should another attack hit."

"Good thinking." Rosemary sounded relieved at having a plan. "I'll call everyone. Come as soon as you can."

I signed off and consulted with Caelus, who had remained embodied above my arm for the call.

"What do you think?" I said. "Are we ready for this if it comes to a showdown? Either the women will be safe as houses locked away in the building, or the mastermind will regard this as a perfect opportunity to get the artifact once and for all."

Caelus shrugged.

"As long as we capture the necklace, I don't care whether the mastermind wins or not."

"Of course, you would say that." I rolled my eyes, something I had never done but seemed to fit my new body and persona. It felt cathartic. "I, however, feel some kinship toward these women. That, and they pay me to keep them safe. I'll do my job, and I'll do it well, as I always do."

My phone pinged again, and I whipped it out.

"Damn Beaky," I shouted at the image on my screen. "I'm going to throttle that flying menace."

When I arrived at Cut Right after a quick stop at my condo—my yoga pants weren't going to wear themselves—it was dark and raining again. I knocked on the door, its closed sign prominent in the window, and a shadowy figure in the back walked toward me.

Rosemary's pinched expression spoke to her worry. She clicked open the deadbolt and let me in.

"I called the motherhood," she said once I slid off my wet hood. "They're preparing the safehouse for us. The coach I ordered should be here in two hours. Hopefully, we will just wait here quietly until then."

"Assuming the mastermind doesn't know that you're all here," I said. "It would be a perfect time to attack the sisterhood. All the necklaces in one place."

Rosemary's round face blanched even paler than usual.

"I hadn't thought about that." She straightened her shoulders. "It's still the best plan. And you're here to help. It's only two hours."

"Keep everyone inside and lock the doors. Nothing should bother you then."

That was assuming the threat was exterior to the sisterhood, which I still wasn't convinced of.

"Have you considered that one of your sisters might be behind the attacks?" I asked. The sisterhood was in too much danger to dance around the issue anymore.

"No," Rosemary said firmly. "And I don't now. We swore vows."

"Okay," I said to placate her. Their vows didn't mean much to me, but they clearly meant something to Rosemary.

Rosemary nodded briskly, then her shoulders drooped.

"The motherhood was making noises about choosing a new sister to lead the sisterhood. They're saying I'm clearly unfit if I can't keep the necklaces safe. I don't know, maybe they're right."

"I don't see what else you could have done."

"I could have taken everyone to the safehouse right away, I suppose. I was just—I don't know. I'm almost ready to age out of the sisterhood, but not everyone can join the motherhood. I wanted to prove myself. I thought that if I could deal with this problem before anyone knew about it…" She sighed. "That was stupid, I see that now."

"Hindsight is twenty-twenty." I patted her shoulder. "It's easy for others to comment on best practices when they're on the sidelines. When you're in the trenches, you make the best decisions you can with the information you have. Don't beat yourself up for the past. Look to the future."

Rosemary nodded with more conviction.

"You're right. I can only do what I can do. Everyone's here who will be. Shu is staying home—Jolene insisted on it, and Shu doesn't have her necklace anymore, so she's not a target—but Wanda and Denise are here to help out, even though they lost theirs."

"Had their necklaces stolen from them," I reminded Rosemary. She shrugged.

"Semantics."

I strongly disagreed—saying the women lost their necklaces put the blame squarely on the victims—but Rosemary rummaged in her pocket before I could comment.

"We're all in the basement," she said. "Here's a key to the outside doors. All the shops are closed by now, Denise shut the coffeeshop early today, so we have the building to ourselves. Do you want to patrol the area to watch for danger? I'll have my phone on."

I pocketed the key.

"Sounds good. Stay inside. I'll check with you every fifteen minutes."

Rosemary disappeared into the back after she locked Cut Right's door behind me. I drew my hood over my hair again and hunched my shoulders against the chill downpour. Caelus popped up.

"All the sisters are sitting with the amulets," he said with a hard edge to his voice. "And we're outside in the rain. Too many water threads for my liking."

"We'll have a look soon," I promised him. "Let's do a few rounds of the building, then we'll finally examine these amulets when we check in. We need to keep an eye on the sisters for trouble, anyway."

Caelus huffed his reluctant consent.

"Keep your eyes peeled for strange threads," I said. My eyes scanned the building as I walked along the sidewalk. "Like the ones we saw at every attack site."

"What a terrible expression," he said with a dainty sniff. "Eyes peeled. Is it like this?"

With his eyelids wide, the threads of his eyeballs unraveled and drifted into the air. It reminded me of worms eating a corpse. My mouth turned down.

"That's disgusting, Caelus. Just look around."

Caelus grinned and molded his eyes back to their usual form.

The streets were quiet, only a few pedestrians striding with their heads down, bent on reaching their destinations with the least amount of rain touching them as possible. The alley was deserted, even after Caelus taught me how to check with more than visual cues.

"Watch the air currents." He pointed a finger near the roof. "See the disturbance? A bird is up there."

I squinted at the roofline. Sure enough, a pigeon waddled

187

along the gutter. Her rusty feathers appeared a dirty orange in the light of a distant streetlamp. A clicking noise drew my eye to the security camera I had installed, and when my phone pinged in my pocket, I recognized the culprit.

"Beaky," I growled. "There she is. I could get her right now."

"We can't interrupt your work for my mission but declaring vengeance on a bird is fine."

Caelus' voice dripped with sarcasm. I rolled my eyes again. It felt good. So uncouth, but I wasn't March anymore. No one expected me to be the epitome of class and restraint.

"Fine," I said. To Beaky I called out, "I'm coming for you one day."

I scanned the rest of the alley. All the air threads drifted randomly, so I assumed no one was down here. Halfway along the alley, a puff of threads indicated movement, but the rat scuttling along the edge of a dumpster calmed my rapidly beating heart.

"I never thought I would be happy to see a rat," I said to Caelus. "But it means the motion wasn't an attacker."

"I prefer the pigeon. Rats are nasty little earthbound creatures."

"They're both pretty low in my books, but an attacker is lower."

After our fifteen minutes of prowling around the building, I opened the back door to Cut Right and whisked inside, careful to lock the door behind me. Rosemary had unlocked the stairwell, and the stairs echoed with my footsteps. When I opened the bottom door to the musty basement, light and the murmur of female voices drew me down the hall.

The sisters were huddled in the narrow, windowless room of their hangout. Joy, Amanda, and Miranda were squeezed on the small loveseat together, and Jasmine sat leaning against it with her eyes on the phone in her lap. Rosemary paced before them, and Joy's eyes followed her eldest sister. Amanda and

Miranda sported the scuffs and scrapes of their encounters, and Amanda's black eye looked painful. I counted the women.

"Where are the others?" I asked Rosemary.

She jumped at my voice and placed a hand on her heart.

"Morgan, you scared me. Wanda and Denise are lying down in another room. Starr's in the bathroom upstairs."

"I need to go, too," Miranda said. She extricated herself from the loveseat. "I'll be right back."

Rosemary nodded and Miranda squeezed past me with an apologetic expression. I beckoned Rosemary closer.

"Can you show me around the basement?" I asked, mindful of Caelus swaying on my arm, invisible to everyone but me. "I want to check for any points of entry."

Rosemary nodded.

"Of course. Come this way." She waved me to follow her through a different doorway. Once through, we paced down a dimly lit hall without doorways that ended in a sharp turn. The musty scent was stronger here, although the floor was polished concrete below scuffed white walls. Rosemary waved at a door on her right.

"That's the bunker. There are no other doors inside." At my incredulous look, she clarified. "The guy who built this place was paranoid. We keep a couple of cots in there in case anyone needs a place to stay in between apartments."

Rosemary turned left, then right, and left again past another hallway. Finally, a door appeared on our right.

"It's a maze down here," I said.

"You have no idea," Rosemary said with her hand on the knob. "I told you the guy who built it was a nut job. It's a good spot to keep our amulets hidden, though."

The next door opened to a short, featureless hallway with a door on either end. Rosemary unlocked it and stopped.

It was a tiny room, no more than an enlarged closet with two other doorways to unknown places. The space was lined with shelves filled with rings, necklaces, cuffs, even a few keychains. To my Caelus-enhanced eyes, the items swirled with colored threads. Each object had a label affixed to the shelf in front of it with a note in neat handwriting.

"Our amulet inventory," Rosemary said proudly. "I categorized everything once I became eldest sister. They were in a terrible jumble when I took over, can you imagine? This way, the sisters can check out the items they want to use, like a library. It's so much tidier."

"Are these all amulets?" My question looked like it was for Rosemary, but I eyed Caelus as I said it. He took the hint and examined shelves with a furrowed brow. After a few moments, he shook his head with a defeated slump of his shoulders.

"Yes, and they all do different things." Rosemary pointed at the nearest label. "See here."

I leaned forward with interest. The simple gold band in front of me would change the shape of the wearer's face. All the user had to do was repeat a simple incantation in Latin, and she would appear as someone else for a short time. I shook my head at the power available to these young women. Were they wise enough for the responsibility? From some of their questionable actions to date, I wasn't sure.

"And the mind-control amulet is still missing?" I asked.

Rosemary found the empty spot where an amulet should have been.

"Yes, it's still gone." She sighed. "Well, there's nothing else I can do right now. We're all in this row of shops. There's no way the mastermind can get any more amulets, and in a few hours, we'll be gone. We'll take the amulets with us."

"That's all you can do," I said. "Although I would recommend locking the amulet room, just in case."

"Why?" Rosemary seemed genuinely perplexed. "The building is locked. Besides, this room doesn't have a key. I usually lock the staircases, but I left them open tonight since we're the only ones here."

I sighed. Rosemary refused to accept that her sisters might

be culpable, and I didn't know how to convince her, so I left the matter alone. I hoped she was justified in her conviction of her sisters' innocence. Unless she was the mastermind, but if she had a motive it was hidden from me.

"Where do the other doors go?" I asked since that was my stated purpose for the basement tour.

Rosemary shuddered.

"Just a few rooms of storage that lead to the end stairwell. I can show you the entrance up top. I hate going into storage—too many creepy-crawlies."

There was something else I wanted to know, and now seemed as good a time as any to ask. Caelus wanted artifacts, and the necklaces might be hiding one, but we couldn't know for sure.

"This necklace, with the Leaf in it, does it have powers like an amulet does?"

"It doesn't do anything by itself," Rosemary answered. She bent to fetch a duffel bag from below the bottom shelf and began placing amulets inside. "Only when it's joined by the Seed and the Blood will the spirit elemental be released."

A thump from upstairs made my heart jolt. Rosemary's head snapped to the sound.

"What was that?" she gasped, but I was already at the doorway and running through the halls. Rosemary pounded after me and shouted directions. When we burst into the sisterhood's hangout, the other women were murmuring and shifting in their seats, but I swept by them and leaped up the stairs.

"Someone's down," Caelus said when I slid into the linoleum-covered upper hallway.

I followed his pointed finger. A figure was slumped on the ground, and I recognized Miranda's slender form. I raced to her side.

"Did she faint?" Rosemary asked behind me. "I knew I should have brought food. No one's had dinner. I wonder if we should risk pizza delivery."

I tuned out Rosemary's babbling and focused on Miranda. A piece of lined paper lay on her shoulder with a handwritten note. I picked it up and read it out loud.

Morgan,

You're protecting the sisters and their precious Leaf, but you don't know the whole story. If the Leaf, Seed, and Blood come together, the spirit elemental will be released. The Book of Souls spins it to sound joyful and harmonious, but connection with all living things means that humans can control them all. We don't deserve that kind of power. We've already messed up Earth enough, and this would be a hundred times worse.

Please, join me and use your powers to take down the sisterhood, so we can hide the Leaf for good. Help me in this, and I will give you as many amulets as you want to make your life easier or even to take out your enemies. To show you I'm for real, I planted an amulet on Peter Teunis for you. You want him punished, right? I've been following you, and I know more about you than you think. If you say the following words out loud and hold this connecting amulet, Peter's face will be disfigured forever.

I didn't read the Latin incantation aloud.

"Who's Peter Teunis?" Rosemary demanded, then she cursed. "Miranda's necklace is gone. Another one down."

"Peter is someone from my past," I said absently, my mind whirling. How had the mastermind followed me to his house undetected? What did she know? Memories of a slender figure in a green hoodie surfaced. I had seen her when I met with Anna and when I left Peter's house. A chill ran down my spine. If the mastermind knew about Peter, did she also know about March?

I picked up the gaudy opal ring that lay on Amanda's shoulder under the note. It swirled with multicolored threads, indicating its amulet status. This ring, when paired with the words in the note, had the power to damage Peter from afar. A numb buzzing filled my head at the thought. Did I want to punish Peter like that?

"Is that possible?" I asked Caelus in a low voice. He emerged from my arm and nodded.

"Looks like it. Quite a tricky little rendering. Peter's face will essentially melt into a new shape."

I put my hand on my suddenly molten chest reflexively. I could disfigure Peter with a few quick words. The torment of my early adult life would finally be put to rest. It would be justice for the pain he had caused me.

No, my rational side protested. It would be vengeance. I didn't need that, nor want it. Peter was my distant past, and his hold on me was long gone. Wasn't it?

The rage throbbing throughout my body disagreed. Again, I couldn't tell whether it was genuine. What did I truly want?

"That means that someone got into the building," Rosemary said with a hysterical edge to her voice. "But I'm the only one with the building key. Or that one of my sisters is the mastermind. How could that be?"

I twisted the ring in my finger, ignoring Rosemary's words. I could have my revenge right here, right now. The mastermind had given me the instrument of Peter's destruction and invited me to join her. By using the ring, I signaled my intent to betray the sisterhood I had promised to protect. One small amulet could have such a far-reaching consequence.

But my hatred of Peter had burned hot decades ago, and my promise to the sisterhood was only days old. Surely, what I owed to myself held more weight? Despite my years of peace, rage toward Peter had recently rekindled with vicious need. Security for the sisters was merely a job, after all.

But it wasn't. I had accepted the role of sisterhood protector not for the money, but because I believed it was the right thing to do. I was helping my fellow women in the face of nameless male attackers, the same as I had done for years with the women's center. That goal was a key value in my life as March and as Morgan, and I couldn't give it up.

But for a shot at Peter, should I relax my principles? Would it be worth it?

"Who is it?" Rosemary said with a whimper. "I trust all my sisters with my life. How could one of them betray us like this? I don't understand."

The inferno in my heart managed to squeeze a drop of sympathy from the molten rage. Rosemary's dismay over her sister's betrayal was real and painful. One of her sworn sisters was deliberately targeting the other women by controlling random men to violently attack and steal the necklaces. How could she look herself in the mirror after?

My reluctant suspicions were now confirmed, but it didn't bring me any gladness. Was female solidarity only a concept in my mind? But it was obvious now, to me and finally to Rosemary. The knowledge of where each sister would be, the stolen amulets, the attacks when sisters didn't have their phones to call me, it all pointed with neon lighting to a sister's familiarity.

Rosemary's blind spot threw into question my current conundrum. Was I blinded by the strange rage of this new body and ignoring the evidence of Peter's reform? Was he truly repentant of his past actions, and his donations to my charity done in good faith? Could his wife and daughter truly love him?

At the thought of his daughter, my hand tightened on the ring. I couldn't knowingly hurt Peter's daughter, even if I wanted my revenge. If she loved him, and I ruined him to satisfy the exhumed desires of my old life—and, to Peter, losing his looks would be his ruination—would I be any better than he was when we were together?

And there it was: the real crux of this matter. I was still stuck in the past. I might have a new body, but letting go of the shackles of my previous life hadn't been that simple. I had refused to accept that the hatred wasn't mine because it was familiar. I had nothing else to hold onto, not looks, not home, not friends. If I let go of my past, would I cease to be me?

Or would I become someone better?

New Morgan, new life. No regrets. It was time to let March go forever.

CHAPTER XVII

I stood, startling Rosemary who looked at me with tears streaking down her face. I let the ring slide from my fingers. It dropped to the tiled floor, pinging as it bounced.

"You have shown no consideration for the lives of your sisters," I bellowed down the hall. If the mastermind were upstairs, she would hear me. "And I will not help you. Your gift is worthless. I'm coming for you, and I won't let you hurt anyone else."

I raised my booted foot, hesitated for a second to strengthen my resolve, then brought my heel down on the fragile ring with force. A cracking, crunching noise made my stomach twist, but my heart felt light. I lifted my foot. The ring's multicolored threads drifted away from the cracked opal. The amulet was broken, and Peter was safe.

A bad taste rose in my mouth at the thought that Peter would forever go unpunished for his crimes, but my heart felt free. The decision to leave my past in the past, as difficult as it was, brought with it a sense of liberty that even the body switch hadn't accomplished. For the first time, I truly, fully, completely felt like Morgan Leigh Feynman. March was now a distant memory, placed among the shadowy recollections of my past lives where she belonged.

I turned to Rosemary.

"Who would it be?' I said urgently. "Think, Rosemary. Who would be behind the attacks?"

"I don't know," she said tearfully. "They're all my sisters. I trust all of them!"

"Don't consider your feelings. Who has already been attacked? Unless the mastermind was extremely devious to put us off the scent, she wouldn't have attacked herself."

"Right," Rosemary sniffed back her tears. "Let's see. It isn't Miranda, obviously. Not Denise, or Shu, or Wanda."

"Or Amanda."

"There aren't a lot left. Jasmine, Joy, and Starr. That's it."

"And you." I looked at Rosemary with consideration. Her eyes bugged in horror.

"You can't honestly mean that."

"Not really. I was with you when Amanda was attacked. Although if you had a mind-control amulet, would it have mattered?"

"It wasn't me, I swear. Why would I?" Rosemary looked terrified, as if she were being accused by a jury on death row.

"Your motives are your own. But I'm going to assume it wasn't you for argument's sake, although I will be keeping a close eye on you." I turned to Caelus. "Can you tell if she has an amulet on her?"

Rosemary looked confused by my words. Caelus turned his gaze on Rosemary. After a moment, he pointed.

"There's one in her pocket. Get her to pull it out and we'll see what it does."

"Turn out your pockets," I ordered.

Rosemary looked cowed but so far hadn't shown any signs of guilt, only fear. She shoved the amulet, a keychain with a smiling beaver on it, at me.

"It's only for the rain," she said in a pleading tone. "I always keep one on me this time of year. It keeps my hair from getting frizzy."

"She's telling the truth," said Caelus after a moment. "Unless there's an amulet hiding in her shoe, the mastermind isn't her."

"So, it's Joy, Jasmine, or Starr." I drummed my fingers on my arm then whirled toward the staircase. "Let's find them and end this."

It was a good plan. Unfortunately, Amanda chose at that moment to run screaming toward us, a knife in one hand and an amulet in the other.

"Damn it," I shouted. "Rosemary, get Miranda out of the

way."

I planted my feet and gathered what air strands I could in the still hallway. Caelus bared his teeth.

"Blast her now," he said, and I threw my strands.

Amanda stumbled as the weak force pushed against her torso, but it wasn't strong enough to stop her. I cursed.

"What next?" I said to Caelus as Amanda looked at me with glazed eyes.

"She's flimsy," Caelus said. "Aim the next blast at her legs, knock her over."

I couldn't disagree—Amanda looked like a strong wind might blow her over, which is what I intended—and I gathered air strands while Amanda raised the amulet. Quickly, I released my handful before she could perform whatever magic she was attempting.

Amanda's feet shot out behind her, and she collapsed to the floor with a shriek. I raced forward and deftly plucked the maroon strand off her hair. Her body relaxed, then she pressed her hands on the cement and breathed heavily. I kneeled next to her with a firm grip on air strands in my fist. I liked having a contingency plan in case Amanda's mind-control hadn't been fully cured.

"Amanda? How are you feeling?"

"Woozy," she murmured. "What happened?"

"The mastermind forced you to attack me," I said. "Do you remember who did this to you?"

"No." She looked up with a confused look and put a hand to her forehead. "The last thing I remember is sitting with Joy on the couch. I think I went to another room? Then I can't remember anything until right now."

I sighed. It wasn't unexpected, but I had hoped that Amanda would provide a clue.

"The mastermind is one of your sisters, and it looks like she won't hesitate to use the mind-control amulet on you."

"No," she whispered. "Who? I don't believe it."

198

"Believe what you want." I stood and held out my hand. Amanda hauled herself up. "Come on. Let's find Rosemary and get you somewhere safe." Louder I shouted, "Rosemary? Where are you?"

Rosemary's head peeked out from a doorway behind me.

"Psst," she said. "In here. Is Amanda herself again?"

We hurried to Rosemary. She ushered us into a tiny room, this one filled with brooms, buckets, and bottles of cleaning fluid. Miranda moaned from her seated position on the floor. When we squeezed in, Rosemary shut the hallway door.

"Yes," I said. "About this amulet, can it be used from afar, or does the mastermind have to touch the victim?"

"Touch isn't necessary." Concern crossed Rosemary's face. "But the amulet has to be fairly close."

"So, the mastermind could be standing in the next room and make Amanda attack us again."

Rosemary nodded, misery etching lines beside her mouth. Amanda crossed arms over her chest in a defensive posture.

"Can I stop it somehow, if I know it's coming?" she said with a trembling voice. "I don't want to attack anyone."

"There is an amulet that might protect," Rosemary said. "It's downstairs." She looked terrified at the thought of venturing out of the relative safety of this broom closet.

"I'll get it," I said. "What does it look like?"

"It's a silver ring with green jade. It should be on an upper shelf. The label will say 'protection for the mind'. But shouldn't we all go together?" Rosemary twisted her hands.

"I'll be quicker by myself." I wanted to sneak downstairs and grab the amulet without being observed, which would be difficult with a parade of women traipsing behind me. "But is there only one amulet? That isn't going to do us much good, unless it works for multiple people."

"You need it," Rosemary said without a shred of hesitation. "If the mastermind took you over, we'd be screwed. You have far more power than the rest of us combined."

The thought calmed me—I was powerful now that Caelus and I were working together—and I nodded without arguing.

"Can you check something while you're there?" Rosemary asked. "We used to have two mind-control amulets in our inventory. One is gone—the mastermind has it—but take the other one for safekeeping. The motherhood borrowed it last week, but they mailed it to me yesterday and I returned it to the basement. If the mastermind gets it, anyone without a necklace can be controlled, and three at a time."

My heart sank.

"Three people controlled at one time?" I said. "That would be bad news, indeed. Okay, here's the plan. You three stay here. If Amanda or Miranda start acting oddly, Rosemary should run, since she has the only necklace here. If Rosemary looks glazed and tries to leave, the others should stop her from going to the mastermind and giving up her necklace."

"Every necklace has a few minor spells of protection for the wearer, including protection from mind-control," Rosemary said. "That's why the mastermind had men attack the sisters instead of making them give up their necklaces themselves."

"Okay, watch out for these two." I jabbed my thumbs at the other women, who looked sheepish. "I'll find the amulet."

Rosemary nodded with a jerk, and I opened the door and peered out. The hallway was silent, and I slipped out noiselessly. The broom closet was at the opposite end of the stairs we had ascended, but an alternate stairwell beckoned to my left. Maybe I could quickly find the amulet room without anyone noticing me. It was worth a try.

I recalled the maze below my feet but shook the dismay away before it could take hold. The basement was only so big. I could find one room in it. My plan was a weak one—find Joy, Jasmine, and Starr, and hope that my intuition about Rosemary's innocence was correct—but I didn't have any other ideas.

Self-doubt crawled into my head and spoke in Peter's voice.

Decisions aren't your strong suit, doll. Let wiser heads deal with the details. Who knows what would fall apart if you were in charge?

This was the voice I pushed through every time I walked into a board meeting or spoke at a conference or made an executive decision for one of my businesses. Every time, I took a deep breath and ignored it. Some days were easier than others, especially as the years wore on, but times of high stress brought out my demons.

I stalked down the cement stairs, trying to push away the voice. My stomach roiled with self-loathing. I could have dealt with Peter once and for all. The mastermind had given me a loaded gun and told me where to point it. All I had needed to do was pull the trigger. Why had I been so weak? After all Peter had done to me, why was he allowed to walk free while I was tormented with indecision?

Caelus emerged from my arm.

"I can hear your thoughts, you know," he said conversationally. "They're very loud sometimes. And I thought you figured this out already. Peter is your past. Morgan is your future. Don't sully your fresh start with all that baggage. Don't you remember your reasoning?"

I took a deep breath and released it.

"The anger in this body is so powerful," I said hoarsely. "I don't know what Fiorella went through in her life, but the imprint of her trauma echoes loudly through mine. Thanks for keeping me steady, Caelus."

Now I had another voice in my head, in a way, but a far more reasonable one. I had considered Caelus a burden to bear, but between his abilities and counsel, he was turning into an asset.

"I still have to discover who to target," I said. "Is it Joy, Jasmine, Starr, or Rosemary? How do I figure it out? More importantly, how do I do it without making a terrible mistake? I now have a track record of attacking innocent people. And with the mind-control amulets, how will I know who the true villain is before I become a villain myself?"

"You think too much," Caelus said. "If someone attacks you, deal with them. We've practiced plenty of defensive maneuvers. Just don't aim to kill and figure the rest out later."

I took another deep breath and put my hand on the doorhandle at the bottom of the dim stairwell.

"You're right. We've got this."

Caelus grinned.

"We certainly do."

The door creaked as I opened it, and I winced at the noise. Hopefully, I was far enough away from the other women at the end of this long building that no one would hear me sneaking around. Tiptoe in, grab the protection and mind-control amulets, then find the mastermind. Dead simple.

As long as "dead" wasn't the operative word here.

I stepped into an entirely black room. None of these basement rooms was above ground level, and windows were only a memory here. I groped on the wall, hoping for a light switch, and my heart thundered loudly with relief when my fingers found a tiny lever. At once, a single incandescent bulb flickered to life on the ceiling.

It illuminated a large room piled high with random junk, and I thanked my lucky stars that I hadn't stumbled my way in here without a light. Broken coffeeshop chairs, old tables, bent clothing racks, and other discarded equipment from the shops upstairs littered the floor and hid any exit. Was this a dead end?

Why did I keep thinking the word "dead"? Phantom hands brushed my neck, and I shivered at the memory of my recent near-strangulation.

"Keep going," Caelus whispered. "There must be a door."

I picked my way through the mess with distaste—I'd always considered an untidy house to be a sign of an untidy

202

mind, although in a communal space, I wasn't sure who to pin the blame on—but froze at the sound of a click.

I kneeled behind an overturned table with a broken leg and waited to see who the intruder was, but Caelus was cleverer. He drifted up from my arm and surveyed the room from near the ceiling.

"It's Wanda," he said out loud since I was the only one who could hear him. "She looks controlled. The eyes, you know. She's looking around for you."

I did know. How could I stop her without hurting her too badly? If I were the mastermind, I would have two goals: one, to collect all the necklaces, and two, to take me out of the running. I needed to be wary.

"Morgan?" Wanda's voice traveled through the room, her words slurred like the man in the alley's had been. "Are you in here? I only want to talk."

I almost stood at that comment. She sounded so reasonable. Had the other controlled people been that sensible? But Caelus shook his head and darted back to me.

"She has amulets," he hissed. "I can't tell what they do. Watch yourself."

I hesitated, but I couldn't get past Wanda while I crouched behind a budget table. I gathered air threads in my hands and clutched them tightly as I stood to face my opponent.

Wanda was ready for me. With a triumphant smile, she held up an amulet clenched in her fist. I wasn't idle, and my blast of charged air shot toward her. I didn't have time to be nervous of whatever her amulet did before I blinked in confusion.

The woman across this strange room dodged a swirling mass of silver strings. That was odd. Who was she, again? I felt as though I should know her, but her name eluded me. And what was I doing in this junkyard? I could really use a lemon tart right now.

"Morgan!"

A silver face made of those same strings appeared before

mine, and I jumped in fright. Was it a ghost? Were they real? Had I always been able to see them? I wasn't sure about anything anymore. The ghost's expression was both angry and fearful. Maybe he had unfinished business to attend to. Could I help? I opened my mouth to offer, but before I could speak, he shook his head in exasperation and melted into my arm.

I lifted my arm and looked underneath it. Where did the ghost go?

I twirled toward the other woman with a jerk, but my body was not my own. I tried walking, but the resistance was too great. What had happened? Had the ghost taken over my body? The notion sounded familiar. I wanted to be frightened, or even indignant, but it was hard to muster energy from the confusion that filled my fuzzy head. I watched my arms lift and my fingers rake silver strings into huge clusters. The other woman had recovered from her fall on the floor and was rushing toward me. Was she angry at me, or did she only want a hug? Maybe we were close. I couldn't remember.

With a throwing motion, my arm tossed silver strings at the other woman's hand. The ring that she clutched between her finger and thumb flipped through the air and landed in a messy pile of coat hangers.

With the contact broken between Wanda and the amulet, my mind snapped into place, as sharp and focused as ever. Caelus reappeared above my arm.

"Thanks, Caelus," I said grimly. "That was quick thinking."

"Someone had to think since you clearly weren't capable of it." Caelus looked pleased with himself. "Watch out, she's got another one. Get the amulets away from her."

I narrowed my eyes and collected air threads. Wanda had taken away my agency, and that was something I couldn't abide. I reminded myself that Wanda's will was not her own—her glazed eyes made that clear—but it was hard to ignore my desire for justice. I shook my head and threw the air threads.

Wanda, who had been in the middle of raising a keychain

in midair, buckled as my blast hit her. She twirled three times with her arms soaring around her like a ballerina performing a pirouette. Her landing wasn't as graceful, and she slumped to the floor, the amulet skittering out of her reach.

I paced forward, ready to tie her up and move on from this obstacle, but she whipped her hand around and shot a venomous glare at me with her arm outstretched. The amulet in her hand was the last thing I saw.

The room darkened, starting from the edges, until a tunnel of blackness closed when the last pinprick of light winked out. My heart thundered in my chest, and I groped to the side for anything to ground me in this nothingness. Panic licked at the edges of my mind.

"Caelus?" I shouted, my voice even higher pitched than usual. "Caelus, what's going on?"

"You can't see," he said. His voice was calm. "I suggest protecting yourself. Wanda is coming."

My heart, which had slowed marginally at his serene tone, galloped back to full speed.

"Quickly, now," Caelus said.

I glared at the blackness, certain that Caelus would see my thunderous face, and raked my hands through the air around me. Slippery, smooth threads passed through my fingers. Instead of grasping them, I spun my arms around my body to stir the air into a frothing windstorm around me. Faster and faster I flung my arms around, and the whistling of wind in my ears convinced me that my efforts were paying off. Great cracking and thumping noises had me worried, but when nothing hit me, I ignored the sounds.

My vision flickered back, and I blinked watering eyes against the now unbearable brightness of the single bare bulb. What had happened? Was Wanda preparing some new attack?

When my eyes had adjusted, I squinted around the room. Junk was littered in haphazard piles. So, not much had changed. It was like the tide had come through and rearranged

205

the furniture.

Where was Wanda? I lifted my hands, ready to defend myself, then a pair of running shoes captured my attention. When I paced forward, Wanda's supine form lay senseless on the dirty cement floor. A gash along her hairline dripped blood in a slow stream.

"Looks like she's down for the count," I said to Caelus. "I had no idea these amulets were so powerful. Can they do anything?"

"Anything to do with living beings," Caelus replied. "Nothing elemental."

"You sound like such a snob when you say that." I grinned at Caelus. "Thanks for saving my bacon back there."

"We're in this together, like it or not. We succeed or fail together." Caelus pointed at the dark opening past Wanda. "Onward, body buddy."

I chuckled at Caelus' new nickname for me—he was loosening up, which I appreciated—and walked to the opening. I left Wanda's slumbering form where it lay. She was still breathing and out of the running, and I had bigger fish to fry. I still had to find the amulet room and give myself the protection I needed to fight the mastermind. Could I access it from this staircase? It must have been possible because Wanda found her way.

The opening forced me to the right. I had a moment of panic when I wondered if my vision was retreating again, but it was only the pitch blackness of the room beyond. I groped the walls for a switch, but there was nothing.

"Watch the air currents," Caelus suggested. "They'll tell you everything you need to know."

"What am I supposed to glean from them?" I peered around the dark room, lit only by random glints of silver threads floating in midair.

"Walk forward, and if there are more strands than usual, you're approaching an obstacle rebounding the air currents your body creates when it walks." Caelus shrugged, his glowing threads not bright enough to illuminate the space beyond. "You'll get the hang of it."

"My shins are already wincing in anticipation."

I sighed and shuffled forward. As I watched silver threads drift around the room, the dimensions of the space became clear. Luckily, this wasn't a junk room like the previous one, and my feet were free to maneuver.

Where I was going, I had no idea, so I set a course for the far wall. When an increase of air threads bouncing toward me indicated an obstacle, I put my hands out to touch smooth plaster. A smile spread across my face. Again and again, Caelus' abilities in our shared body filled me with confidence. If I could navigate in the dark, I could tackle anything.

My hands slid along the wall, searching for a light switch or any feature of interest. A rough edge sparked hope, and I felt around until a door handle presented itself. My eager fingers turned the knob, which stuck and then released with a snap.

The next room was just as dark, but my groping hands encountered a light switch within seconds. Illumination took the form of another bulb in the ceiling, although someone had covered this one with a cheap lampshade that looked like a translucent bowl. The light didn't hold my attention the way the rest of the room did.

I had found Rosemary's amulet inventory. My lungs heaved a sigh of relief, and I shut the door behind me. The darkness outside pressed in like a living thing, and I was on edge enough without worrying about who might be creeping around in the blackness. Distractions would cost me time, and time would give the mastermind more chances to steal necklaces and attack sisters.

My eyes skimmed over the labels written in Rosemary's neat writing, and my heart sank at the empty shelves. More than half of the amulets were missing, and my memory wandered to the handful of amulets in Wanda's hand. The mastermind had already armed herself.

Two labels marked 'mind-control' caught my eye. Both were unaccompanied by amulets, and my lips tightened at the news. Not only could the mastermind control another, but she could also control more than one at a time. In theory, four sisters could attack at once, one with one amulet and three with the other, if they were divested of their necklaces and all in the same room.

I searched frantically for the protection amulet. If I could find that, then at least I would not succumb to mind-control. Manipulated for too much of my life, possessed by an elemental in my former existence, and body-sharing with another currently—I'd had enough of control. I didn't want the mastermind to jerk me around like a puppet as well.

On the second shelf from the top, only an arm's length away, the word 'protection' caught my searching eye. There it was, a ring with a polished jade stone embedded in tarnished silver filigree. Multicolored strands swirled around the stone so that I could only catch glimpses of brilliant green.

Protection for the mind. Say "tegmentum" three times out loud once the ring is on.

I reached toward it.

"Helping yourself to our stash?" a voice behind me said.

CHAPTER XVIII

I whirled around, my heart in my throat. Joy stood before two doorways at the end of the small room. Why did this tiny space need three doors?

She smiled with her lip curled, and the expression was so different from Joy's usual guileless happiness that my stomach clenched.

"You think you're so clever." Joy's unctuous voice curled with malice on the words. "But I'm in a room full of amulets that you don't know how to use. I do. Your move, Morgan."

Was Joy the mastermind? I glanced at her neck, but no necklace lay on top of her ample chest. A closer examination of her eyes revealed their glazed expression, despite her mostly clear words. Maybe the mastermind was getting better at controlling her puppets' speech.

"Get her," Caelus said loudly. "Blast her down."

I raked my hands through the air and gathered strands with my swift strokes, but Joy was quicker. With a vicious smile, she twisted a bracelet in one hand.

I let go of the air strands with a scream. My skin was on fire. Not literally—there were no flames—but it was as scorching hot as if I stood in a furnace. I slapped my arms and torso in a panicked attempt to stop the agony, but nothing worked.

"Make it stop!" I begged Joy, but she only laughed.

"Is it warm in here?" she said. "No, I think it's just you."

I wanted to leap in a lake, preferably one with chunks of ice floating in it. I needed to cool my skin, and I needed it now. What else besides water would work?

Could I blow away the heat? Feverishly, moans escaping my lips with every movement of my burning limbs, I gathered silver threads and pulled them toward me in a steady stream. Air blasted my skin like an arctic breeze.

Little by little, the heat abated. I opened my eyes, which streamed from the pain, and glared at Joy. She looked at me with confusion.

"It's not working anymore?" she said.

I didn't answer her with words. Instead, while one hand continued to pull blissfully cool air across my skin, the other folded and twisted strands into a dense blade. Caelus looked down in approval.

"Perfect, just like we practiced. Go on, knock the amulet away from her."

With a flick, I tossed the air knife at Joy. Caelus was right— we had practiced that trick in the park, although circumstances had been far more favorable—and my aim was true. With a shriek, Joy dropped the amulet and held her now-bleeding hand to her chest.

I didn't let her recover. Now that my skin had cooled from the break in Joy's connection with the amulet, I threw air threads at her. I wasn't aiming for accuracy. All I wanted was to catch her off guard so I could overpower her.

Joy's feet lifted off the ground and her mouth opened in a comical "o" before she smacked against the wall between the two closed doors. I panted, still trying to recuperate from the pain of my overheating, but Joy was too fast. She grabbed an amulet from a bottom shelf and pointed at me, her glazed eyes furious.

My hands lifted of their own accord and slammed my thighs hard enough to bruise. I winced with the impact, then my blood boiled with rage that was a righteous mix of body and mind. Joy was taking control of me? I didn't understand how, but I sure as hell wasn't going to stand for it. Where was that protection amulet?

My fingers twitched, and I had the overwhelming, uncontrollable urge to harm myself. Part of my brain watched, horrified, as my fingers twisted and rolled air threads into flat blades of deadly sharpness. The other part was wholly focused on my hands' task.

When the blades were complete, my hands lifted again. Each silver knife was the length of my finger, but as sharp as the cutting wind that finds cracks in coats during freezing weather. I could only watch, my breath coming in gasps with anticipation of the pain to follow, as each blade swept down in a flashing arc and buried itself in the muscle of my thigh.

I screamed in agony, and Joy released her hold over me. The silver blades dissolved into the air they were made of, and blood leeched out of each wound. I wanted to collapse with the pain, but I couldn't let Joy win. My hand grabbed the nearest shelf for support as my legs buckled, and my eyes frantically skimmed the jumbled shelves.

"You don't even know how to use these," Joy taunted. "Give up, Morgan."

There it was. The jade protection ring was pushed against the back wall in a cluster of other jewelry. I reached for it, but a hand grabbed my hair. My injured legs gave up their quest to support my weight, and I overbalanced and fell to the cement floor.

"You're too much work if you're not on my side," Joy said. "Get moving."

She dragged me by my hair to the leftmost door on the far wall. I let out a yell of distress as she almost scalped me, then I hobbled on my knees to follow her. Tears ran down my face as stabbing pain lanced through my legs with every movement.

Joy threw open the door and pushed me inside the empty, windowless room. I curled into a ball on the cement floor, trying to protect my legs without touching them.

"And stay in there," she said. She put a hand to her chin. "On second thought, I might try an amulet. I've always wanted to know what it does, but Rosemary never let me."

I didn't know if the mastermind spoke through Joy or whether it was Joy herself speaking, but I was past the point of caring. Joy slammed the door shut and the darkness was absolute except for my own swirling threads.

Caelus emerged from my arm. His face was worried.

"I'm sorry I wasn't more help," he said. "Joy was quick with the amulets, and the one that forced you to harm yourself was too powerful for me to contain."

My only answer was a sob. I touched my knees, which were sticky and wet.

"Hmm," Caelus said. He examined my legs. "You'd better hurry up with your healing."

"Oh," I gasped. Of course. How could I forget I could remove this fiery pain? I gazed at the snarls of faintly glowing burgundy, green, and silver threads that were entwined above each thigh, then I gingerly picked a knot.

"Faster than that," Caelus said with urgency. "You're losing a lot of blood. I know you want to stop the pain but focus on the bleeding first. You can handle pain, not blood loss."

"Says you," I muttered, but I changed the knot I was working on to focus on one that Caelus pointed to with his silvery finger. I worked quickly, and the bleeding had mostly stopped by the time I realized I could see my wounds. I sat up, wincing at the continued sharp pain.

"Where is the light coming from?" I said.

"I don't remember those spikes on the wall," Caelus said slowly. "Wasn't this an empty room?"

Rusty metal spikes longer than my foot were spaced at regular intervals on every wall and from the ceiling.

"What the hell?" I murmured. "It looks like a medieval torture chamber."

At my words, the walls shrank toward me with a creaking, scraping noise. I cursed and shuffled my bottom to the center of the small room.

"The room is shrinking!" I yelled. "Caelus, how do we fight this with air?"

"I don't know!" Caelus sounded as panicked as I felt. His emotions, usually so carefully hidden, spilled into my head. He was terrified that he would lose this body before his mission had even started, and without any artifacts to show for it. The threat of dormancy, whatever that meant, loomed large in his fears.

Strangely, Caelus' terror calmed my own concerns. I ignored the walls closing on me and studied the door, which was the only spike-free surface besides the floor.

"The door," I said. "It's our way out. We need to escape. Caelus, can you help me make a serrated air blade again?"

Caelus' overwrought emotions retreated from my mind as he considered my idea.

"Yes, of course," he said. "Quickly, now."

I nodded briskly and set to work, Caelus doling out increasingly agitated advice as I went. The groaning creaks of metal sliding against metal grated on my psyche, but I shoved my crudely created blade into the large keyhole and wiggled.

When spikes pressed against my back, I shuffled forward and kept jiggling my blade, sweat beading on my forehead. A spike touched the crown of my head and I hunched into my shoulders. This had to work. After everything I had survived, I refused to be skewered like a chicken kebab.

With a click, the handle turned. I almost wilted in relief, but instead I pushed the door open with a bang. Joy stood on the opposite side, her glazed eyes indifferent. Without warning, without thinking, I threw a blast of air at Joy. She fell to the ground, and I leaped on her. My legs pinned her arms, thrusting spears of pain through my thighs as I did so. With quick fingers, I plucked maroon strands from Joy's temple.

The haze in her eyes faded, and she blinked in confusion.

"Morgan? What are you doing? What's happening?"

My shoulders slumped in relief, and my legs throbbed incessantly now that the immediate danger had passed.

"The mastermind had you in her grasp," I said. "Mind-control. Nasty stuff." I turned to Caelus. "Can we tie her up with the threads?"

"Yes. Twist hers together with any on the ground." His mouth twisted with disdain. "The earth ones coating the floor will do. They will hold her for a short while. Don't mind the sticky feeling. I hate dealing with earth."

"Tie me up?" Joy frowned. "Who are you talking to?"

"I need to make sure you won't follow me and attack again." I picked up a few brown strands littering the cement floor. Caelus was right—they were oddly sticky and thick compared to the air threads I was used to handling—and I twisted them together with Joy's strands. "The mastermind has both mind-control amulets now, and the one she just stole can control more than one person at a time. I can't take the chance."

"Will you come back soon?" Joy bit her lip, and her eyes grew moist. "I don't want to be down here forever."

"I will," I assured her. "As soon as I find the mastermind. And the rope won't hold for long."

Caelus nodded in confirmation, and I stood. My eyes passed over the open doorway to the windowless room Joy had locked me in, and they widened in amazement. The room was empty once more, and no spikes poked out from shrinking walls. I whirled around to Joy.

"That room. It was covered in metal spikes a moment ago. They were going to impale me. How is it normal again?"

Joy glanced at the amulet on the floor, and her face cleared with understanding.

"Hallucination amulet. It was all in your mind."

I shook my head, recalling the pounding of my heart during my frenetic escape, and feeling the bone-tired weariness that had settled on me now that adrenaline drained from my body. I glanced at the jade ring on the nearest shelf.

"All in my head. Of course." I glared at Caelus. "You could have told me."

"It affected me, too," he said. "We share a body, remember? Same eyes."

I snatched the silver ring and shoved it on my finger.

"Tegmentum, tegmentum, tegmentum," I said.

The threads of the ring pulsed once then spread over my body like an armor of rainbow yarn.

"Okay," I said to Joy. "Relax. I'll be back soon."

Joy's face showed nothing but misgiving, but I couldn't spare any more time placating the younger woman. The closed door beside my temporary prison beckoned, and I limped to it, opened the heavy door, and shuffled through.

My legs ached and burned terribly, but I didn't have time to heal myself fully. I wasn't bleeding out, and that was the best I could manage. I needed to find Jasmine and Starr, and the last I saw, they were in the sisterhood's hangout.

The hallway I entered was mercifully lit—with dim bulbs, but I welcomed any illumination after the fearful dark of before—and a partly open door at a T-junction beckoned. I limped to it and peered quietly in.

A cheerless cement bunker greeted my eyes, although someone had taped brightly colored sarongs on the walls to enliven the cold rectangle. Two cots were pushed against a wall, and a small table with an electric kettle sat on the other side.

Denise was on one cot, her elbows on her knees and her face forlorn.

"Denise?" I said quietly.

She glanced up, and her eyes lit when she saw me. She jumped to her feet.

"Morgan! I'm so glad to see you. Wanda left a while ago and no one else came. I would go to the hangout, but it's so creepy in the hallway, I thought I'd wait a little longer."

"I'm trying to find Jasmine and Starr," I said. "One of them—or maybe Rosemary, I haven't ruled her out, she still has her necklace too—is the mastermind. Whoever it is has two mind-control amulets, so anyone without a necklace could attack at any time."

"Even me?" Denise's dark skin lost its warm glow in the dim light, and she gulped. "Take me with you, please. I don't want to be alone down here."

I sighed. Was it more dangerous to bring Denise along, where she could attack me at any time, or leave her here, where I couldn't keep an eye on her?

"Come on." I waved her forward, and she bounded to my side. "Let's find your sisters. Lead the way since I have no idea where I'm going in this maze."

"It's close," she assured me.

We turned a few corners until a closed door capped the end of the hall. When Denise opened it, I saw the familiar sight of the sisterhood's hangout and its tiny loveseat. Denise stepped inside and frowned.

"Where is everyone?"

My heart sank. Would I have to keep searching this damn building all night, afraid of random women jumping out at me, with each step bringing me fresh agony? I was almost ready to call it quits and go home—I didn't really care about these necklaces—but one look at Denise's face reminded me of my promises. The sisters needed my help, and I couldn't abandon them.

At the sound of thumping footsteps, my heart jumped into my throat. Denise clutched my arm with a vice-like grip.

"Someone's coming," she hissed. "Down the stairs. Come on." Denise thrust me to the side of the door and stood beside me, her arms in a defensive posture and her face determined.

"Ambush them?" I said, forcing my words past the waver in my voice. "Let's see who it is before we attack."

The footsteps stopped, and the door creaked open. Denise's eyes were wide with the tension of waiting.

Rosemary stepped through the doorway and stopped short when she saw us.

"Morgan! Denise. That's where you are. Come on, girls. Let's stick together."

She ushered Miranda and Amanda after her. I breathed a sigh of relief, and Denise released my arm with a huff of frantic laughter. I rubbed my sore muscle, adding it to my list of bodily complaints.

"I'm so glad to see you," Denise said. "Where are the others? What's going on?"

"Yes, let's do a reckoning," Rosemary said. She held up her fingers to tick off each sister. "I'm here, as well as Miranda, Amanda, and Denise. Shu is at home, she just texted me to see how we were."

"Joy is tied up in the amulet room," I said. "And Wanda is out cold in some junk room at the far end of the basement." At Rosemary's shocked expression, I said in defense, "They attacked me. Joy doesn't have her necklace anymore."

"Joy isn't the mastermind." Rosemary said, her lips pursed in thought.

"I can't believe it's one of us," Amanda whispered. Miranda hugged her shoulder. "How could it be?"

"Whoever it was," I said with a sigh. "She feels very strongly that your mission to release the spirit elemental and bring harmony to all living things will end in disaster. In her way, she's trying to save you all."

Rosemary shook her head briskly.

"Normally, I'd say she's entitled to her opinions, but in this case, she vowed to protect the Leaf. I made the same vow, and I intend to uphold it. Only Jasmine and Starr are unaccounted for. Has anyone seen them recently?"

The other women shook their heads with glum resignation. Denise glanced at me, then spoke to Rosemary.

"Morgan said that anyone still with a necklace is a suspect. Only Starr, Jasmine, and you have one."

Her eyes flickered to Rosemary's neck, where a gold chain glinted in the dim light. Rosemary flushed.

"I might be the mastermind, you mean? It's true, we shouldn't rule me out." She lifted the chain off her neck and stepped toward me. With a gentle motion, she draped the necklace over my head. "My only concern is keeping the Leaf safe. If that means giving it to the most powerful woman here, so be it. Morgan has a much better chance at saving it than I do."

"You're trying to prove that you're not the mastermind, because she's collecting necklaces and you're giving yours away." I nodded. "Color me convinced. I'll do my best to keep it safe."

Rosemary's smile brightened her strained face.

"Thank you, Morgan." She turned to the others. "Okay, the three of you should wait in the bunker. If one of you starts to act strangely, the others should restrain her, okay?"

The others nodded with pale faces. One by one, they heeded the instructions of their eldest sister and traipsed through the door Denise and I had recently entered. Rosemary turned to me.

"Let's go to the amulet room. I need to gather supplies if we're to stop the mastermind."

I sighed. The basement was large, and my legs were aching worse than ever, but Rosemary was right. We needed whatever ammunition she could muster to fight the mastermind. I gestured to the door that led to the rest of the basement.

"After you."

The instant we stepped through the doorway, Rosemary tripped over her own feet. My legs tangled in the flailing woman's descent, and I fell hard next to her. Pain lanced through my injured legs. I choked back a scream and twisted my head to look forward.

Denise and Miranda, both with expressions of glazed concentration, stood in the way of our advance. Rosemary and I glanced at each other with identical looks of wide-eyed fear. The mastermind was near, and she didn't want us to reach the amulet room.

"Damn it," Denise shouted. "It's not working on her."

Had Denise tried using an amulet on me? I glanced at the jade ring with new appreciation.

"Get Rosemary, then!" Miranda yelled. "I'll do Morgan."

Rosemary reached up and grabbed her own hair. With a shriek, she yanked on a fistful, dragging her head with it.

"What are you doing?" I shouted. "Stop it!"

"I can't!" she cried. "They're making me."

Denise had a cruel look of satisfaction on her face so unlike her usual honest expression. Miranda lifted her hand, a bracelet grasped in her fingers, and whistled.

I pushed myself to my feet on shaking legs, unsure what was coming next but not willing to meet it on the floor. A rustling, scuttling noise gathered in the hallway behind Denise and Miranda. I gathered air threads to prepare an attack, then dropped them in horror.

An army of rats and spiders flowed around the others, coming straight at us.

CHAPTER XIX

Miranda laughed, high and cold and cruel.

"Death by a thousand bites," she crowed. "How poetic."

"I think you need to go back to English class," I yelled, gathering air threads in hasty bundles. "You clearly have no grasp of poetry."

I threw silver strands at the floor where the vanguard of crawly critters scampered. With a volley of squeaks, the frontmost rats and spiders blew away, their legs wriggling in midair.

But more came. Rosemary shrieked and scrambled to her feet with fingers still entangled in her hair. I threw another blast that deflected the floor creatures, but insects scuttled on the walls, coming closer every second. Giant hairy house spiders ran with legs moving almost quicker than sight. I shuddered and tossed another blast of wind.

A sharp sting on my ankle made me gasp out a startled cry. I lifted my pant leg and shook off a spider, its shiny bulbous abdomen marking it as a black widow. I swallowed in fear. This was an attack that the protection ring couldn't halt. Bites weren't deadly, but I was in for a lot of pain. When would symptoms start showing?

"Get the women," Caelus shouted at me. "Forget the bugs."

"Easy for you to say."

I blasted another pack of rats from reaching my feet, then heaved a jet of air at Miranda. She screamed when the concentrated blast hit her arm, and she dropped the amulet in her hand.

The rats and spiders didn't stop moving, but now their directions were random instead of targeted. I didn't know if that were better. Now, creatures darted in every direction, and we still had rats running over our feet and spiders on the ceiling.

I gulped and limped forward as quickly as I could while the other two shrieked their dismay as their plan backfired. I wrapped a bundle of air strands around my fist then clocked Miranda on the head with it. The threads softened the blow on my hand, but Miranda's eyes rolled in her head and she slumped to the floor like a marionette whose strings had been snipped.

One down, one to go. Movement behind Denise caught my eye, and I cringed. Then there were two. Amanda ran toward us with a glazed look and an amulet swinging from her hand. She thrust it at me while Denise continued to make Rosemary attack herself. The poor woman was currently scratching her own cheeks until they bled.

I gathered threads, then my legs buckled. I dropped to the floor, all strength in my limbs vanished. What had Amanda's amulet done? It must have affected my body instead of my mind, and the protection ring couldn't stop it. Amanda's satisfied giggle brought the heat of anger to my face, and I twitched my fingers that still gripped air strands. I couldn't do much from my weak position on the ground, but I didn't need much motion to create a large effect. As Caelus had drilled into me, intention was the largest piece of the puzzle. My eyes narrowed in concentration, and I twitched the silver threads again.

I couldn't see what was happening, but Denise and Amanda's screams of pain brought a smile to my face. I leaped up, my strength returned with Amanda's loss of amulet, and I grabbed Rosemary's arm. Her face was a bloody mess—somehow, she had avoided her eyes, but the surrounding skin was ripped to shreds—but she had stopped attacking herself.

"Quick, they're getting up again," she hissed, and we fled through the far door. Adrenaline gave my injured legs more speed than they should have had, and I knew I would pay for it later when this was all over. As we pounded up the stairs, a scream from above pierced the night. Rosemary threw an agonized glance back at me.

"Will this nightmare ever end?" she panted.

We burst through the top door. I was instantly enveloped in bitter cold, bone-shaking cold, Antarctic cold. My joints seized with the sensation, and I painfully turned my eyes to Rosemary. She stared at me in horror, then her eyes grew angry and she whipped toward the figure in the hall.

"Jasmine," she yelled. "Stop it, you little bitch!"

"She's not in control," I rasped out. Jasmine's eyes were glazed, and her throat was free of her usual golden chain. I didn't know if Rosemary had heard me, but she charged toward her younger sister with furious determination.

When Jasmine plummeted to the ground, the icy cold broke and I sucked warm air into my lungs with grateful gasps. The two sisters rolled on the ground, but I could only think of one thing.

Starr was the mastermind.

Starr, the youngest of the sisters, only seventeen. Starr, with her badly dyed green hair. Starr, the embarrassment of the tennis team. Starr, with her controlling boyfriend.

The puzzle clicked together. Starr had been listening to Trent's diatribes of resisting authority and thinking for herself. She must have taken it to heart, truly thought about what the sisterhood's mission would mean for humanity and come to her own conclusions.

Correct or not, I didn't know. Not taking rules at face value was an ideal I could endorse, but there were ways and there were ways. All I knew was that Starr was hurting her sisters and me, and she had to stop. Change was sometimes necessary, but violence wasn't the way. Not at first, anyway.

A door leading to the alley flung open and three men raced inside, bringing with them December cold and the scent of rain. Each one sported a fine set of glazed eyes, and all three looked like they meant business. I gritted my teeth and positioned myself between the three men and the two grappling women. Rosemary was busy with Jasmine, so these three were mine.

"Caelus!" I shouted. "Plan of attack?"

"Blast them all while we figure it out," he replied.

I gathered strands and flung them down the hall. The men stumbled, but they were heavier than the young women downstairs, and none was flung off his feet. The two in the back tangled with each other, but the front man in a red coat recovered first and resumed his relentless jog down the hall.

I had a moment of panic. All this magic use was wearing me down, my legs screamed at me, and a strange lethargy dragged at my limbs. I glanced at my ankle. Was the spider venom already affecting me? How long did I have before it pulled me under?

The man reached me before I could muster a defense, and he forced me against the wall. His hot breath, reeking of beer, filled my nose with sickening closeness.

"I got you," he said with a sneer.

I tilted my head in thought.

"But do you, really?"

I squeezed air strands near his waist and concentrated on what I intended to do. It took three full seconds, then the man's eyes bugged. He released me and stepped back with a howl. His hands beat at his skin, where pinpricks of silver threads stabbed him repeatedly.

I didn't have time to gloat, because the next two men were on me. They ignored their fellow, who writhed in the hallway with his painful skin malady. One pushed me to the ground and sat on my legs while the other gripped my hands and forced them to the floor. I was pinned like a specimen in a museum.

Panic flared. This was almost worse than being possessed by an elemental. At least with Caelus I had a chance at fighting back. Here, I had no recourse. Even my fingers were immobile in sweaty hands. A too-familiar feeling of helplessness, of worthlessness, swept over me. I gritted my teeth to fight the feeling.

"You can't get away this time," the man said.

"Are you a betting man?" I said. "Come closer. I have a secret to tell you."

The man, idiot that he was, leaned in. I lifted my head to narrow the gap between our mouths. When he breathed out, I opened my mouth and let the silver threads of his breath filter between my lips.

Then my teeth snapped onto the strands.

I concentrated and yanked the threads as hard as I could with a twist of my neck. The man's eyes bulged, and he jerked upward to get away from me, but that only pulled more strands from his lungs. His hands flew to his throat in the universal gesture of choking.

My arms were free, but I didn't release his strands from my teeth. Instead, I gathered threads at his hands and yanked them together. With a few twists that made him twitch in pain—I wasn't trying to be gentle—I contained him enough to ignore him. My mouth opened and, with a gasp, air flowed into his lungs. He choked and retched, but I had no more attention to spare the gagging man.

"Watch out!" Caelus shouted.

The man locking my legs to the ground rose and swung a ringed fist at my face. I turned to avoid it, but his knuckles still grazed my jawbone. My teeth jolted together with an explosion of pain, and I hoped nothing was broken. The sensation was uncomfortably familiar, even after all these years. I had a brief pang of regret that I hadn't disfigured Peter when I had the chance. I hastily squashed the errant thought, born of my new body's trauma.

I was out of my depth again. My mind flitted to Jerome, even as I scrambled out of the way. Jerome had helped me out of a sticky situation before, but there was no way he would saunter by at this time of night. I spat blood out of my mouth, dodged the man's grasping arms, and threw a bundle of silver strands behind me with a haphazard toss. He grunted, so I guessed I had hit my mark.

I didn't need a man to save me. Putting my trust in Jerome would be foolish. I barely knew him. Why invite that uncertainty into my life? This situation might be a fiasco, but I wasn't down for the count yet.

I swung my gaze at my attacker again, and my eyes widened with recognition, even as I threw a blast of air that flung him onto his back. It was the man who had shouted in the car outside Upper Crust, the same who had attacked Miranda. How had he recovered from my treatment of him?

My lip curled. Did I really need to hold my punches with this one? The other men were unknowns, but this man probably deserved whatever I dished out. I was too hurt and drained to be careful with him, and I probably didn't need to be.

I wove a blade of air and brandished it at the man. He didn't notice, which was understandable since the blade was invisible to him. Invisible, but still deadly. I stepped forward, and something in my face must have convinced him that I meant business, because he scrambled back like a crab. I adjusted the blade in my hand, ready to strike.

Then I remembered Joy's sneering face when she was under control, and Miranda's taunts. I didn't have enough information to punish this man. For all I knew, that argument in the car had been perfectly innocent. Did I have the authority to dish out punishment without just cause?

Starr was the culprit behind all this. Starr was the mastermind, and it was Starr that I needed to bring to justice, not these men who weren't in their right minds.

The man panted with fear despite his glazed eyes, and I slashed at his forehead. With a twitch of my fingers as I brought the weapon down, it changed from a blade to a club. With a blow from the air bludgeon, the man fell unconscious. I breathed heavily, my stomach churning from more than just nerves. Was the black widow bite affecting me? Cold sweat beaded on my forehead.

"Morgan!" Rosemary's urgent voice woke me from my post-battle focus. "I need more amulets to fight with. I'll be right back, okay?"

I nodded, and Rosemary tore off, leaving Jasmine trussed up with her hands tied behind her back with Rosemary's belt around her wrists. I examined her for a minute, but Jasmine's injuries appeared superficial, even to my thread-enhanced vision. The girl moaned.

"Hang tight, Jasmine," I said. "We'll find Starr soon."

"No need to search," a light, youthful voice called out.

I spun on my heel, wincing at the pain in my thighs and a growing spasm in my leg from the spider venom, and peered down the hall. Starr stood at the far end with her arms crossed in a typical teenage can't-be-bothered-with-anything posture. Around her neck draped a cluster of necklaces. Eight, if I had to guess. The ninth weighed heavily on my neck, along with the hope and trust of Rosemary and the sisterhood.

"Why are you fighting me so hard?" Starr said. "Did Rosemary sell you the party line? Do you really believe in all the harmony mumbo-jumbo?" She shook her head. "Rosemary and the others were brought up with that junk, same as me, but I'm the only one who really thought about what it all means. I can't follow blindly anymore—even if I'm by myself, I have to stand up for what's right. It's horrible if you imagine what could happen. Think of all the animals that we could control. Haven't we done enough to make their lives miserable? The world would be a way worse place, and it's bad enough already."

"There's a right way to do things, and a wrong way," I said, stepping slowly down the hall toward Starr. My legs twitched with cramps from the spider's venom, and I grimaced. "Hurting and almost killing others is rarely the correct solution. Did you try talking about it with your sisters?"

Starr scoffed.

"Yeah, I brought it up. They're so stuck on the story in the Book of Souls that they can't even imagine a different reality. They're hopeless. I'm the only one who can stop this brand of crazy. There's only one person I can trust, and it's not a sister." She tapped her foot. "I really can't convince you to hand over the necklace, can I?"

"No." I planted my feet in case Starr whipped out an amulet and attacked. "I was hired to protect these women and their mission, and I keep my promises."

"Whatever." Starr stepped aside. A door clicked closed, then a figure strode from the stairwell behind Starr. A blank-faced Rosemary held amulets in each hand, and Starr smiled. "Then go nuts."

Before I could react, Rosemary thrust out the amulet in her right hand. My body erupted in painful, uncontrollable itching. I couldn't think of anything except the sensation crawling on my skin and my desperate need to scratch every inch of exposed skin. I was vaguely aware of Rosemary pacing closer, but I couldn't spare any concentration for my opponent.

When my feet flew out from under me, my head smacked against the polished cement floor. Stars flashed in my eyes from the impact, and I lay stunned. Caelus appeared in my vision, his expression panicked.

"Get up!" he shouted. "She's coming."

When I didn't move, he melted into my arm and flowed over my body. I let him take over, too stunned to stop him. My arms twitched, but Caelus must have felt the same physical shock that I was experiencing, because he popped out of my arm with frustration.

"Snap out of it," he ordered. "You're human, you can shake it off quicker."

I would have laughed at his failure if the results hadn't been so dire. Rosemary stood next to my body, and I stared at her silhouette against the dim hall sconce. She raised an amulet.

CHAPTER XX

I wiggled my fingers, and Rosemary frowned while she shook one of her feet. Heartened that my small movements had an effect, I pulled harder. Rosemary stumbled. With a gargantuan effort that made my head spin like the gusts of a hurricane, I sat upright. Rosemary glared at me, but I lifted my leaden arms and threw every silver thread I could reach at her.

Rosemary flew off her feet and twisted through the air then hit the wall. Now was the time to make my getaway. Walking wasn't an option, not with the world still pitching and yawing around me, so I crawled on hands and knees to the closest doorway.

The scents of floral shampoo and acrid dye assaulted my beleaguered senses. I must be in Cut Right. I was in no shape to fight until I had fixed my head. Lethargy weighed my limbs with excessive gravity more commonly found on Jupiter, and I crawled further, desperate for somewhere to hide. Rosemary wouldn't be down for long, and Starr was right behind her. Starr didn't seem interested in doing her own dirty work, but that could change at any moment.

I tucked myself under a corner sink and considered my options. My poor brain scrambled for coherent thought while my muscles twitched uncontrollably and my stomach roiled.

I needed help. This was beyond my skills, and all my allies were attacking me, one by one. I was alone, and that wasn't good enough anymore. Who could I call?

Anna. She had been unreliable of late, but she was still my oldest friend. She would come through. I pulled out my phone and dialed her number. Caelus blossomed out of my arm.

"Work while you talk," he snapped at me. "Start untangling those knots on your head."

I shoved the fingers of one hand into the cool smoothness of my own strands. I couldn't see what I was doing, but massaging the knots under my fingers removed my headache, little by little.

The phone rang and rang. Eventually, Anna's sultry voice spoke into my ear, her recorded speech inviting me to leave a message. I hung up and my lips tightened.

Anna was a bust, again. I felt very small. I could only rely on myself, but that was getting old. I was tired of being alone.

There wasn't anyone else to call. The police, maybe, but I shied away from exposing myself again to their notice. I didn't know if Fiorella had been in trouble, and my government identification was still in the works. What would come of opening that can of worms? Surely, I could find someone else to help.

Jerome crossed my mind again. It was the middle of the night, but he told me he often worked on his wedding cakes at night when the bakery was closed. He might answer my plea for help. But did I want to involve someone else for Starr to control?

"Morgan." Rosemary's voice echoed through the dark salon. "I know you're in here."

Rosemary's shadow stalked between chairs. She unlocked the front door and looked out but was apparently satisfied that I was still in Cut Right, because she twirled on the spot with a sly smile.

"I'll find you soon enough."

My fists clenched with my agonizing decision. I was at the end of my strength, but the burning in my gut from Fiorella's unknown ordeals said I didn't want a man's help. I didn't want to rely on anyone else. Calling Jerome felt like a betrayal of everything I had stood for as March, everything I had worked so hard to achieve: strong will, independence, power.

But I wasn't March anymore, and this body wasn't Fiorella's. I was Morgan.

New Morgan, new life. No regrets.

With shaking fingers, I texted Jerome while Rosemary

paced ever closer.

At Cut Right. Need help. Please come.

I shoved my phone in my pocket, hoping against hope that my text wasn't too late. My movement must have caught Rosemary's eye because her voice grew smug.

"I see you, Morgan. Come out and play."

I gritted my teeth, preparing myself for the next push. My thighs throbbed with incessant pain, the muscles in my legs trembled with strong spasms from the venom coursing through my bloodstream, and all I wanted was to lie down and close my eyes. I didn't know how much of my lethargy was from my use of magic, from the spider venom, or from my injuries, but it didn't matter. The only positive was that my thread-massage had cleared my mind enough to ignore the ache in my skull. I gathered as many air threads as I could reach, took a deep breath, and launched myself from under the sink.

Rosemary jumped back with her eyes wide in the bloody mess of her scratched face. I threw my threads with intent, and they jetted across the room and knocked Rosemary down. The other woman cried out, then my body erupted in uncontrollable itching again.

This time, I was prepared. I resisted scratching with all my iron will and pulled threads toward me. The air rasped against my skin, relieving the itch, and I threw another jet of air at Rosemary. She was halfway to her feet, but my blow twisted her around in a whirlwind of woman, hairbrushes, and shampoo bottles. She shrieked once, then I ceased the whirlwind and she dropped to the floor, unmoving.

With her loss of concentration, my insatiable itching stopped. I took a deep breath, then strode to Rosemary's side and snatched the amulets from her unresisting fingers. If she woke up, she wouldn't have magic to use against me.

I hobbled toward the hallway, where light streamed through the open door. It was time to face Starr. No sisters forced to fight for her, no human shield of men, nothing but her and me.

I needed to stop this jumped-up self-proclaimed savior. She had already hurt too many.

One step into the hall, and my legs locked together. I fell with a brain-shaking jolt, my hands the only brace against the hard floor. I writhed and twisted my legs, but they refused to separate.

"We call it the mermaid curse," Starr's voice drifted to me. I turned my head so fast that my neck clicked. Starr sauntered down the hall. "Funny, right? Don't know if it helps you swim. I'm kind of tempted to try."

"You think you know everything," I spat out. "But what makes you believe you know better than the sisterhood? There's no proof either way. They might be foolish, but you're the one hurting everyone."

Starr shook her head.

"I can't let them release the spirit elemental. The consequences are too huge. If I'm wrong and I destroy the Leaf, then the world continues as it is, no big deal."

"Depends who you talk to."

"If I'm right," Starr continued, ignoring my comment. "Then I've saved the world. Come on, you have to admit that either way, I'm the good guy here."

My heart squeezed in recognition of her words. It was so easy to see oneself as the righteous one, and so hard to admit one's faults. Starr, for all her idealism, was blind to her flaws and the consequences of her actions.

"I can lay assault and attempted murder at your feet," I replied. "Not to mention the questionable ethics of mind-control. Does that not bother you? Against your sisters and innocent men?"

Starr's mouth twisted.

"My boyfriend always says you can't make an omelet without breaking a few eggs. Once my sisters know what I saved them from, they'll understand."

Starr was parroting Trent's words again. I shook my head,

more as a distraction from my hand gathering threads than an indication of my thoughts. I was vulnerable on the floor. I needed to attack, and soon.

"I'm as guilty as you of Machiavellian tendencies." At Starr's confused look, I clarified. "Where the ends justify the means. I grant you, sometimes it's true. But to base your actions on an ancient legend, and to start solving problems with violence instead of talking? That was your mistake, and one your sisters will find difficult to forgive."

I threw the air blade I had crafted at Starr. It was as sharp as any I had woven yet. It felt wrong to attack the girl—more than wrong, it went against everything I believed—but she needed to be stopped.

I still aimed at Starr's leg—I had no intention of murdering a girl, I wasn't a monster—but my eyes widened in shock as the air blade, so deft and deadly against the controlled men and sisters, bounced harmlessly off Starr. She grinned and held up her wrist, which was encircled by a silver bracelet.

"Protection against wind elementals." At my incredulous stare, she laughed. "Yeah, I figured it out. All you use is air stuff, it wasn't hard. You must have a deal with a wind elemental, or maybe you're part-elemental yourself? The Book of Souls has all sorts of crazy stories, even if we sisters are only allowed to see part of it. You think I'm too young to know anything, but I know more than you think."

"I can't help you." Caelus sounded flabbergasted. "This girl foiled us. I'm sorry, Morgan."

He melted into my arm and his silver strands writhed in a loose cluster at my stomach.

I looked at the amulets in my hand, stolen from Rosemary. I had no idea what each of them was and no clue how to use them. They were useless to me. And now, with my wind-powers hamstrung, I had nothing.

Starr walked forward and stood near me. I reached for her, to do what, I didn't know. Pull her down and claw at her face?

232

It was all I was capable of now. Even that motion took too much effort. My leg muscles spasmed from the spider venom coursing through my system, and my arms were so tired that I could hardly lift them. A long-familiar feeling of helplessness washed over me. It felt wrong to be caused by a slip of a girl.

I tightened my lips and tensed my jaw. No. I would not fall into that trough of helplessness. That was long-ago March. That past was not Morgan's, and I refused to let it touch me. Never again.

But what could I do?

Starr crouched next to me and held out an opal ring with her right hand. The protection bracelet on her wrist winked in the hall light.

"Do you know what this does?" Starr asked. I shook my head, gazing at the multicolored threads swirling lazily around the ring. "It's a memory eraser. In a minute, you won't remember any of this. You could have joined me, you know." Starr pursed her lips in annoyance, and the expression reminded me how young she truly was. "I wish you had. Oh well, the memory eraser will work out better. Then I can walk away with the Leaf, and no one will follow me."

She reached out with her left hand and wrenched Rosemary's necklace from around my neck. The chain scraped against my cheek and I winced. With another swift movement that I couldn't prevent with my lethargic muscles, Starr ripped the protection ring off my finger.

Now, I had nothing. Not the necklace that Rosemary had entrusted to me, not the jade ring to protect against mind-control, and not Caelus' air powers. Starr could do whatever she wanted to me. I had no more recourse.

With a bang, the door to the salon crashed open. Jerome stood blinking in the light, his huge form filling the doorway. Starr looked up in surprise.

With a speed born of desperation, I grabbed Starr's wrist and slid off the anti-elemental bracelet. Despite Caelus' scoffing, amulets had power far beyond their magic: they gave the dubious power of overconfidence. Starr thought this amulet had the power to protect her from me, just like she thought the ring connected to Peter had the power to convince me to join her. But relying on the supernatural had its downfalls. Greater power came from trusting others.

Before Starr could do more than open her mouth in surprise, I grabbed silver threads from near her lips and pulled.

With a choking gasp, Starr's hands flew to her throat. The mermaid curse released my legs, and I scrambled out of her reach. I pulled harder and winced as Starr's eyes widened as round as the tennis balls she loathed. Manipulated, convinced that she was in the right, acting with righteous justification for her dubious actions—she was too much like me for comfort. Starving her of air was like choking my younger self, and it hurt. A necessary hurt, but still painful. Starr's body writhed and spasmed, but without air, she grew steadily weaker.

"What are you doing?" Jerome yelled.

I shook my head.

"Please don't interfere, Jerome. I promise, she'll be fine."

"She's just a girl."

"I thought that too, and that was my mistake." I pulled the threads harder, and Starr arched her back once before slumping to the floor. "But I need to stop her before she hurts anyone else."

Starr's head slumped to the floor as she fell unconscious. My legs gave out, and I sat on my bottom, breathing heavily. Starr was defeated. This was the so-called "mastermind", a girl barely old enough to be called a woman, behind all the attacks. She had convinced herself—or allowed her boyfriend Trent to sway her opinion—that the purpose of the sisterhood was based on lies, and that the completion of their task would result in destruction.

I couldn't say one way or another. All I knew was that Starr had been hurting her sisters, and I couldn't condone her actions. Sometimes the end justified the means, but without proof on either side of the artifact's power, the pain Starr had caused was unnecessary.

All I knew now was that I was exhausted, my stabbed legs throbbed with incessant fire, and my limbs wouldn't stop shaking. Jerome squatted next to me, his face scrunched with worry.

"What was all that about? Are you okay?" He looked at my thighs, and his brow wrinkled even further. It was endearing, and my betraying gut writhed with affection despite my injuries. "That looks nasty."

"I'll be okay," I said with an attempt at a smile.

"If he gave you a moment alone, we could heal you." Caelus reemerged from my arm and studied the wounds with a critical eye.

"Could you please check the other women?" I asked Jerome. "There should be nine of them, including this one." I prodded Starr with my finger. "And three men in the hallway. Make sure they're all still breathing. Rosemary can figure out the rest. There's no danger now that Starr is down. Some are in the basement. I promise, I'll explain all this later."

Jerome nodded and rose without question. When he entered the stairwell and the door clicked shut behind him, I breathed a sigh of relief that hitched when my diaphragm spasmed.

"Okay, Caelus, how do we stop this infernal pain?"

Caelus guided me through healing my legs, which wasn't much more involved than untangling the knots above the wounds. Removing the spider venom took longer. I had to pluck electric green strands from all over my body and deposit the wriggling things on the floor.

"I have the hang of this," I said after a minute. "Not a big deal, really. Ow!"

I had pulled a strand too hard, and my whole leg lanced with pain. Caelus grimaced.

"Take it slow. Humans are so fragile."

235

"You're as good as one of us, now," I said through gritted teeth as I wiggled a strand free. "Better get used to it."

"When you're quite finished, hurry up and grab the necklaces," Caelus said with repressed excitement. "I want that artifact. This could be the first one. My mission won't be a waste."

I looked at the knots still tangled over my final leg, then at the almost closed wound. I shrugged.

"Good enough. I can finish later."

I shuffled closer to an unconscious Starr. Carefully, so she didn't wake, I lifted the nine necklaces off her chest and over her face. One chain caught in her green hair, and I tugged it free with a wince. Starr's face twitched, but she remained asleep.

"Now, what?" I said. "Rosemary will wake up any minute, and she'll want them all accounted for."

"Open each one until we find the artifact."

Caelus' threads quivered with excitement until his entire form vibrated. My lips tightened to prevent a smile, but my heart sank at my upcoming task. I had worked so hard to help the sisters, and their mission in life was to protect this artifact. Now, I was stealing it from under their noses.

But I owed Caelus. We had brokered a truce, and he had kept his end of the bargain impeccably. He hadn't once tried to take over our body since our agreement, and he'd taught me how to use his powers. What was more, he'd turned into a friend of sorts, and I valued both his advice and his company. An artifact was within his grasp, and his relief was palpable. I couldn't refuse him.

I laid the necklaces on the floor. With my fingernails, I pried open one.

A rolled leaf, dry as dust, was tied with a tiny green ribbon inside the locket, which was sealed with a rubber gasket. One solitary strand, a pale green, drooped from the dead leaf. Caelus swooped over to look, and his face fell.

"That's no artifact. Try another one."

I opened the next with difficulty—it had clearly last been opened years ago, if ever—and the same sight met our eyes. Caelus grew frantic as I pried open locket after locket.

"Keep going," he hissed. "Rosemary will be here soon."

I pushed my fingernails through the second-to-last locket. Instantly, I knew this was the one even without Caelus' gasp of delight. Multicolored threads twined around the dead leaf, fresh and vibrant in a way the other limp strands couldn't hope to emulate. The magic imbued in this artifact was undeniable.

"Quick," Caelus said. "Hide it. No, first wrap a cushion of air around it for protection. I want to examine it later intact. Here, let me show you how."

Caelus sank into my arm and eagerly pushed for control of the body. I allowed him, because I knew how important the artifact was to him, although I chafed at the helpless feeling. Luckily, it took him only moments to wrap air threads around the artifact until it resembled a hairy ball of silver yarn. When he let go of the body and reemerged from my arm, I shoved the artifact in my pocket.

"We can't leave the locket empty," I said. "What if Rosemary checks? I don't want her after me."

"We can make a replica," Caelus said. "It won't last long, but a few hours is all we need. She'll check right away."

"Just make a replica?" I raised my eyebrow. "No problem. How, exactly, would I do such a thing?"

"Study it, pull air threads toward you, and shape them together." Caelus waved his hand as if his instructions were perfectly adequate. "With intention, of course."

"Of course," I muttered and stared at the leaf from another locket. With fingers trembling from exhaustion and the aftermath of adrenaline, I tugged gently at loose air threads. When I had enough, I attempted to weave them together while thinking of the dead leaf and hoping I could make something similar enough to fool Rosemary.

With a twitch, my cluster of silver threads rippled into a dead leaf. My mouth dropped open.

"Don't forget the ribbon," Caelus said.

I swallowed my surprise and glared at Caelus.

"I'm working on it. Honestly, you're demanding."

"I can hear footsteps." Caelus turned toward the salon's door. I hastily grabbed another thread from the air, wrapped it around the new leaf, and hoped desperately that it would turn into a green ribbon. To my surprise, it did. I shoved it inside the empty locket, gathered the necklaces together, and was holding them all in one hand when Rosemary ran into the room. Her eyes in her bleeding face went straight to the lockets swinging from my hand, and the look of relief on her face was almost comical. She hardly spared a glance at her unconscious sister on the floor as she strode to grab the necklaces from my offering grasp.

"You did it," she breathed. "Morgan, you figured it out and saved the necklaces. Words can't express my gratitude."

"As long as my wages drop into my bank account, we're square." I smiled to show her I was joking. A cash infusion wouldn't hurt, now that I had no other source of income, but I didn't really deserve it, not now that I had stolen the Leaf. "Are you okay?"

"I'm fine," Rosemary assured me. "No lasting damage."

"What will you do now?"

"Find a new sister, for one." Rosemary curled her lip at Starr. "There are a few candidates from former sisters who had daughters. Starr will be handed to the elders for punishment."

I swallowed, fearing for Starr. Who were these elders? Would she be slapped on the wrist, or something far worse? Exactly how old-fashioned were these women?

"She truly thought she was doing this for the best." I felt bound to present the facts to Rosemary so that Starr had a fair assessment. Starr took the wrong path to achieve her goal, but I had no idea if her goal was valid. It might well have been.

Rosemary shrugged, her eyes tired.

"She might have to spend time with the motherhood to sort out her priorities," she said. That ominous euphemism made me wonder what the truth was. "Or she'll have her memory erased and be given a new identity, maybe. It's out of my hands, now."

CHAPTER XXI

After that disquieting discussion, Jerome returned. I said goodbye to Rosemary, who was busy applying a healing amulet to her sisters' wounds, and limped out of Cut Right into the now-dry night with Jerome holding my elbow. Leaning on him for support felt wrong—I should be able to take care of myself—but also very comforting. Maybe I wasn't as alone as I'd feared I was.

"Thank you for coming," I said after it was clear that he wouldn't speak until I did. "I needed your help."

That took a lot for me to say, but I was rewarded by Jerome's swift grin.

"You had it mostly under control, by the looks of it. I was a distraction, nothing more."

"But a valuable one. That chit of a girl was hurting the other women to get what she wanted. I'm not the only one with a few tricks up my sleeve. I wish I could tell you more, but it's not my secret to tell." I patted his hand on my elbow. "What did I drag you away from? Are you working on the wedding cake tonight?"

Jerome's face fell, and he turned away from me.

"Yeah, I was."

I pushed my arm into his side.

"What's wrong? Is the fondant not smooth enough?"

"It's fine." He shrugged. "Well, it's not, but there's nothing I can do about it now. And I don't regret anything," he said fiercely.

My stomach plummeted.

"What's going on?" I put on my sternest, no-nonsest voice, the one to quell even the most stubborn board member, and Jerome's shoulders wilted.

"The wedding is tomorrow." He checked himself. "Later today. I was finishing the cake tonight, but there's still a lot to do, and the bakery opens too soon to finish it in time. I'll have to call the bride and apologize. She's not expecting the cake until ten in the morning, but there's nowhere I can do it properly." He wrinkled his nose. "She'll be devastated. And she went out on a limb for me, as a new baker. My career is over before it's begun." He blew air out of his mouth explosively then tried to grin. It wasn't genuine. "It was a pipe-dream, anyway."

I gazed at him, my mind a whirlwind of thought. He glanced at me then looked away, his shame and sense of failure palpable.

"A wedding on a Wednesday?" I murmured.

"They're on a budget," he said. "Midweek venue rentals are much cheaper. That's why they hired me, probably."

"Pack up your cake and equipment," I said. "Meet me in front of the bakery in twenty minutes. No questions."

"But—"

"No questions," I repeated firmly. "Go."

With a frown of confusion, Jerome let go of my arm and loped away. I smiled at his back. March might be in my past, but my air of authority was eternal. When he was out of earshot, I brought out my phone and started my calls.

When I finally limped to Upper Crust, Jerome stood on the sidewalk with a large Tupperware container in his hands and a duffel bag at his feet. The orange streetlight lit his puzzled features and my traitorous heart jumped. I quelled it with a stern thought.

"What now?" Jerome asked when he noticed me. His face fell. "Morgan, I'm sorry. I forgot you were hurt. You shouldn't have walked all this way."

"It's not that far," I said. I could handle a little pain, and Caelus had assured me that with a few minutes of untangling, I would be fully healed. It was easier to bear discomfort when there was a quick fix. The rumble of an engine made me turn my head. "Ah, good. Our ride is here."

"Where are we going?"

I suppressed my smile and tried for an enigmatic look. I wasn't sure I succeeded.

"You need to finish your cake. I can provide you with a kitchen, but the hard work is up to you."

The look of disbelief and fragile hope on his rugged face had me tightening my lips again to hold back my mirth. Before he could say anything, I pointed at the idling taxi.

"In you get."

We stopped at my condo, and I instructed Jerome to wait in the taxi while I hobbled to the elevator. I stared longingly at my shower, but we didn't have time for luxuries like cleanliness. Instead, I threw on a shirt that wasn't wet with sweat and jeans that didn't have holes in their thighs. A fluttering at my balcony window caught my eye, and I crept closer to investigate.

I blinked, worried that my overtaxed body was hallucinating. Those rust-colored feathers were too familiar from the dozens of photos now on my phone. Beaky was here, on my balcony, tucked against the wall like she owned the place. I huffed with incredulous laughter.

"Squatting, are we? We'll see about that. Luckily for you, I have better things to do right now than evict rat-birds from the premises."

Beaky opened one eye, gazed at me beadily, then closed her eyelid again with poised indifference. I shook my head and shuffled to the door to rejoin Jerome in the waiting cab.

We drove to the neighborhood of Kitsilano, which was silent in the darkness of early morning. I directed the taxi to drop us in front of a small shop covered with a neon green awning, although everything was gray in the orange streetlights. I led Jerome to the back, where I entered a code into the door's keypad. We shuffled through a darkened hallway and into a commercial kitchen gleaming with stainless steel. I found a light switch and flicked it on. Jerome whistled as he gazed around the illuminated space.

"I can really use this?" He turned to look at me with awe in his eyes. "It's exactly what I need. Is this the kitchen of that cupcake shop? How did you get us in?"

I shrugged. As March, I had owned many businesses. This was one of them.

"I know someone who knows someone. No one is here until eleven-thirty, and your cake is due at ten, right? So, do you want to gaze rapturously for a little longer, or do you want to take this opportunity to finish your cake?"

Jerome jumped and hauled on the zipper of his duffle bag. Out came his utensils—turntable, spatulas, rolling pin, and pastry tips—and I wandered into the dining area to find a chair. By the time I had dragged it to a corner of the kitchen and sat heavily in it, Jerome had donned a black chef's apron and was placing his first layer of cake on the turntable. His eyes were narrowed in concentration, and occasionally his top lip would disappear under his bottom teeth with his focus.

I finished plucking spider venom out of my bloodstream with Caelus' guidance, then I called a few more people. I had been bone-tired, but after my healing, I felt much better.

"What's the password to edit your website?" I called out.

"Doughboy fifteen," he said absently, then he glanced at me. "That wasn't very secure of me, was it? Why do you want to know?"

"No, it wasn't," I replied, tapping at my phone. "Luckily, I'm trustworthy."

"You're not going to tell me why you wanted it, are you?"

"Nope."

Jerome huffed with laughter and bent over his cake once more. I smiled and continued my own work.

When my phone rang at seven in the morning, waking me from a light doze slumped against the counter, I hastily answered. After a brief discussion with the caller, I covered the speaker.

"What time will you be done?" I asked Jerome, then my breath caught. He stood, arms crossed, gazing at his finished cake on the stainless-steel counter. It was a three-tiered affair. The top layer was covered with smooth red fondant with a cluster of geometric outlines made of chocolate. Up the sides of the bottom and second layer crawled a dizzying pattern of fondant triangles in black, red, and white. A gold strip around the base of the top and bottom layers completed the look.

"I'm done." His mouth quirked. "I think. I hope."

"Right away," I spoke into the phone. We said our goodbyes and I hung up. Jerome continued to stare at his creation with a frown.

"Is it missing something?" He ran a sugary hand through his hair, making it stand on end in sticky spikes. I moved closer to evaluate the cake and stared at it in silence for long enough that he glanced at me with a worried expression.

"It's a masterpiece of creative decoration," I said finally. "The fondant is slightly uneven along the top corner, here, and you probably could have used a bigger tip when piping the gold ribbon. But those are deficiencies that will never be noticed by a glowing bride and her loving groom, nor will the excited guests see them. To them, your cake will rise as a testament to the bride's vision and your skill."

Jerome's jaw tightened and he nodded. Then his brow furrowed.

"It's totally uneven there," he muttered. "Damn it. How did I miss that?"

I laughed and linked my arm through his. My mind tried not to notice the firm heft of his bicep that my body eagerly felt.

"Have the photographer take photos from the right angle. He's a professional, he'll have some ideas. And the chances of the camera picking up a detail like that are minimal."

"What photographer?"

"He'll be here shortly. I couldn't have you using your

phone for website pictures. That's the face of your business, and professional photos will show your customers that you are a professional. I took the liberty of a few design touches on your website, as well. I hope you don't mind."

A knock on the glass of the shop's front door startled me, and I jerked my hand out from Jerome's arm.

"That will be your clothes. Hold on."

"My clothes?" Jerome called out behind me as I walked with measured strides to the front. A yawning courier held out a clothes bag.

"For Morgan Feynman?"

"That's me."

I accepted the bag and retreated to the kitchen, where an endearingly confused Jerome rubbed his eyes.

"If we're having the photographer come, I figured you might as well get your photos done for the website at the same time, so I had clothes delivered. I hope I got your size right. The joy of photography is that we can pin extra fabric in the back if necessary."

I held out the bag. Jerome took it with hesitation.

"I don't understand," he said. "Why are you doing all this? You could have gone home, slept, cleaned your wounds. You're spending so much money. I can't repay you."

"It's called an investment," I said. "I believe you have the skills to turn your business venture into the real deal, but you need a leg up. I happen to be excellent at running businesses, and I can spot potential when I see it."

"If you're 'investing' in me, does that mean this is a loan? I don't know if I can promise to pay you back. This is only my first gig."

"Investment in the loosest sense of the word." I hesitated, then took one of his large hands in both my own. "You befriended me at a point in my life when I was lost, and when I called for help, you answered without hesitation. That's worth a lot to me, and if helping you get started on your business is the only way I can think of to repay you, then I hope you will let me. I have the funds."

I tried to let go of his hand, but he gripped it tightly.

"Thank you," he said, his voice hoarse. "It's been a very long time since anyone has believed in me."

I gave him a smile and a squeeze of his hand, then turned to the clothes bag lying on the counter where Jerome had set it down, anxious to avoid getting too emotional. I unzipped it and flipped through the offerings.

"That is not the color green I requested," I said with a shake of my head. "No one looks good in that. Oh, this buff-colored one is nice." I tugged out the short-sleeved buttoned shirt with a relaxed collar and held it up to Jerome's neck. "Understated but brings out the warmth of your skin well."

Jerome shook his head with a jerky motion. His sandy strands flared out. In discomfort? Caelus and I would have to talk about better identifying emotions that affected the movements of people's threads.

"I'd rather have a tighter collar." He slid out the next shirt and held it up. "What about this one?"

I eyed the shirt critically. It was long-sleeved, a crisp thick cotton in an eye-popping cherry red.

"Yes, it fits your brand perfectly. Simple yet eye-catching. Good choice." I picked up a pair of charcoal slacks and shoved them at him. "Go on, give them a twirl before the photographer gets here."

Jerome looked dazed as he retreated to the bathroom to change. I chuckled and tucked unused shirts back in the clothes bag. I felt like the host of a makeover shows but for a business. Maybe that could be my new job. I wondered if I could get a producer interested.

A knock at the door interrupted my frivolous musings. A short man with unkempt hair that desperately needed a good trim waited outside, a large camera bag hanging from his shoulder. I opened the door and welcomed him in.

"Thanks for coming on such short notice," I said. "I appreciate it."

"And I appreciate the bonus fee that came with it." He grinned at me. "And when such a pretty lady asks, how could I say no?"

With March's history and Fiorella's body, that sort of comment would have provoked a biting response and a reduction in the fee he was looking forward to. I took a deep breath. How should Morgan react to such a remark?

The question was, what did the man mean by it? Was he a chauvinistic pig, or was he essentially harmless and simply needed a gentle reeducation?

"Thank you for the compliment," I said carefully, my tone pleasant but with an undercurrent of steel. "But I'd appreciate you not commenting on my appearance. It has no bearing on your job."

The man looked taken aback.

"No offence meant, miss. I apologize."

I smiled sweetly at him. He would bear watching, but maybe he was clueless. If so, I was happy to help.

"Apology accepted. Please, come this way to see the cake. Did you bring any props?"

The photographer immediately went to work setting up a backdrop for the cake. While he was busy, I peered into the hallway to find Jerome. The bathroom door was open, so I peeked inside.

"How do the clothes fit?"

Jerome turned with his hand at his collar. I looked him up and down, and my disgustingly hormonal body thrilled at the sight. If only I could reeducate it on how to properly react to a handsome man, I wouldn't have to fight the flush threatened to take over my cheeks.

He fit the slacks perfectly, hints of muscled thighs pressing against the charcoal fabric in a pleasing way. His shirt sleeves were the right length, and the shirt followed the line of his narrow waist and not-so-narrow pectorals. Was Jerome a gym rat? *How disappointingly boring*, thought my mind, while my body sang a yodel. I shut it down with iron force.

"It doesn't button up high enough," he said quietly.

I frowned.

"I didn't ask them to bring a tie—far too formal for a baker. You can't just leave the top button undone?"

"I'd rather not," he murmured.

I considered him. There was something he didn't want anyone to see, and I recalled the fully buttoned polo shirts he wore even when the bakery was stiflingly hot, and the tattoo that had peeked out of his collar. I nodded.

"I think there was a safety pin with the clothes bag. Give me a minute."

Jerome's face washed over with gratitude at my suggestion and my seeming lack of curiosity. I promised the photographer that we were almost ready to transfer the cake then found the safety pin attaching a note with my name on it to the clothes bag. When I returned, Jerome had only moved to stare at his reflection.

"I don't know, Morgan. I feel like a fraud. I don't think I've ever worn a button-up shirt before."

"There's a first time for everything," I said brightly. "As for the fraud comment, it's called imposter syndrome. Nearly everyone feels it at some point unless they are pathologically narcissistic." A certain ex-husband sprang to mind, but I banished him easily. Peter had no role to play in my life anymore. I wouldn't let him. That ghost was exorcised, and good riddance.

I beckoned to Jerome in the mirror to turn around and let me help him with his collar. "Fake it until you make it. It always stood me in good stead."

Jerome gave me a weak half-smile but kept hold of his collar. I waved the safety pin at him.

"The photographer is waiting."

248

Jerome hesitated, then he let the collar go. I carefully schooled my face into a bland mask, determined not to let whatever Jerome was hiding affect my expression. I reached up and pulled the collar back to attach the safety pin to the fabric's underside.

A swirl of blue caught my eye. Was that his tattoo? It was only the edge, so I couldn't see what it depicted, but my curiosity burned. I didn't let it reach my expression and finished my task without mentioning my discovery. Jerome searched my face when I finished, but I merely patted his chest—his firm chest, my body noted before I could curtail it—and waved toward the kitchen.

"Come on, the photographer's waiting."

Nine-thirty found Jerome and I in front of the cupcake shop waiting for a taxi, the cake on a large tray and an uneasy expression on his face.

"Could you come with me to give it to them?" he said. "You look great. Just what they're expecting."

"What do you mean?" I was puzzled. "My hair is a mess, and I'm pretty sure I have dried blood on my arms. Anyway, they know you."

"Not as such." He looked sheepish. "We've only communicated via email, and I sign off as my company name, Butter & Scotch."

"Why?"

"I'm not what people expect from a wedding cake decorator. I don't want to give the wrong impression."

I stared at Jerome. He was deadly serious, and I wondered what had happened in his life to make him feel that way. Sure, he was big. And muscled. And threw a mean right hook. But that didn't mean he couldn't bake.

But I understood, all too well, how the perception of

someone could skew their understanding. I had been guilty of that exact sin.

"No," I said at last. "I'm not going to do that. You march in there and own your creation. The time for hiding is over. Your cake speaks for itself, and if the bride had any misconceptions about what a 'proper' wedding cake decorator looks like, she will be swept away by the product you present. Understood?"

Jerome gave me a tight nod, but his shoulders straightened.

"You've got this." I patted his shoulder quickly enough that my stomach merely gave a half-hearted swoop. I was so tired after our all-nighter that even my hormones were sleepy.

"Thanks, Morgan." His face twitched in a half-smile, then he opened the front door and carefully folded himself inside a waiting taxi with the cake tray on the seat beside him. I smiled as his head turned to glance at me from the back window.

Finally, I arrived home. The little condo had never looked so welcoming.

"Bed," I moaned, and barely took off my coat before flopping on my bed and collapsing into a dreamless sleep.

Hours later, I awoke, groggy and confused. Why did my body hurt so much? Why was I damp and dirty? Caelus blossomed out of my arm and regarded me with a paternal air.

"You'll feel better after you finish healing yourself properly," he said casually. "And have a shower. Humans like that, don't they?"

"This human certainly does." I sat with a groan and looked at my aching legs that were covered in dried blood. "They look terrible. I thought I'd finished the stab wounds last night? I guess it wasn't permanent. I'd better get to work."

Caelus let me take the reins on my healing, merely providing pointers for best practices, and within fifteen minutes my legs were fully healed and the various bruises and cuts from yesterday forgotten. I almost skipped to the bathroom and turned the shower faucet as hot as my skin could handle.

When I was sufficiently lobstered and ensconced on my soft couch with a steaming mug of tea, I turned on my phone and scanned a news site to amuse myself while I drank.

The big local news was Jordan Prang's fund infusion into the women's centers of Vancouver. My heart squeezed with confused emotion. Seeing Peter's false name, the one commemorating my old life, brought me some pain, but a far greater measure of composure that I had expected. Had I truly buried March's past and Fiorella's anguish? Was I fully Morgan now, able to put my past behind me? I thought so. I hoped so.

My phone rang, and I answered the call with a smile.

"Hi, March," Anna's voice rang out through the speaker. "I saw you called late last night. Everything okay?"

"Everything's fine," I said. It wasn't a lie—everything was fine now. I had needed her last night, but then I'd learned that there was another person I could rely on. Anna and I had history, and I wouldn't give up on her, but she had other things going on in her life right now and that was okay. I could give her time.

But I did need to get one thing straight.

"It's Morgan now," I said. "My name is Morgan."

"We need to hide the Leaf," I said to Caelus once I finished my call with Anna.

He emerged from my arm looking grumpy.

"Hide? Why? Let's destroy it right away. It's disrupting the balance. Are you getting in the way of my mission again? I thought we had an agreement."

251

"Caelus," I said through his disgruntled chatter. "Calm down. I'm not reneging on our agreement. I only think we should take things slowly. We don't know what this Leaf will do when combined with the other artifacts. Don't we owe it to your mission to have all the information? What if having the Leaf is crucial to finding the Mother's Seed and the lost Elder's Blood?"

Caelus made unhappy murmuring noises, but he didn't disagree. I wanted artifacts back in Caelus' world as much as he did—it wasn't a stretch to imagine the dangers they threatened—and he knew what was in my thoughts. We were on the same page, as far as collecting artifacts went.

"We need to keep it safe," I said, pressing my point. "I'll buy us a safety deposit box at a bank downtown, and we can get it whenever we're ready to destroy it. How does that sound?"

"Will it be safe there?"

"Perfectly so." I stood. "Let's do it right now."

The bus ride downtown was long and slow, and houses whisked by my darkening window in the gloomy afternoon. We passed a road that led to my old neighborhood and my old house, and I had a lingering desire to see it again.

The desire passed as soon as it came, and I smiled at my reflection in the window. I was growing used to Morgan's face and Morgan's life, and March felt more and more like a dream. The old house was not mine anymore, and neither were the cares of March.

As the sun drifted closer to the horizon, it shot one brilliant ray through a gash in the stormy clouds. It was so bright that I squinted against the shine, but I couldn't keep the smile off my face.

New Morgan, new life. No regrets.

ALSO BY EMMA SHELFORD

Magical Morgan
Daughters of Dusk
Mothers of Mist

Immortal Merlin
Ignition
Winded
Floodgates
Buried
Possessed
Unleashed
Worshiped
Unraveled

Nautilus Legends
Free Dive
Caught
Surfacing

Breenan Series
Mark of the Breenan
Garden of Last Hope
Realm of the Forgotten

ACKNOWLEDGEMENTS

Thank you for my wonderful reading team: Wendy Callendar, Steven Shelford, Dave Roche, Cat Kennedy, Stella Jorette, Anna McCluskey, and Danielle Taksron. Deranged Doctor Designs produced a wonderful cover. And thank you to my lovely Fantastical Lair, who helped brainstorm with me (especially Dawn McQueen Mortimer, Red Ravenwood, Léon Lémieux, and Krista Danielle Casada).

ABOUT THE AUTHOR

Emma Shelford feels that life is only complete with healthy doses of magic, history, and science. Since these aren't often found in the same place, she creates her own worlds where they happily coexist. If you catch her in person, she will eagerly discuss Lord of the Rings ad nauseam, why the ancient Sumerians are so cool, and the important role of phytoplankton in the ocean.

Emma is the author of multiple urban fantasy series, including Magical Morgan, Immortal Merlin, Nautilus Legends, and the Breenan Series.

Printed in Great Britain
by Amazon